MURDER
IN THE
VILLAGE
PROPER

MURDER
IN THE
VILLAGE
PROPER

AN IT'S NEVER
TOO LATE MYSTERY

DONNARAE MENARD

First published by Level Best Books 2023

This novel is entirely a work of fiction. The names, characters and incidents portrayed in it are the work of the author's imagination. Any resemblance to actual persons, living or dead, events or localities is entirely coincidental.

Author Photo Credit: Klementovich Photography, North Conway, New Hampshire

First edition

ISBN: 978-1-68512-372-7

Cover art by Level Best Designs

This book was professionally typeset on Reedsy.
Find out more at reedsy.com

To all the men and women who reach out their hand in the aid of someone, something else.

Praise for Murder in the Village Proper

"DonnaRae Menard welcomes us to Katelyn Took's home in small town Vermont where we smell cookies baking and homemade meals simmering. But all is far from peaceful as Katelyn solves the mystery of the vicious murder of a local businessman. Not until the well-crafted final pages do we guess the killer's identity. A memorable visit to rural New England where all is not as it appears."—Marlie Wasserman, author, *Path of Peril*

"*Murder in the Village Proper* perfectly captures Vermont in the mid-1970s from its December blanket of frosty white to the insular vibe of its small-towns. Along with comfort taste treats and toboggan rides, author DonnaRae Menard serves up a trove of secrets surrounding a five-year-old open murder case. Young heroine Katie Took relentlessly pursues information to unmask the killer and help her elderly friend Ruth, the murder victim's widow. Katie realizes only the truth can clear Ruth's debilitating brain fog and her name. An enjoyable cozy."—Linda Lovely, author, HOA Mystery Series

"Quirky characters and small-town mystery make for a heartfelt, fun, and twisty read. Can you get away with murder in a town where everyone knows the darkest secrets? Kaitlyn Took uncovers how far some will go to keep them hidden."—James L'Etoile, award-winning author of *Black Label, Dead Drop*, and the Detective Penley series

"*Murder in the Village Proper* deftly creates the feel of a sleepy New England small town - where everyone knows everyone else's business and long buried secrets abound. There are definitely a lot of secrets for Katie Took to sort thru to find the truth of who really killed her good friend Ruth's husband years ago. The characters' relationships—especially Katie and her girlfriend Marlie—are the highlight of this book. I look forward the next book in the series!"—Deb Wells, Digital Strategist

Chapter One

When the phone rang, Katie knew it was an animal pick-up call. Why else would anyone telephone at nine o'clock after a long working day and on a snowy evening?

Rick beat her to the phone. Handing it over, he said, "I'll go start the truck to warm it up."

"Miss Took? You're the animal control officer, right? This is Carl Terreault. I'm sorry to call so late, but we've got these three small puppies in our barn, and the mother has disappeared."

"Your dog is lost in the snow, Mr. Terreault?" Katie asked.

"She's not our dog. She showed up here around three weeks ago, already in labor. A small, wire-haired terrier mix. We found her in the barn when we went out for the milking. My wife and boy made her comfortable, and we asked around but haven't found the owner. Has someone reported her missing?"

"I haven't received a call on a missing dog," Katie said.

"Well, she had several puppies, and lost all but three. She's been taking real good care of these," said Mr. Terreault. "I saw her this morning when I went out to milk, but she was gone at nine when my wife took her out a bowl of scraps. She ain't been back all day. The puppies are cold and hungry. I just brought them in the house, but we can't keep them."

"I'm on my way," said Katie.

This was the first time since taking what had been Irma Roser Moore's job that Katie had been called for abandoned puppies. Irma, Katie's maternal grandmother and the person who had raised Katie since age three, had lived her entire life in Parentville, and after the death of her husband, Fred, supported herself by her wits.

As the per diem animal control officer for the town of Parentville, she usually got calls for feral cats, raccoons, skunks, and Walker, an ably named basset hound. She got out a cat carrier and tucked a piece of blanket and a hot water bottle inside. Ruth, the crazy old lady Gram had taken in, and who then had turned into a roommate and housekeeper, was standing by the door, her red coat leaving a gap where skinny kneecaps and shins showed between the coat's hem and her boot tops.

"You don't want to go, Ruth," said Katie. "It's cold, and you're not wearing pants. The snow is deeper than your boots."

"I'll stay in the truck," said Ruth, yanking her gloves on in a manner that left no space for arguing.

Rick was standing beside her, frowning. But if she was determined to go, then so be it. He tugged his winter hat with its long fur ear flaps down on her head. Since selling his mobile home and moving in as handyman and renter, he had taken on the role of, if not head of household, protector. Even though Ruth had long ago chosen another to wed, he still carried a sparking torch for the small woman.

"Tie it under your chin." He told her. When Ruth finished, he wrapped one of the long scarves she knitted around her neck, securing it in the front.

"I can't breathe," she said with a giggle.

"You're fine," he replied. "I'll mix up some baby formula and set up a nursery box while you're gone. Be careful."

The Terreault farm was on the other side of Parentville, near Monkton. Ruth knew all the roads, and Katie had only been back for a short time. The sixty-year-old directed them from one dirt road to another. "If we go through the village proper, it will take longer."

In the hours since the snow had stopped falling, the plow trucks had done their business. The roadways were clear, with tall, peaked snowbanks on either side. The wind was gusting, sending light, swirling sprays of glitter across the road in front of their headlight beams. Just before they arrived at the Terreault's, Ruth remarked how it looked like they were driving through

2

a fairy wonderland.

"Yes," Katie agreed. "It is magical."

Mrs. Terreault met them at the door. Her two teenage boys stood behind her, each holding tight to an inquisitive hound.

"I'm so sorry," she said. "It's just that with me working and the boys in school, we couldn't have taken on the puppies."

When Katie first saw the two Plott hounds, she thought she might have found the daddy. Once inside, she realized one was a female and the other a neutered male.

"We only knew the other female dog was in the barn because Ginny found her," said one of the boys. He was rubbing the female Plott. From the whipping of her tail, Katie could tell Ginny was thrilled at the attention.

Katie looked the puppies over while transferring them to the carrier. Two females, one male. Their bellies were nicely rounded, and they weren't whimpering as if in need.

"Are you sure the mother hasn't been here?" she asked, rubbing the belly of one puppy.

"We've been watching," said Mr. Terreault. "My wife warmed up some canned milk and Karo syrup, and we dribbled it into their mouths."

"They were so thin, and just shivering into pieces," said Mrs. Terreault. She gave the babies one last soft and lingering look, as if this was one of her own she was sending away.

Katie thanked them for keeping an eye on the young dogs and slid the carrier across the bench seat next to Ruth, who wrapped a protective arm around the plastic crate. As they pulled out of the long drive, Katie looked skyward. There had been a thin crescent moon showing earlier. Now it was gone, hidden behind more clouds.

"Well," she said. "It doesn't look so much like a Tinkerbell village now. I'm not liking the cloud cover. Let's hope we get home before the snow starts to fall again."

"The forecast isn't for snow." Ruth pointed out. "But the wind is picking up."

Her words were right on. Earlier, small gusts had sent wisps of snow in a whirling dance. Now heavy sheets of dense white blew across the road. Katie and Ruth felt the truck's tires snag on drifts dumped across their way by the heavy blow.

For crying out loud, Katie thought, gritting her teeth. *I can barely tell where the road ends and the snowbank starts.*

As though laughing at her fear, the wind rose still more. Instead of a gust that hid everything and instantly disappeared, they were driving ahead into a blinding wall of snow. Katie slowed down. Their loss of forward momentum meant that upon hitting a solidly packed snow drift hidden by the gusts, there was enough play for the front wheels to veer. In a split moment, the truck was tumbling.

Ruth cried out in fear. Katie, who was clutching the steering wheel, came up hard against it as the truck stopped abruptly. The right front end was down in a ditch far enough so Katie could feel herself sliding down the bench seat toward Ruth. Twisting quickly, she moved her legs, bracing her feet against the hump where the transmission traveled forward under the cab. Her quick movement allowed her to hold herself from crushing the pet carrier into the old woman.

"Are you okay, Ruth?" Katie asked, sounding a little unsteady.

"I'm alright." Ruth sounded small and even more shook up. Katie peered at her friend in the dashboard glow. "I hit my head on the window, but this big hat of Rick's softened the blow." She gave a nervous laugh.

"Well, that's good," said Katie. "I'm going to get out and see what this looks like. Do you know where we are?"

"I have no idea." Ruth sounded less chipper than she had only moments earlier.

Getting the door open proved to be a chore, as Katie needed to push it up as well as out. Long ago, the old pickup had developed a hitch in the driver's door where, if it was pushed so far, it would catch and require a solid pull to close it. Every time Katie inadvertently opened the door to that point in the past, she would complain about the strength needed to shut it again. At that moment, she was thrilled when she heard the metal creak and snap holding the door against the wind.

Thank goodness. I don't know how I would have gotten it open to get back in, Katie thought. She stepped onto the running board, then reached her foot out for the road or the bank of the ditch. Instead, Katie fell into powdery snow up to her thigh. Holding onto the truck with both hands, she inched toward the back, climbing the ditch bank as she went. The rear wheel was lifted off the ground, and, even worse, the tailpipe located on the other side of the truck was out of sight, buried in the snow.

This was a no-win situation. Only by creeping back toward the front of the truck, ducking under the door, and crawling up the hood, was Katie able to get back into the truck. Metal squealed on metal when she heaved the door closed behind her. By that time, all the heat in the cab had escaped.

Rather than get her snowy pants and jacket against Ruth and the puppy crate, Katie lifted the hemp grain bags that covered the cracked vinyl and rolled them over Ruth's legs. Once settled, she turned the heater fan on high.

"I don't know where we are, Ruth. I do know I'm not going to be able to back us out of here."

"Are we going to have to walk?" Ruth asked.

"Okay, well, let's talk about that." Katie wasn't sure where to start. "We're in a ditch deep enough so that if you step out, you'll be up to your waist in snow. You have on low boots, and your legs are bare. That's an issue. I don't remember seeing a house, and neither one of us knows which way to go to find one *if* we can keep on the road. Without a shovel, I would have to stamp around to pack down a path for you."

Ruth gave a shuddering sigh. "I guess that means we stay here until someone comes along."

Both she and Katie were considering the fact it was a Sunday night, and they were on a dirt road, not the main street.

"Ruth, there's also the fact the tailpipe is in the snow. We need to make sure the exhaust doesn't back up."

Ruth sniffed, then reached out to open the vent window. One of the puppies whimpered.

"Oh, the babies!" Ruth pulled off her mittens and opened the crate.

One by one, she lifted the small dogs out of the piece of blanket. Opening her jacket, she tucked them inside her sweater. Katie watched until Ruth had her jacket buttoned again and her mittens on.

"This will keep them warmer," said Ruth.

Katie nodded. "When the cab gets warm enough, I'm going to have to shut the truck off."

Unsnapping the latches that held the top and the bottom of the crate together, and stacking one inside the other, made it small enough to shove up onto the dash. Katie slid down the seat until she was right next to Ruth. Wrapping her arms around the older woman, Katie pulled her close, careful not to crush the puppies.

"Well," said Ruth. "This would be a good time for tea and conversation."

"I'd like tea right now," said Katie, with a small laugh. They were silent, each in their own thoughts. Katie worried about how she was going to protect Ruth from the cold. "If I leave you here, I could walk to a farmhouse and get help."

"No! Katie! Don't leave me!" There was an edge of hysteria in Ruth's words.

Katie hugged her closer. "I've got you. I'm right here. We'll wait. It might get cold, but we'll wait." *We need to stay awake*, she thought. "You said this was a good time for conversation. Why don't you tell me about you and Gram?"

"What about us?" asked Ruth.

"You know, when you were young." Katie cuddled Ruth closer.

"We met in first grade. I was the looker. She was the brat." Ruth continued in a low voice, talking about two country girls in a small school. One, a village kid, and the other a farm girl. If she noticed when Katie shut the truck off, she never said a word.

Eventually, Ruth left the antics of small children and early teens behind and began talking about the lives of young, budding women.

"I didn't know what I was going to do after high school," she said. "Your gram went to nursing school. Did you know that? Yes, she made it about halfway through, then the money ran out. It was a two-year course. She had to come home. The plan was to earn enough money for the second year and go back, but your grandfather came along, and as they say, que, sera, sera."

"And what did you do?" asked Katie. She had been listening with half an ear, knowing she was going to have to go for help, but concerned about Ruth. She touched Ruth's cheek. The skin was very cold.

"Well, let's see. I made it through high school, even though my parents didn't think I would. They said I was too flighty. But I had a teacher in school, Mrs. Pelletier, I'm surprised I can remember her name. She was a tartar, I tell you. She taught math. Early on, she must have realized I was good with numbers. Mrs. Pelletier got me extra books and taught me math the other students weren't learning. She had some big college degree for it. Oh, and she made me learn to type. We all took typing. Mrs. Pelletier just made sure I got lots of practice. Your gram used to complain awfully about it, but I thought it was like a game. I got to be quite fast. Anyway, I knew college wasn't in my future, but by the time I graduated, I was ready to get out there and make it on my own. My two brothers were in the army. My oldest sister was married and moved off to Rutland, so just Vera and I were at home with my folks."

"Where is Vera now?" Katie asked.

"Florida, the last I heard."

Ruth reached up, wiping the frost off a small patch of window. The snow had piled up, and nothing could be seen. Katie slid over and depressed the clutch to start the truck again. There was a rasping cough, but the engine caught. She opened the vent window on that side before moving back toward Ruth.

"Was Rick in your grade?" asked Katie, thinking it would be a safe topic.

"Actually, Rick was ahead of us. He and your grandfather were of an age, same as my brother. That's how I met Rick, through my brother."

"If the Moser family lived in Charlotte, how did you meet Gram? Wouldn't she have gone to school there?" asked Katie.

"Her father was a farmhand on one of Arthur Fortin's farms. They lived in a small tumble-down cottage on the property. It wasn't until Irma's grandparents passed that they moved to the other side of Lover's Lane, up over the ridge in Charlotte, you know?"

Katie smiled in the dark. "As a matter of fact, I do."

"Yes," said Ruth, with a touch of sadness. "Your gram said it was supposed to be better, but I guess it wasn't. They were dirt poor. Taxes and the like were squeezing them out. Only the orchard kept them alive, and the beef cattle. Anyway, Irma came back from that one year gone to nursing school, a different person. She had bloomed into this pretty and smart young woman. Fred, your poppa, your grandfather, just fell over and never recovered."

The women laughed, and Katie shut the truck off again.

"Anyway, they were off together, all googly eyed," Ruth said. "I had a couple of boyfriends, and then there was Rick, suddenly Mr. Friendly. It was funny, really. I thought he was keeping track of me because my brother asked him to; seems he had his own ideas. But he didn't share them with me. Girls made him shy, I guess. Beauregard's general store had just jumped into the hardware and feed business, you know, besides groceries and mercantile. They were in competition with Baldwins Feed and Hardware for a while, but it didn't work so well for Beauregard's. I got a job there helping old Mrs. Beauregard with the books and all. One day, I was working in the office and had to go up front with something for Mr. Beauregard. There was this tall, slim young man standing like a spear in the light coming in through the big front window. He was wearing a pair of pressed trousers and a shirt as white as all this snow." She laughed.

"I almost fell over my own feet. I knew who he was, but when he left town for the army, he had been a gangling farmer-looking sort of fellow. And I had been a snot-nosed schoolgirl, four years younger. You should have seen him then, Katie. He stood there among those farmers in their coveralls and boots. All slick. He told me later on that the army was like the prison system. You got one last haircut and a close shave before you hit the road. George Beauregard, the son of the house, had come home. Did I tell you he left a good job in the army? He was some kind of assistant to a highfalutin brass guy. Traveled all over, developed a sheen other guys couldn't match. He and his father went outside to look at a car he had bought just the day before. I wanted to follow him so bad it was awful. But he never saw me. Just the pride in his old man's eyes. They were a lot alike." Ruth stopped talking for a few minutes. A heavy sigh finally released her from the past, and she spoke again.

"A few days later, he was back in the store. His dad wanted him to work with him, but George wanted something else. He came right out and told his father; he'd stay for a bit and that was it. His younger brother, Christopher, was all about the store. There was some subtle competition there, and they didn't get along. But the old man wanted his shining star son to be standing beside him. Christopher just sat back and waited. He knew George was all flash in the pan. George didn't last two weeks in the store before he was off getting hired at the furniture factory. They told him at the hire that with his military record, he'd be a supervisor in no time. He never made it past planer, scrubbing the rough off of planks day in and day out. Mrs. Beauregard seemed to know as well that George wouldn't stick to anything for long. After George started calling on me, she warned me that he wasn't the best I could do. I didn't listen. He saw me in the store when he started working with his old man. The few weeks he worked there, he didn't do much besides shake hands with people and talk about all the things he had seen and done. I would watch him follow his father around while Christopher did all the actual work. After that first time, George said hello to me, it seemed like every time I turned around, he was there. He smoked these little cigars; he called them cheroots. They smelled like cherry wood, sweet and heavy on the tongue. He talked his father into carrying them in the store. George wouldn't live with his folks and bought this little two-bedroom house on Mechanicville Road. It was just inside the village proper. He didn't want to live outside of town. His wingtips were always shined, shirt and pants pressed. He had a girl that came in to do all that and clean the house. I bet she did more too, but no one ever said a word to me. If they had, maybe when things got horrible, and I kept getting slammed around, I would have been better prepared. I might not have been the one found holding the knife when George was murdered."

After that, Ruth got quiet. Katie stared at the back side of Rick's heavy winter hat, unsure what to say but feeling as though Ruth needed comforting. There was also a lot of confusion in Katie's thoughts. When she'd met Ruth, the older woman had said her husband had been murdered, and though she had been right there when it happened, she was innocent. Just now, Ruth said she'd been holding the knife. Then, too, before Ruth had been defiant, now she sounded sad.

Is it because she was there and couldn't stop it, or guilt because she killed him? Katie wondered. *Why, if they had gone their separate ways, was Gram so quick to take Ruth in? Where is the rest of Ruth's family?*

Katie inhaled the smell of wet wool and cold exhaust, exhaling slowly. She needed time to think. The small space was closing in on her. The white mist of her own breath rose before her eyes, sending her sliding over the seat to start the truck. Knocking it into neutral, she left it to idle. Ruth was shivering. If she had to venture a guess, Katie might have thought the older woman was weeping as well. The inside of the truck cab wasn't getting warm fast. It was time to make a decision about going for help.

"Ruth," Katie said gently. "We can't stay here. This isn't going to work. I have to go for help."

"You said you wouldn't leave me here," whispered Ruth, forehead still on the frosty glass.

She sounded small and old. A moment ago, Katie's heart had hardened at Ruth's words. Now, she felt the need to protect her gram's elderly friend.

"If I wrap you in my jacket, maybe I can get you out on the road. But honey, it's so cold. How far will you be able to go?"

Ruth shifted around in the seat and leaned against Katie, nodding in agreement. Katie thought she heard one of the puppies give a little whine.

Suddenly there was a sharp rap on the driver's window.

"You stuck?" asked a solidly masculine voice.

* * *

The farmer and his family, on their way home from visiting relatives and delayed by the storm, happened along just as Katie's foot touched the brake pedal. The flash of red from the rear braking light caught their attention, and like all good people in the rural community, they stopped to check it out.

Room was made for Katie and Ruth in the family station wagon. Children were ousted from the middle seat, sent over the back to sit among the parcels in the cargo area. From the nearby farmhouse along the telephone party line, Rick was summoned. The women were actually within minutes of the Parentville/Charlotte Road, and, therefore within walking distance of home. That is, if it had been a good day.

* * *

"You should take a hot tub," Rick said to Ruth, as soon as they walked in the front door. He watched her shiver as she shucked her red coat.

The huge house, once a stagecoach inn, was never more than the lowest degree of warmth, around sixty-five degrees, even with the addition of the shrouded furnace Rick and his friends had gotten secondhand and installed in the basement. The tin hood was the size of a two-seater outhouse. The blower sent a stream of hot air up to the single four-foot square grate in the living room, but from there, only the natural rise of heat lifted it through the ceiling vents into the second floor. Constructed square on the foundation with four enormous, high-ceiling rooms on each floor, it was an impressive, but uneconomical residence. An ell added to the western side held the kitchen and bathroom. The cat room was a later addition when the carriage garage had been converted.

"I've got to get these puppies fed," Ruth replied.

"Katie and I can do it."

"Katie can have a bath first. I'll feed the puppies." Ruth's bottom lip came out. Without looking at either of the others, she took the small saucepan down off the warming shelf where Rick had started baby animal formula. She collected baby bottles from the cupboard and stubbornly walked away.

Leaving the two older people to argue, Katie went to run a bath. Her feet screamed in pain as she lowered them into the hot water, but soon she was toasty all over. She walked out of the bathroom with a fresh tub running, just as Ruth tucked in the last puppy. All around the room, cats perched at different heights. The language of ears told Katie how accepting of the canines each cat was. But Sasha, who mothered them all, leapt gracefully into the cardboard box to clean the first drowsy face she came to.

"I knew she would do that," said Rick.

"No, you didn't," said Ruth. Passing Katie, she whispered, "He's already named them all. We're probably getting a dog." The bathroom door closed behind her with a loud click.

"They've already got names?" Katie asked casually, pouring water into her teacup. A kettle boiled perpetually on the kitchen wood stove.

"Yeah, the big female? She's Sassy, the little one is Sophie. And this little fellow," Rick scooped the chubby-bellied male out of the box. "He's Solomon."

Sasha made a phrrpt noise at Rick. Standing up in the box, she reached out a paw. After all, she had just gotten them all cleaned and ready for bed. Rick gave the sleeping puppy a nuzzle and set him down with his sisters.

And it looks like Sol is going to be sticking around. Katie took her tea and headed for bed.

Chapter Two

They were all a little late rising in the morning. Rick and Katie slid into work at the last possible second. Katie was behind the cash register up front, and Rick was in his fairly new job. A switch from loading trucks for customers in the feed shed to driving around local deliveries.

"It's way warmer than working in the feed shed," he had told Katie.

The job had opened temporarily when another employee got nabbed for driving while intoxicated over the Veteran's Day weekend. When it came to going back to his former job in the shed, Rick had played the seniority card and stayed on as the local delivery driver. It worked well with all the side jobs he had, legal and not.

"You may have thought it would be warmer in the cab of the truck," Stan Baldwin, owner of Baldwin's Feed and Hardware, and both Katie and Rick's boss, said, as he walked up. "But with another weather front coming in, you're going to be running your butt off today."

Rick bit back on his lip. His plan had been to get his buddy, Philip Carwell, to bring his wrecker out from the garage on the Mechanicville Road to where Irma's pickup was still in the ditch. It would take the two of them to pull it out. Using the phone in Stan's office, Rick called the garage.

Philip's wife, Arnelle, was manning the phone. "Philip has been out since the middle of the night," she said. "He's got a mess of calls waiting. He's got Frankie with him. We've even got Jason out in the old wrecker doing jump starts. But don't worry, as soon as Phil gets back to me, I'll tell him about the truck. Did you leave the keys in it?"

"I knew I should have called him last night," Rick told Katie after relating Arnelle's words.

It was already so busy at the cash registers that Katie could only listen and nod her head. Not only had the sudden storm the day before alarmed residents, many of whom had moved into the new housing developments from the city, but another was on its way. There were only thirty more days before Christmas. People had been waiting outside when the doors opened at eight, and there was no end of the line in sight. Stan's voice came over the intercom, telling Rick and Dwayne, the bulk feed truck driver, their rigs were loaded and ready to go.

The whole day ran together. Katie worked through her breaks and took only enough lunchtime to go to the lady's room. Between customers, she sipped from the thermos and bit from the sandwich hidden on the shelf near her knees. Cindy, Stan's wife, had come in and worked at the second cash register, freeing the other clerk to do as much restocking as he could. WJOY played on the radio, sending music and news through the feed store, and out into the barns. Frequent interruptions by the weatherman gave him bragging rights to have had called how bad the storm would be. Now, he was predicting a northeaster and possible loss of power in the outlying areas.

"You have to know, he means us." Cindy groaned. "I am not looking forward to being storm-bound with three small kids, and a husband who's chaffing at the bit because the store is closed."

Katie laughed, but she, too, had concerns.

* * *

The store closed for the day. The last customer was sent out into the early darkness with wild bird seed in one hand and a snow shovel in the other. Katie sat in the tiny break area, watching out the window of the back door. Behind her, the furnace was closing down for the night, ticking as it cooled. Each metal click reminded her of time passing, urging her to decide what she was going to do for Christmas. If she should shop, or sit out the holiday in defiance. This time last year, she had been in Illinois, alone with no one.

14

The summons to settle her grandmother's estate had meant there would be no reconciliation with the woman who had raised her. After the summons, Katie pulled into town, intent on selling, splitting, and partying until the money was gone. Ruth met her at the door of the farmhouse, suitcase in hand, ready to turn over the cat chow and leave. But she hadn't. Now, they were a family; Katie, Ruth, and Rick, who had loved Ruth for years but couldn't get to first base, and a mess of cats.

Outside of the feed store, the big parking lot lights were still on, lighting up the front of the storage buildings across the way. While Stan finished up the daily worksheets, he allowed her to stay inside instead of waiting in the cold feed barn. She and Rick had ridden to work together. Though his truck wasn't locked, he had the ignition keys in his pocket. Just as the first flurries of snow drifted down, Rick backed the box truck, used for local deliveries in beside its big brother, the bulk feed tanker.

"I'm leaving, Stan. Goodnight," Katie called out as she left the building. The wind caught the door, almost yanking it free from her mittened grasp. "Crap." She slipped backwards and had to use the door handle to pull herself up enough to push the door tightly closed.

"It's getting slippery," Rick called out, hurrying toward his own vehicle.

"I know! That was me almost splatting into the parking lot gravel." Gritting her teeth, she bent forward, pushing against the wind.

Where other people had left their places of business, some hours early, and gone directly home, Katie had fielded a call from Arnelle, stating the pickup truck was back on the dirt road, parked right next to where it had slid off. They were going to have to deviate in the dark and snow to pick it up. The aged and well-driven truck was always temperamental. Katie could only hope that after spending hours tipped on its right front corner, the truck would start smoothly and travel safely home.

Her prayers were in vain. Turning the key got a hoarse ruh-ruh, but nothing else. Rick pulled up alongside to attach jumper cables from the battery of his truck to hers. Branches knocked together, like a rattlesnake's tail, a death knell to any critter or person who dared venture out. The flurry of snow had already mounted to a much heavier downfall, even as the wind

15

rose high enough to squeal through the barren tree branches. The result was both a sharp jab of icy needles to exposed flesh, and a roaring in their ears. With the addition of juice from Rick's battery, Irma's old pickup caught and revved up. Katie exhaled, relieved to be able to head home. Unfortunately, after the first hundred feet, she hit a slick spot, fishtailing slightly. The narrow dirt road was domed with packed snow and ice. She hadn't driven in winter weather in years. It was not an enjoyable experience, and trying to pry her shoulders apart made her more aware that she had lost what knowledge she had previously held.

By the time they turned up the hill on Fire Lane 61, her body, beneath its layers of flannel and wool protection, was slick with sweat. Her fingers ached where they clutched the hard steering wheel. At the top of the rise, the truck slowed slightly. Katie had the urge to press down harder on the accelerator. "Steady," she whispered to herself. "Hold it steady." After only a slight spinning of the rear tires, the pickup crested the hill and pulled into its spot in front of the farmhouse.

"Well, that worked out just fine, didn't it?" Rick said as he opened the front door of the house.

"Watch the cats!" Ruth called out.

Katie looked down around her feet. There were no cats there. Instinct told them this would not be a good night to be outside. All around the room, boxes lined with pieces of blanket held felines, curled and settled. Only LG, Little Girl, approached. She sauntered across the room like she had the same rights given to the Queen of Sheba. Though several cats hopped up to follow Ruth, none approached the new arrivals. It was left to LG. After all, Katie was her human of choice. It didn't matter how Katie felt about it. LG had staked a claim.

"What about Old Tom?" Katie asked. Bending to unlace her boots, she gave LG a little rub and got the usual swat in exchange.

"He's over here complaining," said Ruth. "I added a pint jar of leeks and potatoes to this stew left from the other night. That and the biscuits will be plenty for supper, I think."

There was no wasting here. Katie had returned home broke, ready to sell the farm and leave town again. But Gram, even in death, had been smarter. Her will had been written so that for the property to be turned over to Katie, she had to go along with rules regarding the seventeen cats and the one crazy old woman. Katie had acquired a house which was crumbling down, while the bills left for her to sort out crept up. She had the urge to turn and bolt, until crazy Ruth told the story of Irma's murder, and the cover-up that followed. A lesson in fidelity that must have been woven into Katie's fiber rose. It was okay for her to besmirch her gram, complaining about the old woman's controlling ways, but the rest of the world had better watch their p's and q's. Ignoring the sheriff's bad attitude, Katie had persisted in asking why. Not only did she eventually find the person responsible for Irma's death, but she uncovered the medicinal mistake that kept Ruth fog bound.

While Ruth put supper on the table, Rick lugged enough chunk wood in from the stacks running off from the back door to keep the kitchen stove glowing through the night. Down in the cellar, next to the bulkhead entrance, he and his friends had stacked a couple of cords of sixteen-inch split wood for the furnace. Even if the electricity went out, they would be warm. If they stayed on the first floor, anyway.

By the time Katie had hustled the last of the cats into their crates in the cat room, a repurposed attached garage, it was time to sit. Cats inside at mealtime meant a lot of mewling and reaching paws, and maybe a few attempts at jumping up onto the table.

"If the storm keeps up like this, we can probably plan on the electric going out. We can let the cats into the main house to keep it warmer and sleep on the first floor," said Ruth, laying a platter of cold biscuits between them.

"I'll wait to see if we have to drag the mattresses down later." Rick looked toward the kitchen window, which was coated with lacy frost, hiding the storm.

Dinner conversation consisted of weather-related topics and if any damage had been done to the underbelly of the pickup. Katie stacked bowls in the dishpan. Behind her, Ruth and Rick were chatting about the chickens out in their coop and the puppies in the big box. When she heard the cellar door open, Katie turned.

"What are you up to, Rick?" she asked.

"I picked up some boards from the scrap heap at the dump a few days ago. If I knock together some shelves in the cellar, Ruth can move all the jars you two canned out of the cardboard boxes on the floor."

"Good idea," said Katie. "A little organization will make everything easier to find."

Ruth came buzzing back into the kitchen, a puppy and a baby bottle in her hands. "Put that spoon back, Rick," she ordered.

"What?" The old man looked both innocent and guilty at the same time.

Katie looked from one to the other. Ruth had a hard look on her face, pinning Rick in place until he pulled the fore mentioned spoon out of his pocket and dropped it back into the silverware tray. Only then did Ruth release him from her penetrating stare so he could flee down the cellar stairs.

"What the heck?" Katie asked.

Ruth headed back to her seat on the living room couch and the rest of the puppies. "There's all that apple butter down there we canned. He can scarf down a pint all alone and I've found the empty jelly jars to prove it."

Katie laughed, but as soon as Ruth was out of sight, she snuck two teaspoons out of the drawer and followed Rick down the steps.

"How did you get away with it?" Rick asked, breaking the seal on a pint-sized canning jar.

"She thinks I'm too innocent to be a party to your schemes," said Katie.

While Rick measured and cut boards and Katie pounded nails, they emptied the jar. Thanksgiving was newly past, and the world had just taken on a heavy coating of winter white. It was natural sometime during the evening for conversation to turn to Christmas, which felt like it was racing toward them.

"So, Rick?" Katie asked shyly, cheeks warming with the audacity of her question. "Are you going to give Ruth a ring for Christmas?"

"Nope."

"Really?" Katie stopped, raised hammer in hand. "I thought you two were getting along so good, and well, I kind of expected that to be the next step."

Rick put down the saw, rising to his full five-foot and ten inches. Arching his back, he rubbed a sore spot above his belt line. Even though they were in the basement with a few feeble forty-watt light bulbs overhead, Katie could see his face clearly. There was pain in his features that had nothing to do with a sore back.

"It's not that I haven't asked, Katie. She's the only woman I have ever loved. Way back when she was a junior in high school, I was smitten. Back then, she hadn't even had her first kiss. Then I was too slow. Now, well now, Ruth considers herself spoiled goods. She's got a black thumb crushing her heart. I can't seem to fix it."

This didn't seem to be the moment to laugh and tell him to turn up the charm. Katie took another bent nail from the one-pound coffee can, and, laying it on the anvil, tapped it straight again. All the while thinking of the words Ruth had spoken, when the two of them huddled for warmth.

Without looking up, she began speaking. "Gram used to tell me hunting and fishing were guy things. Making cookies was for girls. It didn't matter that I could bat a ball better than most boys. There was no place for me on the fast-pitch team, but I could play softball with the rest of the girls. I remember I wasn't happy, but it wasn't the worst thing in the world. On the sly, Poppa taught me to gut fish, dig worms, and cast. It was only natural when it came to being time for him to go hunting. I wanted to go with him. I had a good eye, drew a fine bead, and Gram would allow me to go down in the sandpit to practice shooting, but it took a solid argument for me to be able to go with Poppa into the woods. They stood toe to toe. He reminded her that she had learned to hunt, and so had my mother."

Rick laughed. "I didn't know that not everyone in the state of Vermont didn't hunt until I was a grown man. We were a large family and a couple of deer every season made an enormous difference around our table. It seems to me, I remember your grandfather bragging about you getting your first deer, a five-pointer. And that you did it all, including field dressing and dragging the deer out of the woods."

"Yeah, it was a long haul back to the road." Katie grinned. "We had been talking for weeks about where we were going to hunt. Gram said we only had to go as far as the orchard, but Poppa had bigger plans, and we went up to Eagle Drop Ridge. He said there was still plenty of food and water available, and not cold enough for the deer to go lower into the hardwoods and swamps. The deer would still be up there. Instead of walking, we hunkered down in a blackberry bramble and waited."

"How many times did you get stuck on the thorns?" Rick asked.

"Too many to count." Katie sat back on a wooden apple crate, hands in her lap, one wrapped around the hammer, the other holding the nail between grubby fingers. "The day was perfect; crisp but not frigid, clear with barely two inches of new snow on the ground. Poppa whispered we would get a deer that day and a turkey the next. It sounded like a perfect combination. I knew we were going to get the granddaddy of all deer. But nothing happened. After a while, we left the brambles and moved down the ridge on Dean's side. There was a place they had clear-cut out the softwoods. I was so frustrated. We wandered back and forth on the clear-cut. There were plenty of signs, scrapes and trails, but no sightings."

"Happens like that more times than not," said Rick, holding out another piece of lumber.

Katie stood up, taking the piece and fitting it in between the sidewalls.

"You know, Rick. It took a long time for me to realize that when that buck walked into view, it should have been Poppa's deer. He had a better line of sight than I did, yet he motioned me ahead and held my shoulders steady while I took the shot. When the deer leaped ahead, Poppa dragged me with him after it. I must have been in shock. I don't know. I just sort of froze up."

"That's not unusual, first deer and all," said Rick.

Katie thought on about that long ago day in the woods with Poppa. How he had talked her through each step of field-dressing the deer. Even so, it had come as a surprise when he said it was up to her to drag it out. But she wanted to please him, and though her arms felt like they were going to tumble off, she kept on. Near the end, she had gotten slow. To speed her up, he shoved a handful of snow down the back of her jacket. Then stood with his hands on his knees, laughing until every animal for twenty miles was long gone. Back at the house, gram snapped photos while grinning like a jack-o-lantern. Never saying a word about them having gone against her

20

wishes.

"So, Miss Katie," said Rick, reaching over to straighten the board she was about to nail into place. "What has all this jawing got to do with Ruth's feelings?"

Katie readjusted the board to where she'd had it and laid the level on top. Rick had been right, but he didn't say a word when she hiked one edge up another inch.

"I don't know. You and me. Down here. The rest of the world seems so far away. I think about Poppa so much, and you just seem to be the person who would understand about him the most. Then, yesterday, when we were sitting in the truck hoping to be rescued, Ruth and I were talking about Gram. We were all alone. She was talking, you know, about going to school with Gram long ago. Then how they grew up and things changed. Somehow, there was this bit about her meeting George, and for the first time, realizing he was a grown man. But I guess, my point is we all have our memories, some of them are of the same event, and yet, each one is slightly different. Even our own memories seem to change with time."

"I know exactly what you mean. Even about that deer hunt." Rick stacked left-over lumber to the side. "The way your grandfather was going on, you had to be this big, strong Amazon, born with a brain full of wood lore. Somebody who didn't know you would have expected a lot more than one puny girl."

"I wasn't puny." Katie pouted in silence for a few minutes.

"Did she happen to mention me?" Rick asked casually. "Ruth, that is, while you were waiting in the truck."

"Yes, in passing. She also spoke of this guy who was really interested in her, but who couldn't get up enough nerve to ask her out. She called him shy, but isn't that akin to scared?" Katie took a quick peek. It seemed in the light of the overhead forty-watt bulb. her carpentry buddy was blushing.

"How is it you got her talking about George?" Rick asked. He held a piece of narrow planed wood in his hand, rubbing back and forth, feeling the grain. "Usually, she refuses to talk about him at all. Even I can't get her to open up." He laid aside the plank, and taking the hammer, hit in a few more nails before looking at Katie. "You know, when I first met Ruth, she was already darn near the cutest girl in town, but what an attitude! Irma led her into that. I always said so. I was out of school and working at the furniture factory. Suddenly, overnight, she graduated high school, and the next morning, she was one heck of a beautiful woman. Always spit and polish. Hair just so. You know, wearing a bit of jewelry. Her dresses all had these little round, white collars. And she was fond of short fuzzy sweaters. When a couple of the guys at the mill asked her out, I scared 'em off.

"Then the day came that George Beauregard came home from the army. I remembered him from high school. Even back then, he was a rich man's son, full of himself. For all his charm, he had a mean streak. His half-brother was three years younger, and George would go out of his way to make the kid look like a fool."

"Wait a minute," Katie said. "George has a half-brother."

"Christopher." Rick was putting the tools away and missed the confused look on her face. "Didn't you know they're related?"

"Well. Yeah. But I didn't know they were half-brothers. Even Ruth spoke about them like they were family."

"They are really, Katie. Old man Beauregard was married, and he and his first wife had George. When he was barely a toddler, his mother fell off a hayrick and broke her neck. So, Mr. Beauregard married June Tucker. She was the second Mrs. Beauregard. Together, they had Christopher."

"So, Mr. Beauregard had two wives and two sons?" asked Katie.

"Mr. Beauregard, Senior, had two wives, but he had at least three sons that we know of. There's talk there might be more." Rick picked up the pint jar and frowned at the tiny words written on the label. "Truth is, he was known to be quite a dog."

"Rick, Ruth also said she was caught holding the knife the morning they found her George dead."

"That's just a figure of speech," said Rick. "And one she shouldn't use. She was there, blood all over her nightgown. But that knife was buried so deep in George's chest, it took two men to pull it out."

Katie took the pint jar and hid it in the woodpile. "I'll come back for that later."

Suddenly, the lights went out.

"Power's off," said Rick. "You go on up. I'm going to fill the furnace."

Katie found Ruth trying to tug the second mattress down the stairs alone. With Katie helping, a flashlight in hand, they got the last mattress, the one from Rick's bed, into the living room. Together, they got the twelve cats currently in residence in the main room and an ample amount of cat boxes spread around.

"Rick's not going to be happy sleeping with a cat," said Katie.

"If I go downstairs and find another empty jelly jar in the woodpile, I'm not going to be happy either," said Ruth.

Uh-oh, thought Katie. *And here, I thought that was a good hiding place.*

Chapter Three

At 5:30 A.M., according to Katie's windup alarm clock, there was still no electricity. The snow was so deep, she wouldn't be able to flounder through it to the chicken coop.

"Maybe if I'm going to go out there, I should just bring the chickens back to the house with me," she said, then burst out laughing at the look of horror on Rick's face. "Just kidding."

The snow was still falling. They could see the top of the windows and the roof of the coop. The trees on the other side of Fire Lane 61 were invisible.

"After I get the furnace filled, I'll get the tractor running. This is going to be a heck of a lot of snow to move," Rick said.

While he was gone, Ruth remarked about the shelves Rick had built and was now ready for the jars of canned vegetables she and Katie had put up in the early fall. "I won't be able to sort them out of the boxes with the electricity off, not if I have to hold a flashlight in one hand while I'm at it. On the other hand, with the furnace down there, it'll be warm." She looked toward the cellar door, lips puckering together. "He better hope I don't find any empty jars."

Katie immediately remembered the one in the woodpile, but before she could rush down the stairs, Rick was back. On his way to the kitchen door where his coat and boots waited, he passed her the sticky jar which she hid under soapy water in the dish tub. Turning to the stove for the teakettle of hot water, she moved back to the sink to find Ruth, who had taken her place, pulling the jar out from beneath the suds.

"Rick!" Hissed Ruth.

"Actually, Ruth, it was me." The look on Ruth's face caused Katie to bite her lip. "Yeah. I, ah, noticed there was seepage on the side of the jar. I figured the seal wasn't good and threw the jelly away."

"Smart move," said Ruth. "You're already learning."

Rick at the door, wrapped to the bridge of his nose in coats and scarves, raised his eyebrows. Then, without a word, hurried out the door.

Katie picked up a dishtowel. "Ruth, you didn't tell me Christopher Beauregard was George's half-brother." She hoped to get Ruth talking again, maybe have her reveal more information about the event that had occurred while she was far away couch surfing in Illinois.

"It didn't really matter, did it? I mean, I didn't tell you that George and his girlfriend, Mildred Hooper, had five kids either, did I?" Picking up the clean baby bottles of warm puppy formula, Ruth walked out of the room. The set of her shoulders told Katie; she had been told all that would be forthcoming.

* * *

Even though she stalked away from Katie in the state of high dudgeon, as her Irish grandmother had been fond of saying, Ruth's inner workings quaked. It had not been her intent to say a word about George to Katie. Ever. Yet, locked in by snow and buried in a ditch, she had said things that had been squeezing her heart for days. It was like this every year. She would make it through the early part of November, enjoy a good meal with Irma and maybe a few of their friends on Thanksgiving, and then when evening came, darkness would bring with it the ghosts and the evils they had committed.

She wanted to stop talking, but once the words started coming, it was an avalanche. Wanting to take back each syllable she had uttered caused her a physical pain. Then once again she had opened her big mouth, revealing to that poor girl, who already had more on her plate than was healthy, bad things from the past. But all that she had said was a terrible truth. Lifting Sophie, she rubbed the pup's soft fur across her cheek, comforting herself and wiping away the tears.

25

Chapter Four

Irma Roser Moore had left behind cupboards and cardboard boxes filled with papers, notes, and newspapers when she passed away. Over time, Katie had sorted through them, casually discarding most. After finding a few five-dollar bills among odd pages, she had slowed down and flipped through every single one of them. In the midst of everything else were complete Burlington Free Press sections. Katie had read every article about Parentville, separating it from the rest and eventually trimming out anything that could possibly be relevant to the murder of George Beauregard and the questioning of his widow. The attitude of the news story was dependent on the reporter writing at that moment. Much of the information was convoluted and disorganized, leaving Katie even more confused.

When Ruth was first recovering from her medically induced confusion, she had confessed her husband, George Beauregard, had been murdered while they slept in their bed together. She had not offered much in the way of information, but said few people in Parentville besides Irma had remained friendly when the police released her. With no local family, and no place else to go, Ruth had moved into the farmhouse with her childhood friend, Irma Roser Moore. Together they had collected cats and eked out a living.

The pages and articles Katie had cut out were hidden in her bottom dresser drawer. When the day of ongoing snow and no electric radio got long, and Ruth dozed, Katie pulled out the pages. There were a few photographs among the newspaper articles. One showed George in his military uniform. Katie had to admit, he did look dashing. There was another, of a small house, barely bigger than a bungalow.

I've seen that, Katie thought. *I'm not sure where.* She tilted her head to the side. *And maybe a little different.*

While she was trying to work out where she might have seen the house, and put the articles and Irma's sprawled notes in chronological order, Katie came across a mimeographed sheet and forgot all of her other thoughts. The sheet had two punch holes on the top, so it had been in a file somewhere. Both were ripped out, and the page had been folded and crushed. The peculiar crease lines left on the mimeograph paper couldn't be smoothed away. Bold letters across the top identified the page as having been part of an OFFICIAL INCIDENT REPORT. The top third of the sheet was lines and spaces dedicated to identifying information. Katie didn't pay any attention. The bottom of the page was filled with the badly typed description of the incident site as the writer had seen it. The sparsely furnished house, the dead man in the bed, the top end of a thirteen-inch hunting knife that was buried to the hilt in the man's chest, and the hysterical woman in her nightgown with blood, hand-prints on the front.

"That's a heck of a big hunting knife," Katie whispered to herself. "If Ruth didn't kill George, and she wasn't holding the knife, why was she covered in blood? Did she try to revive or save him?" Ruth's description had been brief. George was dead, she was taken for questioning.

While Marlie had still been working as a sheriff's deputy in Parentville, before Geoffrey Ash had insinuated he knew about her sexual orientation and would ruin her if she didn't leave. She had told Katie about her first cop lesson.

On the first day of training, the first thing the instructor said was, Get a small notebook and a reliable pen. Every morning when you suit up, put it in your pocket. It's like your weapon. Carry it with you all the time. You're going to be given a lot of information. Much of it will be garbage. The only way to remember it all so you can sort it out later is to write it down. You'll remember the sensational parts, but the tiny kernel of truth will be lost. Write everything down. Don't be afraid to ask somebody to slow down or repeat what they are saying. Marlie had laughed hardily. *He was absolutely right.*

Sitting snowbound in the stagecoach house on the ridge above the

27

Parentville village proper, Katie's thoughts touched Marlie. Her laugh, love of her job, and now her despair. Katie could feel herself sinking into depression. This was not the time. And that was not the subject she needed to be concentrating on at the moment.

"Shake it off, Katie-girl," she whispered aloud. "Marlie was right. Get a piece of paper, start writing. Make a list of what you know is true, and what is gossip."

In the kitchen junk drawer, she found a three-by-five-inch spiral notebook and a half-chewed pencil.

Good enough, she thought, ripping out the pages of old lists and returning to her seat.

The wood stove in the kitchen glowed with heat, the fireplace in the living room crackled, sending dancing shadows to the ceiling. Outside, Rick played with the Massey-Ferguson tractor like a boy with a new Christmas truck. Katie sat in her rocker, pulled up close enough to the fireplace so she could rest her toes on the hearth while she read and re-read the newspaper articles. Folding them all back together, she looked toward the sofa beneath the living room windows. Ruth was wrapped tightly in a quilt while several cats snuggled around her. In the cardboard box beneath her fingertips, Sasha's ears dipped repeatedly as she washed the puppies. Their whimpering cries did not sound fearful, but content.

You've given me so much, thought Katie. *I never even knew you existed. And you just keep giving.*

Ruth wiggled in her sleep, freeing herself from the weight of the cats and yawning as she woke. Katie rushed up the stairs to hide her papers away again. But returned, determined to discover what Ruth didn't know or couldn't remember. Ruth had put the puppies out on the floor to stretch their skinny legs. Seeing the older woman smiling happily at the trio of gangling little mutts, Katie paused.

That's all, she thought. *I'll just ask around a little. If you come to realize no one blames you, then you will be able to forgive yourself.*

"Aren't they just the cutest little things?" Ruth smiled, unaware of Katie's thoughts.

"They certainly are."

Katie raised her eyes to the window. Outside, the snow was stopping, only an occasional spitting fell from the lead dark sky. Rick and Raymond Dean were both working on the road with their tractors. Rick's as old as he was, and somebody else's throw away. Raymond sitting high on the seat of a shining John Deere. Two men separated by a generation, both of the soil, and both working toward the same end.

Rick came in half-frozen while Katie was frying a cast iron pan full of ham and pickle hash next to a pot where water boiled for poached eggs. She had hand-ground the potatoes, onions, and left-over baked ham before confiscating a few of Rick's coveted sour pickles. Once the ground pickles were added to the mash, it was dropped into the hot skillet by the spoonful. The outside of the patties would fry crisp and brown. Gram had called it the poor man's steak. The gallon pickle jar was still on the table.

"Have you been eating my pickles?" Rick asked accusingly as he unwrapped his scarf.

Ruth came out of the living room tsk-tsking about frostbite.

"Not yet," said Katie. "I made enough hash for sandwiches tomorrow. We've got boiled biscuits to use for bread."

They ate by lantern light and were just finishing when the electric lights blinked back on. The refrigerator began to hum happily, and Rick sighed.

"The cats can go back to sleeping in the cat room," he said.

"And tomorrow, we can go back to work," said Katie.

Chapter Five

T he house didn't heat up fast enough for everything to be put to rights that night, leaving Rick still complaining about cats sleeping on his bed in the morning. Katie, happy to escape outside, dug the pickup out of the drifts to drive herself to work. On the way, she made a quick stop at Beauregard's General Store and Mercantile for canned milk. The three puppies had healthy appetites, which seemed to explode when they had grown big enough to scramble around when put on the floor. Personalities were developing, but all of them whined and chirped when hungry or cold.

In the back of the store, Christopher Beauregard was wiping the glass meat cooler out with a rag and a bucket of bleach wash. Katie stopped, watching him over the top of the case.

"Sorry," said Christopher, not looking up. "The meat counter isn't going to be open until I get done cleaning it out. There was some spoilage while the power was off. Can't have that, you know."

"Yes," said Katie. Then her mouth worked independently of her brain. "To be honest, I was wondering about your brother. You know, George."

Christopher stood up slowly. "What?" His eyes narrowed.

Katie's heart raced up into her chest. She hadn't meant to say anything. The words had surprised her as much as they had taken Christopher back.

"I'm sorry." She blushed until she felt like she was melting inside the horse blanket lining of her canvas barn coat. "What I meant was that while I was in church, I saw the little placard beneath the stained-glass window of Saint Joseph with the lambs. It said in memory of George Beauregard."

Christopher was stone still, one hand on the case, the other holding the dripping rag. He was breathing high in his chest, then with an effort, took a deeper breath.

"I don't remember your brother, but I think the window is a beautiful thing to do in his memory." *Run away*, she thought as his chest expanded with a second deep suck of air, but her feet were planted to the planks.

Finally, Christopher spoke, not particularly chilly, but with a definite rebuff. "That window is actually for my father. He was also George Beauregard. But you wouldn't know that being from away and all."

Katie didn't bother to correct him. She was sure he knew who she was and that she had grown up in this same village. Until that moment, she had not remembered there had been two George Beauregards. The thought that it was possible the ugly memories she had heard were confused between the two ran from one ear to the other through the center of her brain. How much of what had been said was for the younger one? Were both men lousy husbands, or had all the bad she heard belonged to just one?

"But I appreciate your thought." Christopher stared down the length of the aisle behind Katie. His tone hadn't softened, but picked up a note of sadness. "It would be nice to do something for my brother. He was a great guy, always willing to help out. My mentor really, a family man, soldier, one of the solid citizens that built this town."

He went back to cleaning the case. With a quiet goodbye, Katie moved away.

"That was a surprise," she said to herself as she drove towards Baldwins Feed and Hardware. "Maybe all the bad belongs to George, Senior because Ruth didn't say anything bad about Christopher. I was surprised, and it shut me right down, because I thought the stained-glass window was for his brother, not his father. Christopher seemed pretty broken up after he got done being snarky. He didn't say his dad was a good guy, but that George was." She drove along, chewing on her lip. "But on the other hand, Rick sure had an attitude about the younger George." Pulling into the feed store parking lot, she considered that Rick's bad memories could have been caused by jealousy, and all the years of happiness lost.

She was a few minutes late arriving, and the doors were already open. There was a flurry of activity at the feed store. Fortunately, the parking lot had been plowed out well. Now it was filled with pickup trucks and station wagons. Even with the wide-open spaces between snow-banks, Katie had to park far in the back near the sheds. Between the surging rushes of customers, Katie and Cindy helped with the restocking, mopping up of snow-melt puddles, and when given a moment, chatted about life in general. Cindy had a degree in real estate development, but was mostly a stay-at-home mom. She and Stan had three small children. The oldest had just started first grade. When Katie had decided to stay in town long enough to satisfy the terms of Irma's will and not forfeit the farm, Cindy had helped her develop a plan for renting out the sand pit. The deal earned enough money to start paying off the back taxes and help put food on the table.

"Yeah, so now that my mother is living with us, I can leave the kids with her and come down to help out." Cindy sat back on her heels from where she was stocking a lower shelf. "Does that sound terrible? Leaving my kids and mom so I can be somewhere else?"

"Where are you getting adult time besides here?"

"You are so funny, Katie. When you have children, you forfeit your right to adult time for the next twenty years." Cindy's knees cracked and popped as she got to her feet. "Did you hear that? I already sound like an old lady. Anyway, Mom's been camped out in the guest room, but yesterday when we were all trapped inside, Stan and I started talking. We're going to have the garage converted to a mother-in-law apartment. We only use it to store the kids' toys, anyway."

"That sounds pretty awesome," said Katie. "That way, you'll get some privacy, and so will she. I have to admit, I was on my own so long that living with Ruth and Rick can get under my skin at times." *Not to mention there's no way to have Marlie around.* The thought of Marlie caused a yearning burn in the pit of Katie's stomach.

"Mm," Cindy pulled open another cardboard box. "So, what's new at your house?"

Katie sighed. "We had a weird exchange, Ruth and I, while we were stuck in the snow. She was talking about when her husband died. I wasn't living here then. Not only that, but when I ask other people about him, I seem to be hearing a wide variety of descriptions of George."

"Who else has been talking?"

"His brother, Christopher. I thought the new stained-glass window at the church was in memory of the son, but I guess it was for his father. I remarked on it this morning and Christopher went on to tell me what a saint George Junior was."

"A saint?" Cindy guffawed. "I barely knew the man, and I can tell you that's not right. Every time he came in here, he was totally wasted. Ask Stan. He knew. Some farmer would send George in to pick up the order, and even though we always say cash on delivery, George was always short. He'd say that was all whoever his boss, at that moment, had given him. That it wasn't his mistake. A month later, he'd be working for some other poor Joe who couldn't afford better and stealing from him, too."

Katie got to her feet beside her friend. A customer walked up and stood in front of the cash registers, but Stan had come out of the office and was cashing them out. Cindy laid a hand on the younger woman's arm.

"That's not all, Katie. George was a violent man. He hurt Ruth badly. So terribly she couldn't remember what had happened to her. I'm ashamed to say, like other people, we knew, sort of, yet no one did anything."

"Maybe it isn't that she can't remember, but that she won't," said Katie.

"No. I don't think so. As long as I've known Ruth, there was this blank look. If something like that was on her mind, I'm sure it would have shown in her eyes. All the bad stuff that happened with Ruth got worse when George's other family moved into the village."

"What?" Katie shook her head, her brow furrowed. "He moved his trash and kids into Parentville?"

Stan came walking up the aisle toward the women, pushing the two-wheeler with more stock loaded on the platform. "Are you two taking a break here?" he asked. "I just made a fresh pot of coffee. Why don't you go sit down for a bit? The guys from the feed shed are having a break. We'll probably get busy again about three when school gets out."

33

"Stan," Cindy laid her hand on her husband's chest, stopping him.

She's a real touchie-feelie, thought Katie. It wasn't a judgment, just a fact based on seeing Cindy physically reach out to others she was talking with. And remembering the comforting hugs, not a bad thing.

"We've been talking about Ruth, or George, actually." She looked at Katie, silently asking how much more she should say.

"Look, Stan." Katie wet her lips. "I didn't know Ruth before I came back. When I first met her, she was sick, confused in her mind. Now she's better. But something is changing again. There's some fact I don't know that's keeping me from understanding what's going on. I'm afraid I might have triggered it by asking about my grandmother. There seem to be boundaries to what Ruth either can remember or is willing to talk about. I can't recognize them. I just know Rick is also a little off. Is it because of the holidays? Am I overreacting?"

When Katie showed up in town after Irma's death, there was a fair-sized chip sitting on her shoulder. Stan, always gregarious, had laughed at her, not viciously, but in a friendly manner, yanking her back to earth. When it was evident there was a problem between Katie and Sheriff Lewis, without even knowing who she was, the merchant had stepped in, diverting the sheriff's attention and giving Katie time to get out of the line of fire. She'd come back to the feed store looking for a job. Though he had been looking for a strong young man, Stan had taken her on to work out in the feed shed with Rick. Now they were more than employee and boss. His family, and her related-by-a-roof group, were friends. He, as well as Cindy, looked at Katie like a younger sibling just trying her wings, but still in need of occasional guidance.

Stan pointed his wife toward the cash registers in the front of the store, then said to Katie, "Let's sit in the office, have a cup of coffee. I can get some work done while we talk. Maybe if you know the basics, you'll be able to see clearer."

"Gram had a lot of papers which had news articles about George Beauregard and his murder. I saved them. I just can't figure out when everything started to go wrong for Ruth. If she was found not guilty, shouldn't she have gotten better?" Katie sat with her back to the door and the window that looked out onto the selling floor.

"If I'm not mistaken, you're asking for a timeline," said Stan. "I'm not one to gossip and I probably don't know a lot about what happened, but I'll tell you what I have for facts."

Katie nodded, took a sip of her coffee, and waited for Stan.

"Ruth's problem with George started the day she married him," said Stan. "I can tell you this because my father told me. He was in the army at the same time George was. He came back after George. Years later, after I was born, dad was in his cups one night, and I heard him tell my mother that the army was the perfect place for George because he was a narcissistic sociopath. By that time, Ruth and George had been married several years. She wasn't working anymore except as a volunteer at the school and the church. That's where I saw her, at the school. I was a student; she was a teacher's aide. Even back then, there were days she'd come in heavily made up. It seems I remember her talking about being clumsy, falling down, running into something, common stuff like that. No one said anything, but we still heard gossip at home, or here. This is where I spent my time, helping dad and learning the business. The same way Christopher Beauregard did. Anyway, near the end, the older Mr. Beauregard got kind of weird. George was spending most of his time in Bristol with this other woman. I heard there might have been a kid. He had been hired and fired twice at the furniture factory. I don't know how many farmers he had worked for. Then suddenly, a family moved into the little house on the corner of Main Street and Parentville Road. Right across the street from the mercantile. I didn't know them until school started. There was a girl in my grade, her name was Geneva Beauregard. She was the youngest kid in her family. Didn't talk much. Most of the village kids had been told by their folks to stay away from the bunch of them. Geneva's family didn't go to church."

"Let me guess," said Katie. "This was George's other family. He moved them here right under Ruth's nose."

"They were George's children, but he didn't move them here." Stan put his coffee aside. "His father did. I never saw George anywhere near them. Or heard he was either. But the old man introduced the kids to people as his grandkids. I don't think their mother mingled much. The older two worked in the store. Later we heard George Senior, paid all the bills. If his drunken son wasn't going to take care of his grandchildren, Mr. Beauregard would. But that might be just gossip. It's true, however, that June didn't want them in the store. She stopped working when it was clear the youngsters were going to, and that any time Mildred Hooper wanted anything, she would walk in and help herself."

"Mildred was the mother?"

"Yes. So, let me just tick off some things really quickly," said Stan. "There was an episode where the sheriff was called because Ruth kept standing across the street staring at the house. She was gone for a few weeks after that and when she came back, it wasn't often we saw her out on the street. George had a new girlfriend, or maybe a bunch, I don't know. I just know there was a huge row in the middle of the street one night after the Wagon Wheel Tavern closed. Mildred and George were duking it out, I heard. That was Veteran's Day weekend. George was strutting around in his army uniform. He couldn't even get his shirt closed over his big belly. Then Thanksgiving came, and four days later, George was murdered."

"Whoa, wait a minute."

Katie searched her brain. How had she missed the fact the anniversary of George's death had been less than a week earlier? That was the trigger, the reason Ruth was so distraught. Before they could continue, Cindy knocked on the glass. There was a long line in front of her register. Katie needed to get back to work. For the rest of her shift, she looked into the eyes of her customers, searching for something in their minds related to what Stan had told her. But it wasn't until closing time she realized what she should have been looking for was someone who looked like a Beauregard.

Chapter Six

There were two pay telephone booths in Parentville. Katie avoided the one in front of Beauregard's General Store and Mercantile and stood in the dark glass booth at the end of the creamery entrance. The door would barely close because snow had drifted in and frozen. With a pocket full of coins, she dialed Marlie's telephone in Rutland. It was long distance, and they wouldn't have long to talk, but calling on the party line was out of the question. There were just some things no one else could know.

"Hi, Marlie." Katie breathed when her love answered the phone. "I've got about enough money for eight minutes."

"Then tell me you miss me. Everything else can wait until next Tuesday," Marlie said.

"Your boss gave you the day off?" Katie smiled in the dark. Tuesdays were her regular day off, and with Rick at work, she and Marlie might actually get to spend a few minutes together.

"Yes. Why wouldn't he? There I was telling him I wanted to work on Saturday and have a day off that no one in their right mind would ask for." Marlie was chuckling into the telephone.

"Let me tell you about Ruth," Katie began.

"Is it an emergency?" Marlie asked. "If not, tell me about it when I get there. Right now, let's talk about you and me. The stuff we can't say when every pair of ears in town is listening on the line."

"Oh, Marlie. You make me feel good." Katie sighed. "Talking to you makes me feel so much better."

Marlie giggled. For six and a half minutes, they talked about them.

Chapter Seven

Instead of church on Sunday, Rick and Katie spent the morning moving piles of snow from one place to another. Because there were only two farms on the road, the Took's and the Dean's, and it was a fire lane, not a thru street, they were often one of the last for the town plow truck to get to. Instead of waiting, Raymond Dean, and Rick did most of the work by themselves. Raymond and his big John Deere tractor were all the way down on the corner of Fire Lane 61 and the Parentville/Charlotte Road, when Charlie came along with the town sander. Knowing the grade up to the farmhouse would be slippery, Charlie turned the sand truck around and backed up the hill, spitting sand out as he went. That gave the town's heavy dump truck enough traction to keep moving forward in a backward manner.

Ruth met him outside in front of the farmhouse with a hot cup of coffee and a sandwich. While Katie and Rick moved their vehicles so Charlie could drop a little sand in the parking area, he consented to return for dinner that night.

"If I'm not here by six, go ahead without me," he said. "I've been at this for thirty hours straight. I may be too tired to come out." With that, he shifted into first gear and headed back out of the fire lane, leaving more sand in his wake.

"Where is he living since the fire?" Ruth asked Rick as they all went back inside, and she headed up to the second floor. The apartment house Charlie lived in had gone up in flames just before Thanksgiving.

"I don't really know," Rick answered. "But he sure looks rough."

"Is it the thirty hours plowing snow and sanding or the roughhousing?"

Katie asked.

"Don't know. Ruth, Grace is out front blowing the horn," Rick called up the stairs.

A moment later, Ruth came clattering down. She and Grace were going to Williston to do their big every two-week grocery shopping. Even though it was Sunday, the grocery store was open, unaffected by the blue laws that forced other businesses to close. For Grace, with her family and at-home goat cheese and butter business, doing a big shopping every other week was a necessity. Ruth, however, found the excursions that usually happened on a Friday morning an exciting adventure. She always got dressed up for the trip to the Grand Union Grocery Store, carried a list, and paid her fair share when they stopped for lunch at Howard Johnson's.

"You've got your list, right?" Katie asked. "And the extra money I gave you?"

"Yes, yes." Ruth's cheeks were red with excitement. On top of her regular list, she would be gathering the goodies needed for the cookie boxes she and Katie planned on making as Christmas gifts.

After Grace's station wagon crept down the hill, Rick returned to moving snow. Winter had just arrived, and already the banks were high. At this rate, by spring, they would be parking in the street. Katie added fuel to the stove and took on the chore of dragging the mattresses back upstairs. Never far from her mind, while she worked her way through the list of chores, was Ruth. When her chores were caught up, Katie headed down to the Dean barn for some quality time with Bonita Belle, her big girl buddy.

In the barn, the black and white Hampshire pig, now tip-toeing past the two hundred-pound mark, planted her front hooves on the edge of the feeding troth, stretching up to reach Katie. Bonnie had been Katie's first animal pick-up with the town. Some prankster had tied the thirty-pound shoat, or teenage pig, to the back of Sheriff Lewis' cruiser. Though most town folk found it amusing, the sheriff did not. Deemed a rescued pet, if Katie couldn't find a home for her, somewhere guaranteeing she would never grace a dinner table, she couldn't be adopted out.

Right now, that was fine with Katie. Bonita Belle had been right there, throwing her weight into the fray, when Irma's killer attacked Katie. It had been an unfair fight, according to the killer, but neither Katie nor Bonnie thought so. With no heat in the tumbling-down barn behind the stagecoach house, Katie had accepted Raymond Dean's offer of a space in his cow barn until the spring. She and Davey, Raymond and Grace's oldest son, had a working agreement on caring for Bonnie. Not wanting to be forgotten, Katie made it a point to visit the pig every few days.

Katie finished mucking out Bonnie and spent a few minutes talking to her while sharing the carrots she'd brought and scratching the wide black and white back. Leaving the pig snuffling around the fresh bed of wood shavings, the young woman headed up the rise. The sun tickled the banks of white into sparkling, blinding beauty. The dark wood of the barren oaks and lilacs only magnified the intense white. It was as lovely as it was dangerous. *A wolf in sheep's clothing*, she thought.

There was nobody home except Katie. The big old stagecoach house felt like an empty cavern. A few cats prowled around, but most were curled up, paws tucked in and napping. Peanut called for Ruth. When she didn't answer him, he followed Katie. LG watched with a jaundiced eye. It wasn't until Katie shut the bathroom door and filled the tub, however, before LG got noisy about her aversion to Peanut in her spot.

Katie sat in the tub washing her hair while outside the door, LG uttered plaintive meows.

"I hear you," said Katie. "I'm already in the tub. You're going to have to wait."

"Meow."

"You're fine. I'm right here."

"Meow."

Katie laid back to rinse her hair. Totally submerged except for her face, she opened her eyes just in time to see Peanut jump up onto the curved porcelain side of the tub. Before Katie could react, the young cat lost his footing and tumbled into the bath water. Flailing claws caught Katie's legs, and both of them yowled. Scooping Peanut up from behind, Katie dropped him over the side onto the mat before she pulled the plug.

41

On the floor, Peanut coughed and sputtered. His red fur was even darker now that he resembled a wet hedgehog.

"That wasn't real smart," said Katie, stepping onto the mat beside the hapless feline. "No wonder LG is making so much noise. Where were you hiding?"

Wrapping a towel around Peanut, she gave him a good rubbing before setting him aside to tend to the rest on his own. Three thin rivulets of blood ran from her left calf down to the mat. Katie stepped back into the tub to cut down on the amount of mess her wounds created on the floor. She rinsed, and applied Mercurochrome and bandages.

"I haven't had on this many Band-Aids since the training wheels came off my bike," she told Peanut. He was busy trying to lick the water out of his hide.

When the bathroom door opened, LG gave Katie a scathing glare. Tail in the air, she stalked away. Her human would receive no pity today. Katie dropped her pig-stinky clothing into the laundry and made it all the way to the door at the bottom of the stairs before LG appeared again. This time when Katie opened the door and headed up to her room and fresh clothing, the gray/green tiger cat whisked through. On the return trip, Katie had to carry LG back with her or risk closing her upstairs. LG seemed fine with the ride, but once they were on ground level, she leapt away.

Katie made herself tea and toast. Sitting with her back to the kitchen stove, she waited while her hair dried. She was still there re-reading some of Irma's clippings when Rick returned. A car engine was heard in the drive, then the slamming of a couple of car doors. Ruth ran in, kicked off her boots, and with her coat still on, ran through the living room and up the stairs. The armful of bags was a dead giveaway. She had done some Christmas shopping, and she didn't want to share her purchases with Katie and Rick. Together, they stepped outside to retrieve the bags of groceries left at the end of the walkway.

"Seriously, Rick?" Katie groaned. "I thought we said Christmas would be a meal to share with our friends."

"Yeah, we said that." Rick hung his coat on a peg by the door and poured

42

cold coffee into a small saucepan. Setting the pan on the wood stove, he retrieved a diner mug for the quickly steaming liquid. "Ruth said maybe one small thing."

"That looked like more than one small thing," said Katie.

"Well, there's you, and me, Chet, Charlie, maybe Grace, the Yankee swap at church, knitting group, and the library board."

"Phfft. We've got sixteen dozen cookies to bake." Katie swapped her tea for what was left in the saucepan of coffee.

"Something smells good," said Ruth. Peanut trotting behind her. "What have you got going for supper?"

"All I can smell is pig poop," Rick said.

"Be quiet," both women said at the same time.

Among the items in Ruth's bags was an eight-pack of Crayola crayons, which she had brought back downstairs with her. She had been saving brown paper grocery bags, carefully cutting each one open to store them flat. Using the crayons, they would decorate their own Christmas wrap.

Charlie never made it for dinner, but Rick promised that if Ruth made the other man up a plate, Rick would make sure it got delivered first thing in the morning.

Chapter Eight

Even at work the next day, Katie searched the features of customers, practically absolute strangers, searching for somebody who would remind her of Christopher, and therefore, George. It wasn't until late in the evening, when Marlie arrived, those thoughts were pushed from her mind.

Everyone was all smiles as a short, generously endowed woman arrived. Her cinnamon skin glowed with health and excitement.

"Well," said Ruth, also short, as she wrapped their guest in a hug. "I was starting to worry."

Rick pshaw-ed and pulled Marlie far enough into the room to close the door behind her. Both Katie and Marlie stood there grinning, trying not to look at each other or reach out for a caressing touch.

"We've got plenty to keep you busy while you're here." Ruth crowed. "Tomorrow, we're making cookies. Dozens and dozens."

"It's a good thing we have plenty of eggs," Katie said with a sigh. "I made up my room so you can sleep in my bed."

Marlie's eyes flew open, but she was quick to recover. Katie realized the implication of the words she said to her love.

"You know, in my room. I'm going to sleep on the couch with all the fur balls so I can watch the puppies," Katie explained.

"Actually, the puppies are big enough so they can make it six hours between feedings. Would you like to see them?" Ruth asked Marlie.

"I'd be lying if I said no." Marlie allowed Ruth to draw her over to the cardboard box where Sasha and her rapidly growing brood were resting.

44

"They are so adorable!" Marlie gushed. "Don't you just want to keep them all?"

While Rick went on about the prowess of the four-week-old Solomon, Katie studied Marlie.

"You look kind of stressed," she whispered.

Marlie turned to look at the older couple tucking the puppies in for the night, and thereby avoiding eye contact with Katie. She had left a letter at home that might destroy any chance they had of a future. There was no way around it. She was going to have to tell Katie. *Now is not the time,* Marlie thought, but said aloud, "I worked all day. It was a long ride on really messy roads. I think my eyes need a nap."

Everyone agreed it was time to turn in. With Ruth leading the way, and Rick carrying Marlie's small suitcase, they climbed up to the second floor. Only Katie returned. From where she lay on the sofa, cats wandering back and forth on top of her while seeking the best spot, she listened to footsteps on the floor above. She could tell when each person climbed into bed. After a few minutes of silence, she heard Marlie's low words coming through the heat vent.

"Good night, Katie. Sleep well."

Chapter Nine

Katie and Ruth were already mixing cookie dough, and Rick was gone down the road before Marlie roused.

"I'm so sorry," she said, rubbing the sleep sand from her eyes. "I can't believe I slept so well."

"You didn't miss anything. We're just getting started. This is sugar cookie dough," said Ruth. "It needs to chill before rolling. Have some coffee. We're making five kinds of oatmeal cookies next. You can help with those."

"Why would you want five different kinds of oatmeal cookies?" Marlie asked, accepting a plate holding scrambled eggs and bacon from the warming oven.

"Same cookie, different treat inside. You know, chocolate chips, or raisins, walnuts, or coconut." Katie put the tall circular container of Quaker Oats on the table.

They followed the recipes, mixing cookies, and after a spirited debate, elected to use the electric oven and save on the number of burned bottoms on the treats. While Katie and Marlie measured and stirred at the long farmer's table, Ruth moved back and forth, handling all the day-to-day that was needed. But with each pass through the kitchen, she reminded the giggling pair, she would be ready when the frosting work started.

"I bought all kinds of jimmies and sprinkles," she confided.

Much of the time Ruth spent was in another part of the house, Katie spent describing her concerns about Ruth and Rick.

"I wasn't working here yet, when the murder happened," Marlie said. "So, I don't have any firsthand knowledge. I do know that Sheriff Lewis keeps a locked file cabinet in the office of case files. If he has a file, that's where it is. I've never seen it, Katie. Much of what I know is the same as you are discovering. You'll probably end up with more, because you know how you get what you want when you need to find out something."

Katie blushed and looked away.

Marlie reached out a flour-covered hand. "It's not a bad thing."

"How's it going?" Ruth called out as she sailed through to the cat room with Old Tom in her arms, and Peanut trailing.

It was near noon, when on the pretext of looking for something in the barn, Katie was able to get Marlie away. The barn held Irma's hoarding of treasures found at the dump, left at the curb for the taking, or yard sale bonanzas.

"What are we looking for out here, exactly?" Marlie, standing in the cold, swung her flashlight around the interior, which contained mounds of stuff, some of which were salable. There was a lot that was just plain junk.

"A twin bed," said Katie. "But I already know where it is. Ruth will stay busy watching the cookies in the oven and frosting the sugar cookies." She laughed in embarrassment. "This isn't what I expected to do to be able to spend some time alone with you."

Marlie turned into Katie's embrace, murmuring, "It's okay." Again, the memory of the letter surfaced, but hiding her face in the rough fabric of Katie's barn coat, she pushed the thought away, down deep in her mind. "This coat stinks."

"Hey, if it was good enough for my gram, it's good enough for me," said Katie.

"I meant the coat actually stinks, not that it's old. I've been watching Ruth. Are you sure there's a problem? Why are you worried? She looks okay to me."

Katie gave Marlie a more in-depth view of the two of them, Katie and Ruth, being stranded in the truck, the emotional tone of the conversation with Ruth, and the switch up when Christopher Beauregard was talking about his brother. "First, he was all snarly, then, I don't know, sorrowful."

"Don't trust him, Katie," said Marlie. "Or at least, don't turn your back on him. I've never had a problem with either Christopher or his wife, but Sheriff Lewis can't stand the man. He won't go in that store to buy a piece of penny candy."

"You know Lewis is a bigot and a jerk, right?" Katie asked.

"This is different. It's deep-seated. They are of an age, so it might be something that happened in high school. I don't know, but Lewis is downright surly where the Beauregards are concerned."

"Was Brad a deputy here when George Beauregard died?" Katie asked.

"No. I don't know, maybe. He didn't transfer in much ahead of me. There were two slots. The guy got the first one, of course." Marlie snuggled closer. "Is that all we're going to talk about, Katie? Some guy who has been long dead?"

Their time was fleeting. When they were ready to return to the farmhouse, each carried a part of an old maple bedstead that had found a home in the barn. They made a quick second trip back to get the side rails.

"We'll wipe it down and put it in the parlor," Katie told Ruth. "If we can come up with a mattress, we'll at least have an extra bed should it be needed."

Chapter Ten

Marlie stayed until breakfast. Then she, like Katie, had to leave to be at work on time. Ruth was left to guard the cookies from Rick, who had already made inroads in the oatmeal chocolate chip variety.

"What?" He demanded. "Taste testing."

"First, the apple butter, then the cookies." Ruth shook her head. "You had better have something else planned for today, or you're going to spend your day off locked in your room."

Katie wished Marlie a safe trip home and had to settle for a hug while Ruth and Rick stood watching from the front porch. Only the memory of the stern look Ruth had given the old man when she warned him about the unauthorized taking of both sweets relieved the anguish of watching Marlie drive away. It also provided a reason to smile as Katie drove through the tall snow-banks and then the village on her way to Baldwins.

Starting at the post office and continuing through town were wooden cutouts of Christmas trees, wrapped gifts, candy canes, and stars. It had been a group effort between the boy scouts and the volunteer firefighters. The tall wooden stakes had been planted in the ground before the freezing weather, and the previous Sunday afternoon, guys young and old had gone out and installed their creations.

"I hope you guys got compensated with lots of hot chocolate and maybe some brownies," said Katie as she passed a mischievous wooden elf standing on the corner.

Cindy was not working, and Davidson, behind the second cash register, spent a fair amount of time complaining about the Christmas music WJOY was playing. Lack of Christmas spirit did not stop the young man from stuffing his face with all the holiday goodies that were already finding their way to the break area outside the open door to the furnace room. More than one employee spent their break sitting between the door jambs, feet stretched toward the tall, steel-encased furnace. Heat traveled through the duct system, but wasn't retained long on the showroom floor. The large wooden structure of the feed store had virtually no insulation and was built on a concrete slab.

About the time Katie started longing for time to huddle close to the furnace, WJOY played the daily announcements.

"For residents of the Douglas Development in Parentville," said the announcer. "Ida Jarvis is asking for people to keep an eye open for her wandering Basset Hound. If you see Walker, please call 482-1234. Thank you."

"Oh, Walker. You bad, bad boy," groaned Katie. The dog was a frequent animal control officer pick up.

"Katie," Stan called from his office. "Ida Jarvis is on the phone."

"Tell her I'll drive out on my lunch," said Katie.

Twenty minutes later, Katie shivered in the front seat of the pickup, hoping the ancient heater would warm up quickly. Passing through Parentville again, she took a right on the Mechanicville Road. After passing a small area of older houses, and Philip Carwell's garage, she came to the intersection where a right turn would take her to Douglas Development. The small farmhouse on the corner was the residence of Ida, the newer mobile homes installed beyond were set on what had at one time been farm property. Katie left her truck parked in the first driveway she came to, and proceeded on foot. Three trailers further on, Walker lay on the deck of an absent owner, basking in the weak sunshine.

"You are a bad dog." Katie smiled as the basset's thick tail thumped on the wooden planks. "Come on; we're going home."

"I can't tie him on the run, Katie." The elderly owner, wrapped tight in a saggy sweater, pointed to the high line Katie and Rick had strung earlier in the season. "The snow is deeper than his legs are long."

"Keep him inside. I'll see if I can get somebody over here to plow it out," said Katie.

Philip's wrecker was out when she drove past. "I'll have to call Rick," she said to herself. Suddenly, she was tromping on the brake, sending the truck fishtailing. Out the driver's window, she was looking at the house that had been photographed for one of the articles about the Beauregard murder in Parentville.

"It's the same house. I know it is." Katie bit her lip. "White instead of gray. The little deck is new, and the shutters. But everything else looks the same, except the bird feeders and the Christmas tree in the front window. I'll have to ask Rick. No, better Philip, I think."

She spent a couple more minutes staring, then drove back through the village. Once again, a house caught her eye, the small clapboard building on the corner. It was across the street from the four-foot-tall elf, but right in his line of vision. Beyond it was a two-story brick house, big enough to frame the white wooden one with its peeling paint and tilted porch. Though the residence looked abandoned, a thin stream of smoke rose from the kitchen chimney.

In the feed store, Stan told her to take a few minutes to warm up. Katie used the time to call home and leave a message with Ruth about Walker's run.

"Is Rick going to drive his tractor over there?" Stan asked.

"Hopefully, he can get one of the young guys from the fire department to plow it out," Kate said. "Does Mildred Beauregard still live in the house on the corner, across from the mercantile?"

"Hooper, not Beauregard." Corrected Stan. "She died of cancer. I don't know how many years ago. I have no idea who is living there now."

"You'd think this hick radio station would break down, maybe play a little Zepplin." Groused Davidson.

"Foolish boy. Zepplin is rock. This is country." Katie chided.

The line to cash out was gone. Katie waved Davidson away with a flick of her fingers. Left alone to straighten out the racks closest to the front counter, she thought dreamily of her short time with Marlie, ignoring the other woman's edginess. When that train of thought began to depress her, she moved over to wondering how to help Ruth. There was a short list of people to ask for information. Fortunately, Katie was not beyond asking them all.

Chapter Eleven

Without Marlie to help her, Katie ran aground, trying to figure out how to get information. Marlie had agreed that the mimeographed official report page had been torn from a file. "Police and legal binders don't work like the black three-ring binder you had in high school." Marlie had explained. "Instead of flipping the pages back and forth, they are attached at the top by a two-hole metal wing clip. On the right side are all the important pieces, and on the left are the backup or less important notes. In some cases, possibly, but maybe not all the stuff is in there. Sheriff Lewis keeps a second file for connected interviews, third-party observations, and stuff like that. Mostly because there can be a lot of it, and important information would be lost in the shuffle. If the file was his, on the front would be FILE 1 OF 2. He is partial to black magic marker."

With only the page, Katie had no idea who it had belonged to. Knowing Irma didn't believe the law always worked in the public's best interest, she was aware her grandmother could have come into ownership by devious means.

There weren't a lot of places that had a mimeograph machine. The library was too small, the high school wouldn't be a place Irma hung around.

So, she either went to the bank in Charlotte or the town office here, thought Katie. She had business to take care of at the town office. She'd stop in, maybe casually ask about the mimeograph machine. Normal conversation, right?

Janice, the town clerk, had been a school chum of Katie's mother. She was always friendly and had even discretely helped Katie out during the search for Irma's killer. Janice was also the person who collected Katie's chits for animal incidents. After they were processed, she also sent out the checks. Janice flipped through the stack to make sure each chit was signed. While Janice checked out Katie's paperwork, Katie looked over the other woman's shoulder. There was no mimeograph machine in sight.

"Janice, does the town have a mimeo machine, you know, in case I need a copy or something for my, ah, tax guy?"

Janice nodded toward the selectman's office. "Ten cents a copy," she said. "Kind of sparse this month, huh?"

"Yes," said Katie, specifically not pointing out three of the chits were for bringing Walker home. "I'm sure in a few months there will be more calls than I want."

"Mm."

Katie stood still. That mm sounded like a prelude.

Sighing, Janice laid the chits on the counter and crossed her hands on top of them. Looking Katie in the eye, her mother's old friend said, "There is gossip going around that you're out asking questions about the George Beauregard murder."

"How would you have heard that?" Katie asked, startled at Janice's statement.

"Knitting club."

"Do they send you a copy of their minutes?"

Janice raised her hand in the girl scout pledge sign. "Knitter."

Katie's eyes narrowed. "Was Ruth part of this conversation?"

"No. To be honest, Charlene and I always sit down and have a little chat before the group shows up."

A woman stepped through the front door into the lobby; both women twisted to look. The woman greeted Janice, then proceeded into the selectman's office. When Katie looked back across the counter, Janice was gone. The door to the side, which offered entrance to that inner sanctum, opened.

"Why don't you step in here?" Janice asked.

Katie sat in the same chair she had once stood on to be tall enough to eavesdrop on a conversation in Sheriff Lewis' office. The two rooms shared the same vent system.

"Before you get on your high horse about Charlene, you need to know she spoke only in the best interests of both of us," said Janice.

"How's that?" Katie asked. She felt a little twitchy, like Janice was going to play Mother and tell her to back off.

"Well." Janice licked her lips. "We are assuming you are checking around about George, hoping to find out who hated him enough to kill him?"

Katie's ego deflated. She had thought she was being discreet. But apparently, she was not.

"Okay," she said slowly, and then, with more conviction. "Yes, I guess I am."

Janice was also hesitant. "Then you need to know that not all of George's enemies lived in Parentville. I have, or had, a cousin who lived in Monkton. Her name was Edna Barrette. She was known to be quite wild, and while in high school, her parents allowed her to marry a man at least ten years older than she was. He was a mechanic, or maybe some other type of repairman, and worked in Bristol. Anyway, they weren't married long before she figured out that wasn't where she wanted to be and moved back home."

"Though they had let her come there, it didn't work out well for her parents because they couldn't control her. It wasn't until she showed up pregnant that they threw her out. Edna didn't settle down after the baby was born. If anything, she got worse. I didn't have a lot to do with her ever, but because he's from here, when word got out the child's father was George Beauregard, I knew who he was. Charlene mentioned what you were doing in the event I wanted to tell you."

"Is there a reason you specifically would?" Katie asked.

"Edna was a wild child. She just was. Her fate was her own doing. What happened to her broke my aunt's heart, and I loved that woman. Edna left Jim Nattress because of George Beauregard. She got pregnant with Pam because of George Beauregard. I am as sure as I am sitting here right now. She got hooked on booze and drugs, and then finally blew her brains out, because of George Beauregard."

Minutes passed while Katie contemplated the big government clock on the wall and tapped her feet.

"Do you know where Pam is?" she asked.

Janice gave her directions to a house barely ten miles from where they were sitting.

Chapter Twelve

"Has it occurred to you to have a candid conversation with Ruth?" Cindy asked the next afternoon. She had come into town to the store to do the payroll and was sitting behind Stan's desk when Katie called Dr. Gillian's office, asking for an appointment to discuss Ruth's health.

"Yes." Katie replaced the receiver slowly. "It's hard, Cindy. I don't know what I'm really asking. What if I offend her? Or she just won't talk to me?"

"What about getting Grace to talk to Ruth? She's the one who got Ruth to go see Doctor Gillian when she was still sharing a practice in Monkton."

"I'm going to talk to Doctor Gillian this afternoon. Maybe she'll tell me if she thinks Ruth is strong enough emotionally to handle the hard questions."

"Ah huh," said Cindy. As Katie turned away, the seated woman added, "I don't think you give Ruth enough credit."

Katie didn't answer. Her life was complicated. There were so many secrets from everyone, except Marlie. Or at least Marlie knew the big secret. Stan and Cindy had gone out of their way to help Katie save the farm from becoming just another housing development. All over the county, property like hers was being snapped up. Seemingly, overnight mobile homes or tract houses were filling the landscape.

The first day she had met Ruth, she thought the woman was odd, but mostly in an old-person way. As time went on, she realized her first impression had been generous. Ruth hadn't lived with Irma. Irma had taken care of Ruth. With Gram gone, Ruth had become Katie's problem, one that she had planned on abandoning as soon as she figured out what to do with the

57

seventeen cats. Several of the original cats were gone, some to new homes, others lost to advanced age. Ruth, however, was still there. Then there was the alien in the backyard episode, which both Grace Dean and Katie had witnessed. On the day Grace took her boys to Doctor Gillian, she took Ruth. The remedy had been surprisingly easy. The root of Ruth's confusion was a cocktail of drugs her old physician, Doctor Darlpin in Parentville, had prescribed and never altered.

Doctor Gillian had continued to treat Ruth after that first visit. When the young doctor bought the Parentville village practice, Ruth had been standing at the door the first morning waiting to say hello and welcome while holding out a tin of date bars. That was the first thing Katie had taught her to bake and the elderly woman's go-to favorite.

Now Cindy worked on the store's payroll books, occasionally raising her eyes to Katie. When the bell rang, summoning Katie to the front end, Cindy spoke up again.

"Instead of running around town asking questions that might possibly irritate a hidden murderer, you might want to stick to talking to Beauregard family members other than, you know, Christopher."

"Like who?" Katie asked, already hustling out the door.

"Well, Mildred Hooper's grandson works here."

Katie was already moving away, and tried to catch herself, stumbling as she turned back toward the office door. The telephone was ringing, and Cindy was intent on answering the call. The bell for the front end rang again, and Katie hurried to her register beside Davidson's. When the line began to dwindle, she asked him what the names of his grandmothers were.

"The one I know is Lynn," he said. "She used to live not far from here. Now she lives in Fort Lauderdale. I'm going down to visit her over spring break."

"Nice," said Katie. "Have a good time."

* * *

"Well, Katie," Doctor Gillian said as soon as Katie entered her private office.

"I've been doing a little research."

"I bet you have. I heard you walked into a real mess."

"I can't talk about it. The case is still ongoing while the representative to the state medical board, and I go through Doctor Darlpin's records."

"Is it bad?" asked Katie.

"Let's just say there are some places we may never be able to make it right." Doctor Gillian opened a file on her desk. "I pulled all of Ruth's records I could find. The basement is full of case files, so there might be more down there. Shoveling that out is going to take time. What I have started when she would have been in seventh grade. She came in for inoculations. Then there's a big gap. I'm not comfortable sharing it all with you, But I will tell you that about five years into her marriage, she came in about a broken arm. The records say it was a bad sprain. Even back then, Darlpin referred to her as of a hysterical nature. However, there is also a note questioning possible concussion. Ruth came in a couple of times with different ailments and was prescribed. That's where we start seeing the beginnings of the medicinal problems. She wasn't alone. Doctor Darlpin passed out a lot of prescriptions with no end date. She trusted him. If he didn't tell her to stop, she believed she should keep on taking the medicine."

"Grace told me a lot of elderly people are like that. They feel the doctor has an education they don't have, and he knows what he's doing. Like he can remember every pill he passes across the desk."

"Exactly. There's a notation of the incident you were asking about. Ruth was standing in the parking lot of Beauregard's. That's the general store, right? This says she had been there a while. A resident called the police, who brought Ruth into the office. Darlpin wrote that she was distraught, exhausted, and suffering from dehydration. He kept her here for two hours. She did not regain lucidity, but became more agitated as time went on. Eventually, she was transported to Mary Fletcher Hospital for evaluation. He writes she was admitted to Baird 6, that's the psychiatric floor, where she stayed for two weeks. His recommendation was the state facility in Waterbury, but the attending at Mary Fletcher elected not to go that route. When she returned home, her husband brought her in for the shakes.

That's when she was given her first prescription for a sleep aid medication. Unfortunately, when that drug was replaced with something stronger, she still had access to the first."

"And because that quack didn't tell her not to, she took both." Katie surmised. "Does it say how she was transferred to Burlington? Did her husband take her?"

"It doesn't say." There was a hurt look in Doctor Gillian's eyes. "And, Katie, it's not all on the doctor. Even if he is a quack."

Katie was mortified. "I'm sorry, I really am. That's not what I meant. Doctor Gillian, the anniversary of her husband's death, just passed."

"I know," said the doctor.

Cripes, did everybody except me realize it? Katie thought. "Ruth has been a little off for a few days. Not like she's confused. But she will remark on something, or start talking about George. I want to talk to her about it, but I don't want to shove her off a precipice. Any advice?"

"Maybe Ruth needs to talk to a professional. I can get some names for you."

Katie stared at the hollow of Doctor Gillian's neck. She and Ruth and Rick had been all over this before. There was no way Ruth would voluntarily see a shrink. Katie felt so distraught, the skin around her eyes ached. She came here hoping for a miracle trick that would take away Ruth's angst. Then she and Rick, and by extension, Katie would be good.

"Katie?" said Doctor Gillian, reminding her where she was.

"Yes. Maybe a list. We can talk to her, see if she is more open to it now."

"Perfect," said Doctor Gillian, smiling at Katie.

Katie smiled back. Unbeknownst to the doctor, it was more a thank you for her time than an acknowledgment they might have found a solution.

"Oh, one more thing," said Katie, with her hand on the doorknob. "Do you treat any of the Hoopers?"

"I don't recognize the name," said Doctor Gillian.

* * *

Pulling into the driveway at the farmhouse, Katie found a vehicle in her spot that she immediately identified as Cindy's Rally STX van, with the telephone pole bump in the middle of the front bumper still marring the nose.

"When are you going to get that dent fixed?" Katie asked, kicking off her boots.

"I told you if I get it fixed, I'll hit something else. It's a karma thing." Cindy was sipping tea at the table with Ruth and an unknown older woman.

"I've been telling her the same thing, but she says sliding isn't the same as hitting. She doesn't need to fix it." The new woman at the table was certainly Cindy's mother. There was a strong resemblance, right down to the smile.

"You must be Mrs. Fontana," said Katie.

"Donna, please," said the woman, eyes twinkling over her Mrs. Santa Claus' cheeks.

"Rick told me you were baking up a storm," said Cindy. "Mom brought several pints of homemade candied fruit with her when she moved in. I thought we'd share."

"That's lovely of you," said Ruth. She set a plate of homemade oatmeal cookies down among the teacups. Rick was very noticeably absent.

"I told her not everybody likes fruit cake, but she didn't listen." Donna blushed.

"While Ruth and Mom get acquainted, let's look at the puppies," said Cindy. "Are you interested in a puppy?"

"Absolutely not." Cindy moved away from the doorway between the kitchen and the living room. "Let's give them some space. What did the doctor say?"

"Is that why you're here?" asked Katie.

"My mother recently retired. She used to work in the Goodrow Clinic in Burlington. They served the mental health needs of the less financially secure segment. I know I should have asked first, but I wanted her to have a little conversation with Ruth before I tainted her thoughts. Doctor Gillian?"

"The once, but no longer, Doctor Darlpin, is guilty of a lot of things. Bad practice being one. She suggested Ruth meet with a specialist who she could talk to openly. My take on what Doctor Gillian was willing to say is that

Ruth's health is improving, and her mind is clearer. She is questioning what she remembers against what people are saying or what actually happened."

"Who would be talking to Ruth that you wouldn't know about?" Cindy asked.

"Ladies at church, in the knitting group, maybe even Grace." Katie picked up Solomon. He really was a cute baby. *Don't get attached*, she thought. Out loud she said, "It might not be so much a conversation as Ruth is sliding the occasional quick question in. If so, she's only getting bits back, like I am. It's very confusing."

"What's going on in there?" Ruth called out. "Did you two fall asleep?"

Half an hour later, Cindy and Donna left, and Rick emerged from the cellar.

"Let me smell your breath," Ruth demanded, "so I can tell if you've been in the apple butter."

* * *

While Ruth and Rick quibbled over the disappearing apple butter, Katie took the leftover roast chicken carcass out of the refrigerator and broke it apart in a five-quart saucepan. She added water and a cut-up onion and left the pot on the wood stove to simmer until what was left for meat fell off. After separating out the bones, she put the pot and the stewed chicken and water in the refrigerator. The good smell of chicken soup filled the house, and though her inclination was to finish with it then, she went to bed.

Chapter Thirteen

"How many are we expecting for Christmas dinner?" Rick asked.

"The three of us, Chet and Charlie," said Ruth. "That's it, I believe. Philip and Arnelle are going to her mother's house."

"He's going to enjoy that," said Rick, topping off his coffee cup.

"Marlie's coming for Christmas, too," said Katie.

"No, she's going to her grandmother's." Ruth was keeping a keen eye on the oven timer. She had date bars baking and didn't want them to be dry.

Katie stood beside Ruth. "She didn't tell me that."

"You were in the bathroom when I asked her," said Ruth. "Her grandmother asked her to come for the day. Of course, she's going." Ruth turned to Katie. "Wouldn't you?"

Nodding, Katie turned away. *No wonder she acted so tense. Why didn't she just tell me?*

As if guessing her thoughts, Rick said, "She knew you weren't going to be happy when you found out."

She watched her elderly friend cross the room and rinse out his cup. She wondered if he had guessed her secret. The one she shared with Marlie. It was the reason Marlie had left her much-loved job as deputy sheriff. To be able to bring Geoffrey Ash to justice, she had to accept the fact that just as she knew about his secret life; he knew about hers. Now Marlie sold gas and candy bars, hoping for the day she could return to law enforcement.

* * *

63

Living in the old stagecoach house on the ridge above town meant living where the wind would frequently twist and play. Ten minutes before they left for work, Katie or Rick would step outside into the cold and start both vehicles. Rick's truck never hesitated, but being ten years older, the vehicle Katie had inherited from Irma had days it would ruh-ruh a bit before catching. Once sure neither would stall, a walk around to the front to make sure snow hadn't drifted in front of the tires was usually all either one wanted to experience in the early morning chill.

Katie threw the last shovelful of snow aside, then rubbed her foot against the frozen ground to test the need for sand.

"Katie." Ruth stuck her head out the door. "Father Metevier is on the phone. His cat is missing."

"For how long?" Kate called back. "All night?"

The door closed. Kate leaned the shovel against the wall on the porch where it would wait for the next call of duty and stepped inside, nearly colliding with Ruth as she came hurrying back.

"He says she asked to go outside this morning, so he let her. Now he can't find her."

Each animal call-out meant a chit turned into the town for payment. Winter calls were few. The wild critters had found a hidey-hole for their winter nap. Household pets stayed close to home.

"Tell him I'm leaving in a couple of minutes, and I'll stop on my way to work," Katie said.

Elderly Father Metevier had adopted the long-haired, gray, and equally advanced age cat from the brood Irma had left behind. She had gone to be a church cat whose purpose would be to catch mice in the vestibule. It hadn't taken her long to move into the parsonage. When Katie pulled into the dooryard, Father Metevier, in only a sweater with his cassock brushing the tops of his handmade slippers, was descending the front steps.

"Thank goodness you're here, Katie-girl. I'm so worried. The wind is raw, and she's just a baby."

"No, Father, she's a seven-year-old veteran of barn life. You, on the other hand, are in danger of pneumonia. Step inside. Go on."

Katie had brought with her a can opener and a can of mackerel. The strong fish smell was sure to tempt any cat or raccoon in the vicinity. Father Metevier handed a small bowl out the door, and after leaving a healthy helping right beside the kitchen entrance, Katie stepped inside. Once a tall, sturdy man, the cleric was hunched over with age, fingers white as frozen lake water gripped each other. But though drooping and showing the signs of cataracts, his eyes focused on Katie, reminding her of who he had been in her youth.

"Remember last fall when I was trying to live-trap the raccoon that lived under the porch? I told you back then, keeping Boots safe was your responsibility."

"But she so loves to go outside," he said.

"I know. And I caught her in the live trap three times before I caught the raccoon." She put the half-empty can of mackerel in the refrigerator. "Even though it's six-thirty, it's still dark. If she wants to go out during the day, there are rules. Never before daylight, never if it looks like snow or rain, and always back inside before dark."

"Those are good rules," he agreed.

Katie opened the door and scooped up the gray cat whose nose was buried in the bowl of ground fish. "You are the shepherd of her flock, Father. Tend to them."

Father Metevier accepted the cat from Katie's arms, burying his nose in her fur. "Yes, of course you are right." Behind him, the teapot whistled on the stove.

Laying her hand on his arm, she said, "Never be afraid to call me if you need. Better sooner than later. Now, a hot cup of Sanka and the both of you will be fine."

At the door, Katie paused. "Father Metevier, do you remember George Beauregard, Junior?"

"Well, I married George and Ruth, didn't I?" He sat Boots and the near-empty bowl on the floor. "Why are you asking?"

Katie debated for half a second. "I want Ruth to be happy, and I don't think she will be until people stop wondering if she killed George."

Father Metevier looked up, startled.

"I don't think she did, Father. But I am concerned the killer is still right here walking around the community."

The priest lifted the singing kettle off the burner, then reached for two Blue Willow coffee cups. Katie cringed at the thought of drinking Sanka, but it appeared he had something to share. She unbuttoned her coat.

"I knew George as a child. He was about ten when I first came here. Even then, he was a willful boy. Already handsome, spoiled by his father in the way the child of the manor would be. He had a lot of followers and chose who would be his friend from one day to another."

"That's pretty direct," said Katie.

"Have you ever heard the phrase of two minds?" Father Metevier scooped a level teaspoon of Sanka into each cup before adding boiling water. "For people in the clergy, and I'm sure some other careers, it means that I know the same people in two different fashions."

At her confused look, he offered a can of condensed milk and sugar, which she declined before continuing.

"I know you as your confessor. The Keeper of your Faith. In you, I know you are unsure. One day you are here, another you are not. Your heart is generous, but fearful."

Katie blushed. Father Metevier looked solemn, but then he smiled, and his face lit up.

"Then I know you as my friend. A happy, strong girl that I can call upon if there is a need, as can others. I have seen the love you've given to Ruth since you adopted her. It is a good thing."

Blinking at the reference of her adopting Ruth, a woman almost forty years older, stunned Katie. She cleared her throat.

"About Ruth and George?" She choked out.

"Yes, as I was saying, George was the child who always had a pocket filled with candy, leading others who rarely had any. In high school, he was respectful in a belligerent manner. His parents were members of the congregation, always donating with a flourish when others watched. They were not, however, people of solid faith. He went into the army and returned as a hero. I never saw him in church until they were married, and after, he attended for only a few months. Yet, I heard about him all the time."

At Katie's look, he said gently, "There is a lot of dirt under some people's rugs. They empty their souls here, but that doesn't mean they ever alter their ways."

"Ruth attended church with her family throughout her life. They were decent people. Even when misfortune fell, they carried on. Their faith was more easily discerned. Even Ruth, sweet and innocent, had confessions to make that concerned me. However, I was surprised when she appeared at my door with George asking me to post the banns. He was not her type, not really. There were other girls who would have been better suited. But she was a beauty, and trusting."

"Are you saying George took advantage of Ruth?" Katie asked, anger rising.

"No." Father Metevier cradled his cup to his chest. "She saw him as he was. I know she did from things she told me years later. But Ruth believed she could change George, save him from himself. He was a glittering prize for a young girl who had never quite had enough. Or maybe she was just finding her independence and didn't know it came with perimeters."

"Now you're telling me Ruth wasn't a sweet, young thing?" Katie asked.

"Oh, she was young. And I'm sure she was sweet and passive, but she was also independent. She wanted a solid life like her folks had, but she wanted the party part, too. They got married, lived alright, as far as I know, for several years. There were no children, but that wasn't for me to ask why. George was working at the furniture factory. I remember one day we, Ruth and I, were working side by side at a fete. I asked why George wasn't attending. Ruth came right out and said because there was no beer tent. Then she must have realized what she said, because she told me how he was having a hard time at the furniture factory. They had promised to make him a supervisor early on, and nothing had come of it. Shortly after that, there was a bad accident at the factory. A particularly large slab of wood had fallen off the planer. Two men got hurt. One of them was George. Almost broke his back. He was a long time recovering. That was about the time Ruth stopped coming to church on a regular basis."

A plaintive meow drew the attention of both people to the kitchen door. "See, Katie? She's asking to go out," said Father Metevier.

Katie got up and buttoned her jacket. "And you're going to tell her she can. At 9:00 A.M."

Chapter Fourteen

The little clock on the bedside table said three-thirty. Katie was wide awake and cold. Silently she pulled on her clothes and, once at the bottom of the stairs, left the door to the hallway open so more heat would find its way up to the bedrooms. Rick had stacked plenty of wood near the wood furnace and in the kitchen stove wood box. Katie filled them both. To keep the cats silent, she tossed a couple of handfuls of dry cat food across the floor. Searching out the goodies would keep every fur ball that was crowded around her ankles busy. The puppies' box had been moved into the kitchen, but they slept through everything that was going on. Taking the saucepan with the left-over chicken stock and a bowl of green beans from the refrigerator, she sat the pot on the hot stove and chopped the beans into small pieces. When she was through the green beans, she dumped them, along with a couple of handfuls of macaroni, into the simmering pot. The aluminum pan heated quickly, and soon the odor of chicken stock was rising again. Katie stirred, added some chopped celery from the freezer, and filled the metal cup inside the percolator with coffee grounds.

The coffee finished first. Pushing LG off her lap, Katie poured hot water from the kettle into her cup to preheat it, then dumped the water back into the reservoir and refilled the cup with strong coffee. The pasta was tender, and the soup was thick and ready. It didn't matter it was breakfast time, Katie ladled soup into a bowl. For several seconds she sat with her nose near the surface of the soup, allowing the steam and healthy homemade smell to fill her senses. It felt good, like her grandmother. For that moment, she was safe and protected. All the worries that everyone was warm and fed were

69

not hers. Even the cats had quieted down and gone back to napping or the endless bathing. Old Tom showed his acrobatic abilities, wrapping his fat body in a knot to wash his butt.

Rick came through the doorway yawning, flannel shirt buttoned wrong and the hair on the back of his head sticking out all around like the Statue of Liberty crown. After pouring a cup and filling a bowl, he took his seat at the table. The two of them ate in silence, with the exception of an occasional slurp.

Katie had finished and was depositing her bowl in the sink when Ruth came in.

"I hope all the cats are down here, because I closed the upstairs door." Her words were followed by a healthy sniff. "Soup for breakfast?"

Katie ladled another bowl, then swiped a particularly large chunk of onion from the inside of the empty pot. While Ruth settled down to her soup and coffee, Katie filled the sink with dirty dishes and wiped down the counters. Rick watched her warily.

Eventually, she sat across from Ruth. Rick was down to his last sip of coffee and considering the necessity of tending to the wood furnace.

"Ruth," Katie said with a resigned sigh. "You and I need to have a conversation."

Rick bolted.

"Ah-ha," said Ruth, still intent on her soup. "Toast would have been nice with this."

"Later," said Katie. After a few moments of drumming her fingers, she decided that there was no reason to beat around the bush. "I know that when I first came here, we had a few tense moments."

Ruth raised her head, but Katie lifted her hand, stemming the older woman's words.

"To be honest, if I'd had any experience with cats, I probably would have let you go when you wanted."

Ruth looked across the table with sad eyes. Katie fought the impulse to reach for her elderly friend's hand.

"It would have been a mistake," said Katie. "For way more reasons than one. It's true that by the second day, those cats would have been devouring me for breakfast, but beyond that, I never would have known you. Nor would I still be here. Hell, the way I was going, I'd probably be on a slab in some far-off city."

"Don't be foolish, Katie. You're not a dummy." Ruth pushed the empty bowl aside. "Look at all you've done here."

"Don't try to sidetrack me, Ruth. I don't want to talk about me. It's you that we're talking about."

Ruth quirked an eyebrow.

Exhaling noisily, Katie continued. "When I first came here, you told me that something terrible happened to you. Maybe you took the initiative because you knew I'd hear something about it later. I don't know, and I don't care."

"Is there a reason for all this prattle? Because I've got things to do." Ruth asked impatiently.

"Sit down," Katie ordered, showing her own impatience, which she had hoped to keep under cover.

"If you're going to go on about how it came to be that George died and that you're asking questions about it all over the countryside," Ruth spat out, "let me tell you, I'd have to be deaf, dumb, and tied to a chair in a closet not to know what you've been doing."

"Well, that puts it right out there," said Katie. *It's time to take the white gloves off.*

"I love you, Ruth. I didn't want to. I didn't want to care about anyone or anything here. All I wanted was enough money to get far away and maybe not sleep on a park bench for a while. No, don't say a word; just listen. You told me George had been murdered. You told me you were innocent. I wanted to believe you, but there was this little black and yellow wasp in the pit of my stomach that kept buzzing at me, jabbing into my guts. Then one day it was gone. Just like that. Do you want to know why? Because suddenly, I wanted you to be happy."

"I am happy." Ruth sat back, crossing her arms.

"No, you're not. Not in the place that annoying wasp was stinging me.

You're not. There's only one thing that will get rid of what stops you from enjoying *all* of your life. That's the idea that those people out there, in this village, will stop believing you might actually be guilty."

Ruth tried to keep her features stern, but the slide was like snow from a mountain peak. It started with a small tremble, and before she could stop it, her every defense was gone. Tears slid down her cheeks. Katie fought to ignore them, to keep going with what she now knew had to happen. Clearing her throat, she spoke before Ruth had a chance to.

"Ruth, if the law and Doctor Darlpin had done their jobs competently to begin with, your reputation would be free and clear right now. We both know Darlpin messed with a lot of things, and a lot of people. I'm getting the impression that Sheriff Lewis might have dropped the ball again on this one, or maybe he was over his head. I don't think it was because Doctor Darlpin pushed him to overlook the facts. There was other muscle working to keep a lid on who did George in. I'm out there asking questions so that we can clean up the mess regarding his murder once and for all. If nothing turns up so that we can get a lawyer to handle this, then it won't be because we never tried. The way I see it, that's where this is right now. No one tried. It might have been because so many people thought George was just scum. That part doesn't matter. The thing that does is that you got caught in the fray, and when it was over, you were left floundering."

"You can tell me to back off. We both know that probably won't happen. Or, just ignore me." Katie reached out a hand. "The only other thing you could do is tell me everything you remember about those few days. It might stop me from walking up to a killer and asking questions he won't like."

Ruth gasped. Before she could recover, Rick came hurrying upstairs. Grabbing his lunch pail and thermos, he told Katie he'd make sure Stan knew she'd be in late, and ran out the door. Ruth looked up at the clock. It was a little early for him to be going. She watched the truck pull out, frowning.

"I'm not leaving until we get this done, Ruth. So, if we sit here silently for two hours, I'll be that much later for work." Katie reached behind herself and grabbed the percolator off the stove.

72

"What do you want to know?" Ruth asked.

Katie reached for her notebook. "Tell me about the day. No, start with the morning before, and tell me about your day. We'll get to the other stuff later."

Ruth spent a few minutes thinking. Peanut jumped into her lap. "The day before was Saturday. I remember it was rainy and the kind of bitter cold that makes your bones ache. The church had given us a turkey, so because it was just the two of us, we had a mess of leftovers. I was up and working in the kitchen, real quiet like because George had come in terribly late. Way after midnight. I knew he was going to be hungover." She gave a brittle chuckle. "When he finally got up, he wanted a Thanksgiving sandwich. That's what he called it. Toast stacked with dark meat turkey, stuffing, potatoes, and cranberry. I never ate it, the cranberry, because he liked it so much. I left it for him. So, I made him a big sandwich. He drank half a pot of coffee, took four aspirins, and went back to bed. He had a cold and was a little congested. He was dosing himself right out of the pint bottle he had conned somebody out of. When it was empty, he went back to bed and fell right to sleep. I thought he was all done for the day. I spent the rest of the afternoon trying to keep busy. I had a few things I was putting together for friends. That was it."

"Around supper time, George came out of the bedroom. While I was puttering around, I had made soup, thinking it would help his cold. You know, maybe he would eat and go back to bed. He said the soup was lousy and left. I never was much of a cook. As usual, at nine, I took a sleeping pill and went to bed. The next day was kind of the same, except I felt better and walked to church. I'd go every now and again."

Katie was watching Ruth. While she was talking, her hands were working. When she spoke about the pills, she reached toward the salt and pepper shaker. When she talked about George, she rubbed her face. It was some kind of tell. Katie just needed to figure out what it meant.

"Did George go out that second evening?" Katie asked.

"Yes," said Ruth. "Around seven. He was still hacking and spitting out all this green gunk. I was in the bathroom. Somebody knocked at the door.

73

When I came out, George was gone. I don't know if he would have gone if somebody hadn't picked him up because it was raining. Pelting down, actually." She looked up at the ceiling. "I don't know who it was, but not his friend Hank. The muffler on his truck was shot. This one was much quieter."

"Okay, how about after George left?" Katie asked.

Ruth was rubbing her face again. "I remember feeling a little stuffy, like I was catching George's cold. Not long after he left, even though it was early, I took one of those sleeping tablets and went to bed. It seems to me, it was in my mind that if I slept, maybe I could shake the cold off. I was in bed, then I had to go into the kitchen. I can't remember, but there was...." She faded off for a few moments, then refocused. "Later, I guess I was asleep when George came in. Usually, he's so noisy I rouse a little, but I didn't. And he must have come home earlier than normal because he didn't just pass out on top of the covers. He had taken his shoes and pants off. When I woke up in the morning, I had to pee bad. I snuck off to the bathroom. Coming back, I turned on the light in the hallway, meaning to sneak into the bedroom and grab my robe. That's when I first looked at him. He was lying on his back on top of the coverlet, just as straight as if he'd been laid out. And this big knife handle was standing up like it was a tree that had grown out of his chest. I touched him. He was cold." Ruth stopped talking. Her eyes were on a scene from five years before.

"Ruth," said Katie. "RUTH!"

"I'm sorry. I try not to think about it. There was just so much," said Ruth. She turned slightly away, eyes drifting across the floor, following Sasha's exiting steps.

"Blood?" asked Katie.

"No, confusion. I mean, there was blood. But not as much as you'd expect. It's the confusion that gets me. In a couple of minutes, the house was full of people. All talking, all, I don't know, moving around, touching stuff. I'm sorry Katie. I can't sort it out. It was all fuzzy then, and now it feels like I was sitting on top of the dresser watching somebody else moving around."

"Okay, turn away from George, okay, Ruth? Don't look at him. Try again.

Tell me what's confusing you."

"There were so many things, Katie. When I saw the knife, I tried to pull it out. I know I did, because I can see my hands on it and feel the handle. It was wood and had grooved finger grips. But it wouldn't come out. I kept yanking and pulling. And I felt so fuzzy. Normally, once I'm awake, that's it, but that morning I was kind of drunk. Do you know what I mean? I don't know how Sheriff Lewis and Doctor Darlpin got there. Somebody kept pushing me, and I woke up in the hospital."

"Okay, one thing at a time. You couldn't pull the knife out because the flesh created some kind of suction around it, which also explains why there wasn't as much blood as you expected. Marlie was telling me about that. If the sleeping pill affected you differently than normal, are you sure it was the same medicine you took all the time? Or how about, are you sure you only took one?"

"I only had one real sleeping pill to take. The prescription was five or six years old, so I took them all the time. Doctor Darlpin had given me an anxiety one, but I kept that in the medicine cabinet with all the other pills because I only took it now and again."

"But you kept the sleeping pill somewhere else? Like on the bedside table?"

"No, silly. On the kitchen table." Ruth reached out her hand toward the salt shaker again.

Katie saw it in her mind. It was a habit to reach right over there, where the old woman wouldn't have had to make an extra effort to get the medicine. *Or,* she thought, *where anyone else had access.*

"So, somewhere in there, you called the sheriff? Do you remember when?"

"I didn't call the sheriff, Katie. I told you. I don't know how he got there. We didn't have a telephone. I would have had to leave the house, and I wasn't even dressed."

"What? Who?" Katie was stuttering.

Ruth shook her head.

"Who was shaking you, Ruth? Was it Christopher? Or maybe Doctor Darlpin giving you a shot? That's why you don't remember anything about getting to the hospital. He knocked you out."

"It could have been Doctor Darlpin. I don't know about Christopher. I heard him yelling. First, he was all nice and smiling. Then there was screaming. He was pushing Sheriff Lewis around. They had an argument."

Katie leaned back. That didn't sound right. Lewis didn't like to be touched or pushed around.

"Ruth. Why would Christopher be pushing Lewis around? I mean, yeah, George was his brother, but Lewis is the law. He's there to help."

"Because Christopher thinks he can. His dad showed him that. His dad pushed Al around, and when Martin was elected sheriff, old Mr. Beauregard stood up in front of everybody and laughed at him," said Ruth.

"You've got to be kidding!" Katie exclaimed.

"Nope. It was always like that. Al was the poor brother. His mother walked away from George, Senior. That was it. Martin was like his grandmother and his dad. He never asked the Beauregards for anything."

"HOLD ON! Are you telling me that Sheriff Martin Lewis' father was George Beauregard Senior's son? That your George Beauregard was Martin's uncle?"

"You knew that, didn't you, Katie?"

But she hadn't. After that revelation, Katie couldn't concentrate on Ruth's words.

"I need some time for all you've said to soak in," said Katie. "I'm going to work. We'll finish this conversation later." She shoved her arms into her jacket before turning back to Ruth. "If you think of anything else, anything at all, no matter how small, write it down. Okay?"

Chapter Fifteen

Tucked in the back pocket of Katie's work pants was the small notebook and the pencil stub. Periodically, she would take it out and scan her notes. She had started out just scribbling things down as they came to mind. As she read and then re-read, she realized her thoughts were like a hamster in a wheel, going round and round and not making sense. During her lunch, she ripped out a few more pages and started again.

At this rate, she thought, spreading pages on the table, *I'm going to need to buy another notebook.*

She titled one page, About George, another About Ruth, List of people to talk to. The notes were starting to make sense. She went back to work with a short list of people to interview and a specific person in mind to start with. One that might question her motives the least.

* * *

Contacting Dorothea was as simple as pulling into the church parking lot and descending into the basement. On both the upper and lower door was a notice saying that the Saint Jude Thrift Store was open Sundays from 11:00 to 2:00 and Thursday evenings from 5:00 to 8:00. Every person in town knew Dorothea, age eighty-three and Thrift Store Director, an appropriate title according to Father Metevier, and straw boss by her description, would be there any afternoon, noon until five-thirty. That's when Ellen, her grandniece, and a nurse in Burlington would pick her up on the way home.

"Dorothea?" Katie called out as she swung the lower door open. "Are you still here?"

"Is the dang door unlocked?" A crotchety voice from beyond the depths of neatly folded clothing called back. "Dang fool girl."

At five foot four inches, with a dirty mouth and a nasty temper, Dorothea was a force to be reckoned with. According to her, there wasn't anyone in the danged town of Parentville that was worth a danged minute of her time. She remembered Irma and repeatedly told Katie that if her grandmother hadn't been so danged softhearted, she'd still be walking the danged earth. Dorothea and Katie got along like a hand in a glove.

"What are you looking for today, girl?" Dorothea asked. Steam rose from the hot flat iron encircling her head like an ethereal cloud vapor.

"For you to flap your gums," Katie said honestly.

"Well, if you're gonna be standing here, step up to the ironing board. My shoulder's about shot."

Dorothea believed that just because this was a thrift shop, it didn't need to appear poorly. Every item of clothing that came through the door got a good looking over. Seams were mended, buttons replaced, and shirts and trousers pressed. It was one of the reasons volunteers were hard to keep.

Katie spat on the flat iron to verify it was hot and grabbed the top shirt from the pile. "Tell me about George Beauregard."

"Born the same year as me," Dorothea began.

"Eck. Stop right there. The second George Beauregard."

"Well. Cut from the same stretch of cloth as his father. Raised to believe he was better than most. His stepmother tried. She loved him, really, she did. But that love was twinged with pity. He may never have realized it, but deep in his soul, his spirit did."

"So, he was a jerk from the get-go?" Katie asked.

"Actually," Dorothea sighed. "He wasn't. I was an old maid lady living in the same little house Ellen and I live in now, working at the furniture mill. I came across him one day when I was walking home, hiding behind the old high school. He had taken quite a beating from his old man. I don't remember why, but he was only about eleven. I got him cleaned up, shared my supper with him, and sent him on his way. After that, I would come home to find wood stacked by the kitchen door or the walk shoveled. Nothing real big, but there it was."

Dorothea was sorting and folding jeans. Her gnarled fingers stopped for a moment, lying quietly on the denim fabric.

"Then the military called him, and he went off. Came back a different boy. Don't get me wrong, he left a little bastard, but when he came home, something inside of him had been twisted sideways. He and Ruth got hitched. Her mother cried for days. I don't think she ever quite recovered. The one daughter got knocked up and moved away, one son was lost to the military. I heard he died of drugs, but that could be gossip. The other took off running. That left just the two cuties. Ruth and Vera, who also got married. She and that Touser boy packed that boy's automobile and drove south out of this town as fast as they could go."

"Ruth's mother died maybe a couple of years later. Her father followed shortly. Broken heart, I guess. They knew George was a danger, but they died before it came to public knowledge of how bad he was. Ruth didn't have anybody, nowhere to go, and too much pride to tell the law. Not that they would have believed her. George, Senior carried too much weight."

"What about Mrs. Beauregard? Ruth said she was good to her," said Katie.

"June? She had her own devils. We never heard a word about her and old man George Beauregard. But if the apple don't fall far from the tree, you look back at the tree to identify the apple. Other than Christopher, there were no other children there. No daughter. Maybe June would have helped Ruth. But then the old man brought his bastard grandchildren into the store and shoved them in her face. She couldn't bear it, so she just stayed away. Christopher's wife, Tracey, she was the one to throw the biggest stones when Ruth snapped."

Katie hung the shirt on a hanger, buttoning the first and third buttons as Dorothea had directed. Stretching a new shirt across the ironing board, she asked as casually as she could muster, "I hear you went in to clean the house after George's murder." From below her lashes, she saw Dorothea stop folding and straighten to her full height.

"Katelyn Took, what trouble are you getting into now?"

79

Shrugging, Katie moved the steaming iron across the fabric. "No trouble. I'm just sort of checking."

"Like taking a census?" Dorothea asked.

"Sure, like taking a census."

The old woman selected another pair of jeans, shoving her hands into the pocket and pulling out lint. Finding no holes, she continued, folding the pants. "Well, Little Miss Census Taker, what kinda questions you got on your list?"

Katie chewed her lip, undecided about what to ask.

"Katie?"

Looking up, she found Dorothea had moved silently. Now she stood on the other side of the ironing board. Katie bit down harder and jumped at the pain.

"You and I," said Dorothea, "we're a lot alike. Oh, I don't mean we're any different from anybody else living in this town. But there's something from away as well." Faded brown eyes looked toward the exit, cantered up a bit as though Dorothea could see up the staircase and into the distance. "I went away once too, you know. Yes. But I didn't find it any better. There's no place to hide when you are different way down in your core than most." Looking down at her gnarled, ring-less hands, she whispered, "I came back for a different reason than you. I was scared. Here I could hide among people I had known my whole life. There was some measure of safety there. No one need ever know. I would be the odd spinster, maybe too rough, to mean, for any man to lay a claim on." Shaking her head, she moved back toward the tangle of denim clothing, away from Katie's outstretched hand.

"Ask me your questions, Katelyn Took. Now, before I meet my maker and you have no other chance. Let's see if together we can help some other poor soul."

Taking another shirt, Katie began. "I was told you were the first to go inside the house after George Beauregard was murdered, and the police closed it up."

"I was. Christopher came to me, told me he wanted to sell the place, but it would need to be, as he put it, freshened up. He came right out and told me that he thought I was salty enough not to be scared off by any ghosts. Well, that told me he'd asked someone else, and they'd turned him down. Come to find out, it was his wife, Tracey. She was talking about it in church the next Sunday, how it was a gory mess."

"Was it?" Katie asked, almost forgetting the iron until the smell of scorching cotton caught her attention.

"Heck, no." Dorothea shook her head. "I didn't know what I'd find. I tried to get a couple of the other women from the church auxiliary to help, but they were all suddenly too busy. I went back to Christopher and told him; I would be working alone. Would take me a bit. I was, after all, danged old. He offered me a key so I could come and go as my strength allowed. And," her eyes twinkled as she whispered, "a healthy sum to get it done." Cackling happily, she pushed one stack aside to begin another. "Yep, I was happy to oblige. Anyway, with Ellen working in the city, I got Eugenie to drive me down to the house. She worked at the store for years. Christopher was perfectly willing to send her out to tote me around. She'd come back in four hours to pick me up. Worked well for me. Took a whole week, five days on Christopher Beauregard's dime."

"I thought you said it wasn't bad," said Katie.

"Twasn't. I had it done that first afternoon. Two of the young fellows came in with me that first day and lugged the mattress out. That was the worst of it. I bagged up the rest of the linens, cleaned with bleach wash, and had tea before I left. Come about Thursday, Eugenie stopped at the store on the way home. She said Christopher wanted words. I sweat a little, then. I did because she's a gossip second to none."

"He figured you out?"

"Nah, he ain't all that bright. If he were, he'd a'gone in there and looked before he sent me. What he wanted was for me to pack up the house and clean it up for the real estate people. I told him all that would take another two weeks, and I couldn't do a lot of heavy lifting. He said when I was ready, he'd get Arlo, Eugenie's husband, and some other fellas to do the hauling. Every day after that, Eugenie would show up with the back of her car packed full of empty boxes."

81

"Stop right there," Katie said. "When you went into the house to clean, was there blood all over the place?"

"Nope, only in the bedroom," said Dorothea. "There was quite a mess on the bed and some places Ruth must have touched when she was trying to help George. The rug beside the bed was ruined. Oh, and the bathroom which is off the kitchen needed to be cleaned. I think most of that mess came from them folks that came in to help. The house was pretty sparse, but for the most part, it was neat as a whistle."

"No blood or, I don't know, gore on the walls, or the ceiling?" Katie asked.

"Look at me, Katie. How would I have been able to clean the ceiling? Tsk. I'm surprised you'd asked that."

"I don't understand. If George fought back, there should have been some kind of mess."

"What makes you think George fought back?" asked Dorothea.

"Wouldn't you if somebody was trying to kill you?" Katie asked.

Once again, Dorothea moved closer. "I don't think George was in any condition to fight back, and it looked to me like he'd laid down for the night. His pants and shirt were thrown on the chair. His shoes were off. And another thing on the drainboard was an empty bottle of Jack Daniels. That's expensive whiskey."

"Hold on, Dorothea," said Katie, "are you suggesting whoever killed George was drinking with him?"

"I am exactly. I didn't find enough money in that house to buy a cup of diner coffee. Yet, here's this expensive bottle right there, and in the dish drainer, two water glasses."

"You're sure?"

"Right beside a couple of coffee cups. Oh, and whoever puked in the toilet left his false teeth behind in the bowl."

"Do you know who called the sheriff?" Katie asked, trying to shake away the vision of vomit-mired teeth.

"I do. It was Christopher. Eugenie told me. He went next door and pounded the door almost in until somebody answered."

"I don't understand. I thought Christopher and George didn't get along.

Why would he be there early in the morning?"

"According to Eugenie," Dorothea said, "he was taking George some cough syrup."

Katie narrowed her eyes.

Dorothea's chin raised toward the ceiling. "I remember distinctly because she said Christopher had tried to get Arlo to fix a pipe, or maybe a car. She wasn't sure, but Arlo said he was too tired to go. Christopher was carrying on something awful. Eugenie figured Arlo had just screwed the pooch on picking up extra work at the store. But Christopher went off stomping around, cussing about finding somebody else. He took a box of cough syrup and left. The next morning, he followed Eugenie into the store when she opened up. He grabbed another box, and she pointed out that was the last of the stock because somebody had stolen two, and she only kept a few on the shelf. She was all ugly because she thought she was doing her job, and he blew her off, saying it was too danged bad. His brother was sick."

"Dorothea, did you find two boxes or bottles of cough syrup when you cleaned the house?" asked Katie.

"I didn't find nary a bottle, but I didn't inspect the trash."

"Could you have packed it up with Ruth's stuff? Maybe she would remember," said Kate.

Dorothea stopped cold. There was an odd look on her face.

"Katie," she said slowly. "When Arlo and Thomas were loading the household goods into that truck, Christopher pulled up into the driveway. I asked him if he had called Ruth to tell her they'd be dropping off that whole load of stuff." Dorothea licked her lips. "He said, real sarcastic like, why would this stuff go up to Ruth? I got kind of nasty. You know my mouth and besides, he had just handed me my money, and it was safe in my pocket. So, I told him like I saw it. Because, I said, you might own the house, but all the goods within belong to Ruth. You can't just throw her out and then steal her blind to boot. She never came back to me and said thank you for packing all her stuff up nice and neat. That's not like her, is it?"

"No," said Katie, "it's not."

Outside, a car horn beeped twice.

"Unplug that flat iron. Get moving." Dorothea hustled into her jacket and grabbed the cash box. "Ellen is here, and I left a boiled dinner on the back of the stove."

* * *

Katie sat in the truck at the end of the church parking lot, watching the red taillights of Ellen's Chevy round the corner and disappear. All that was left to be seen after they were gone was the single pole light in the sheriff's department parking lot. Beneath the light, Katie could see the dark silhouette of a vehicle. Someone was still there. It could be Angus, who had replaced Marlie, or Sheriff Martin Lewis. Taking a chance, Katie headed up the road to park under that solitary light.

Once in the lot, Katie realized there were two vehicles. One was the ancient black and white Dodge Monaco that had been issued to Angus. It was a dinosaur on wheels, bad on gas, worse in the snow, according to Marlie, who had been the last employee to have driven it. The other was a newer, down-sized version, with a more efficient V8 and better traction. Through the window, she could see Angus at the desk. Behind him, a light shone through the open doorway to Sheriff Lewis' office.

Katie walked in, the jingle of the bell on the door alerting Angus, who tilted his head up, and then just a tad more so that he was looking through the very bottom of his coca cola bottle lenses.

"Can I help you?" he asked.

"It's me, Angus. Katie Took."

Angus blinked behind the heavy glasses, eyes narrowing as he focused. Field sheriffs were hired, went to the academy in Norwich, and came back ready to deal with crime. Administrative employees, which Angus was, were hired, often as a political appointment, and never received more than the minimal training, which didn't include gun safety or the issuance of such. Angus had proved that shortly after the hire, it was safer for him to answer the phone. He would never be more than a desk clerk. Handing him a weapon put anyone in range in danger.

"Did you get an animal call?" he asked, his searching fingers drawing the paperwork on his desk to him. His question told Katie he was on the evening shift and hadn't yet read the log notes left by Deputy Brad. Like the solitary mole, Angus would be working in the dark, above ground, but still in the winter darkness.

"Nope. I'm here to see the sheriff." Katie had the uncontrollable urge to ask him if he liked the job. It had been Marlie's, and she had chaffed at the bit, yearning to be a field deputy. Katie bit down hard on her tongue to muffle the question. It was a good thing, because Lewis appeared in the doorway.

"What do you need, Katie?" he asked, dry as unbuttered toast.

From the moment she had returned to Parentville after Gram's death, she and Lewis had developed a disdain-hate-distrust relationship. At the current moment, they were experiencing a slight truce. But that was about to end.

"I'm looking for some information about a cold case," she said.

"What case is that?" Lewis asked.

Katie looked pointedly at Angus and rubbed her ear. Lewis invited her into the office, closing the door on his newest deputy.

Before he got settled behind his desk, Katie said. "Around this time of year, George Beauregard was killed out on the Mechanicville Road."

"I'm aware of that," said Lewis. "How did you come up with that information?"

"Let's see," Katie said sarcastically. "Oh, yeah, Ruth lives in my house."

She instantly regretted her indiscretion. Lewis, who had been on his way to sitting in his desk chair, changed direction. Now he stood rigid behind the enormous piece of scarred maple furniture. Katie swallowed her pride.

"I'm sorry, Sheriff, that was uncalled for. It's been a long day, and it took me a while to realize you are the person I needed to talk to."

Lewis relented and sat down.

"Why are you bringing this up now, Katelyn?"

His use of her full name was not lost on Katie.

"The anniversary of that event was a few days ago. The trauma has raised people's emotions," she said.

"By people, you mean Ruth?" Lewis stated.

Katie's teeth were starting to clench. *What made me think this was a good idea?* "Among others."

"What others?" Lewis asked.

"I'm trying to understand what happened here so that I can help my friends cope. I know it probably sounds like I'm scrounging for gossip. But believe me, Martin, I'm only trying to help." There was only a slim chance her words had deflected his question regarding Ruth and Rick. She hoped for the best.

"As it is, and you were correct, a cold case and still unresolved, still considered open. I am not at liberty to share with you or any other member of the public either what was found at the site or what the department was able to ascertain."

Katie sat there for a moment, small notebook in hand, considering the smug look on his face and knowing his use of legalese to push her aside was perfectly within his rights. Watching him, trying to hold a blank look on her face as he did the same, wasted three minutes of both their lives.

"Okay, well, how about if you just tell me what you can?"

"I was about to leave for the day," said Lewis.

"There's that much, huh?" Katie smiled and started to rise. "No problem. I can be back here first thing in the morning, and we can take as long as we need."

Lewis frowned, motioning Katie back down in her seat. He said, "There isn't much to tell. We received a call early in the morning that George Beauregard had been attacked in his house and expired. We got there. Ruth was hysterical. The bed was all torn up where she had been dubbing around after she found him. She said she was trying to pull the knife out so he'd breathe again. She went to the hospital; he went to the morgue. We tried to establish if she was the killer. The findings were inconclusive. Her lawyer set up a case that she wasn't strong enough to push the knife into his body as far as it went, into the back of a rib and all. The hospital did a tox test looking for the sleeping medicine. That took weeks. Came back with traces. The expert said she would have had to take three or more for the dregs to still be in her system. Judge Costello ruled her able to have performed the act. That's all I've got."

"Let me get this straight. You, this office, received a call. Not 911. But directly here. There was no telephone in the house. Who called? From where?" asked Katie.

"Restricted information," Lewis said.

"Ruth was trying to revive George?"

"Can't speak to the state of her mind," said Lewis.

"How deep into the bone was the knife?" Katie could feel her teeth holding together while she spoke.

"Restricted information."

"I'm sure you can't share the toxicity test results with me. Can you tell me who the expert was?"

"Nope, sorry."

Katie said good night and left, knowing Lewis wasn't sorry at all.

Chapter Sixteen

The ride home was darker than the previous night's. There was no moon. Katie looked off over the white-covered pastures. They didn't look as pretty tonight, and the black wasn't soft like velvet. It was hard, dull, and angry. Rick had left the feed store, bound for the dump and a meeting with Chet. There was food in his cooler to be dropped off. A Tupperware bowl of beef stew, a couple of venison sandwiches, and, if Rick hadn't eaten them, a tin of brownies. Katie pulled up and backed in beside Marlie's car.

"Hey, you're early again." Katie came through the door, grinning.

At the table, Ruth and Marlie were cutting up old Christmas cards, taking the pictures and stringing them together with yarn to make garland for the Christmas tree.

"Check this out, Katie." Marlie grinned happily. "My mom and I used to do this too. Is it cool?"

"It is for a fact." Katie hung her winter gear on the pegs beside the door. "What's for supper?"

Ruth looked up, all innocent. "Oh, I forgot."

"Liar." Katie gave both women a squeeze and opened the refrigerator to see what was available.

By the time Rick returned from his visit with Chet and unloaded what the older man had saved for him, supper was ready.

Marlie declared she was going to sleep on the sofa. "It's my turn. Last week, you gave up your bed. This week I am sleeping downstairs on the sofa."

Katie tried to talk the shorter woman out of it, but Marlie stood her ground. In the parlor, closed off to conserve heat, the maple twin bed they had carried from the barn to the house had been washed and set up. Now all they needed was a mattress and spring to stack on the fresh slats Rick had cut. Ruth had done her part and scavenged some almost-as-good-as-new sheets and two blankets from the church thrift shop.

"How do you feel about a metal spring for the extra bed instead of a box spring?" Rick asked. "That's what we have upstairs, and Chet's got one at the dump that is in really good condition. If I haul it home, we can wash it down and use it."

"I'm okay with that. Just don't stop and pick up any mattresses or pillows on the side of the road or at the dump." Katie warned. "That's disgusting. After Christmas, we'll check around for some new ones."

"The mattresses upstairs are all over thirty years old," said Ruth. "Mine is almost so thin, I could fold it into a suitcase."

"I know." Katie sat back in the kitchen chair as all eyes swiveled to the side of the refrigerator.

Several different lists were taped on the white expanse. Rick kept track of everything they needed in the hopes it showed up somewhere. Dutifully, he crossed off what they found. Under house repairs, he had drawn a straight and heavy line through the word furnace, remarking as he did so that it gave him great pleasure. The list for needed furnishings was short, but mattresses weren't near the top.

Rick reached over and pulled down the list. Using the carpenter pencil stuck behind his ear, he crossed out 3 and wrote in 4.

"Please," said Marlie, "don't do that for me."

"Don't worry, Marlie." Ruth smiled across the table. "The lists are mostly just to remind those of us with more feeble brains to keep our eyes open."

"As if the stack of bills that comes in practically daily won't," said Katie. Her happy smile flipped over.

Rick's hardy laugh sounded a little forced. "Hey, everybody. It's almost Christmas; lighten up. How about a bit of toast and apple butter?"

Ruth looked like she might cave and agree.

"Actually." Marlie had a mischievous smile. "Sunday, I stopped at a church bazaar and bought whoopee pies and peanut butter fudge." She had left her tote bag by the door, and from it she pulled the desserts and a loaf of cranberry walnut bread. "What do you think?"

"I'm thinking more tea and a big piece of each," said Rick.

* * *

For a while after Ruth and Rick had gone upstairs and Marlie was tucked in, Katie lay on the floor next to the sofa. Her raised hand tucked under Marlie's cheek. They could have squeezed together on the cushions, but Katie didn't dare. Her longing was too great, and she was sure her self-control was lacking.

"Have you heard anything about being reinstated as the sheriff's deputy?" she asked. There was a movement as though Marlie had pulled slightly away, but then the round cheek returned to its resting place.

"I had a couple of meetings with my union rep," said Marlie. "It's a tough call because the job has already been filled, you know? Anyway, I'll, ah, probably have something soon."

When Katie spoke again, Marlie shushed her. Shortly after, she feigned sleep, and Katie rose, gave her a light kiss, and went to her own bed. In the darkness with Old Tom tucked behind her knees, Marlie let tears fall, rolling over her cheeks and being absorbed by the scratchy wool blanket. It was time to talk to Katie about their future.

* * *

Katie came downstairs in the morning to find Rick dressed for work and frying eggs while Marlie, wrapped in an enormously fuzzy robe adorned with gingerbread men, cradled a mug of coffee. Both were laughing, but broke off abruptly when she entered the room.

"What are you two up to?" she asked, retrieving her own mug.

"It seems," Marlie said mischievously, "Rick has an assignment for us, if we have the stomach to handle it."

Katie wrinkled her nose at the thought of what Rick, always out trying to make a buck, would want them to do. She sipped coffee while the other two watched. Finally, she said, "Okay, what is this assignment, and will I need hip boots and rubber gloves?"

"Well, boots. Gloves or mittens might be a good idea as well," said Rick. "I got one of the young guys from the fire station to go out and plow Ida Jarvis' yard the other day. I specifically told him she had to have access to the dog's run so Walker wouldn't run free. He did the plowing. She called and told Ruth to say thank you, but I guess he didn't get out of the truck and shovel any of the banking away from the back door or the doghouse at the far end. I was hoping if you were out today, you'd stop in and take care of it. Shouldn't take longer than fifteen minutes."

"I remember Mrs. Jarvis and Walker," said Marlie. "Sweet little old lady and hobo dog."

Katie nodded in agreement. "One of my most frequent animal control customers."

"Who do you get more calls for than that?" Rick asked.

"Lately, to get Memere Fortin's cat off the porch roof."

"Oh, yeah. Bebe. I forgot about her."

After collecting eggs and restocking firewood, the two women threw shovels into the back of the pickup truck and drove through town toward Mechanicville Road. It was a slow trip because Marlie wanted to stop at every house and get a good look at the Christmas decorations. At the corner of the Parentville/Charlotte Road, they sat at the stop sign. Marlie, sitting on the right, leaned forward to look left at the green and red outfitted elf cut-out, while Katie on the left stared right, taking a good look at the small white house.

"It certainly looks deserted," she muttered.

At her words, Marlie turned to look as well. "I don't think so, Katie. The path has been shoveled out."

In the rear-view mirror, a milk truck was chugging up the grade. Katie checked traffic and took a left, getting out of the tanker's way.

Rick's estimation of time to be spent shoveling was way off. The plow guy had made a total of two broad swipes. Besides the banking pushed back by the plow, there was a wide stretch of pristine snow too deep for either Ida or Walker to wade through, blocking the back steps. At the far end of the overhead run, the doghouse was flat-out buried.

"That bugger." Katie cussed.

"Rick or the plow guy?" Marlie asked.

"Both."

Katie got out, waving to Ida in the kitchen window, and buried her shovel in the closest bank. By the time a path had been cleared and widened sufficiently not to be lost in the next snowstorm, and the doghouse and surrounding area were open, both women were sweaty. Katie's jacket lay on the hood of the truck. She threw the last scoop of snow just as Walker, rattling the overhead chain along with him, scurried past to add his yellow signature to their work.

Marlie, wheezing with the effort of shoveling, was now left more breathless for laughing at Walker's artwork.

"Come in," Ida called from the stoop, wrapped in a long droopy sweater and wearing only slippers. "I made hot chocolate."

Leaving Walker outside to inspect the rest of the yard work and to christen Katie's tires, all three women trooped inside. They sat at the heavy round pedestal table, sipping rich cocoa and eating cookies the Ladies' Auxiliary had dropped off.

I'm going to add Ida to the Christmas cookie list, thought Katie. *Maybe get her over for dinner on Christmas and New Year's.*

At a lull in the conversation, Katie asked Ida if she knew who owned the small house with the maroon shutters up the road toward the village. Rather than say it was the one Ruth and George had lived in, she merely described it. On the way by, she had pointed it out to Marlie, who sat with her mug held high, listening.

"Do you know the one I mean?" Katie asked. "It's really adorable."

"Yeah, I do. The new people did some fine work fixing it up. They keep adding and improving," said Ida. "Used to be when Christopher Beauregard owned it, it was kind of a dump."

"Christopher Beauregard lived there? I thought he was up on Apple Orchard Road," Katie said.

"Oh, he never lived there." The old woman was fussing around with the buttons on her sweater. "He owned the place, but his brother George rented it."

Katie sat silently, waiting. Sure enough, in another minute, Ida was talking again.

"That's where he was living when he died, don't 'cha know. They found him there soaking in blood, slashed to bits."

Marlie choked on her hot chocolate.

"Huh," said Katie, ignoring her friend, who continued to sputter for several minutes.

"Yes," said Ida. There was gossip to be spread. Marlie's needs were pushed aside while she told her tale. "I've known both boys their entire lives. Knew their daddy. People spoke highly of him, while throwing daggers at his back. But he had it all coming until towards the end when he tried to do right."

"But the boys." Katie interrupted, hoping to swing the conversation back to George.

"Different as two could be," Ida said. "It's true they had different mamas, but the same woman reared them from the cradle. Had to be in the blood. When my husband was alive, and I could get around, I'd see them often. Then I was stuck out here, not that I mind, plenty happening now, all those trailers are here. Anyway, did I tell you I saw George just before he died?"

"No," said Katie. "When was that?" Even Marlie was listening intently.

"Well, let's see. It was the afternoon, no, it was after supper, the day before he died."

Katie's throat was so dry, her words croaked out. "The day before, or the same day he died in the night?"

"Well, he was here, then he went home. So, let's see." Ida stirred her chocolate.

Katie and Marlie were inching toward the edges of their seats.

"He died that night," Ida said at last.

"Katie," said Marlie, "I don't think we should be talking about this."

But Katie held up her hand, quieting her.

"Ida, you saw George? On the road, or he came to your house?"

"Well, he couldn't fix the broken pipe out in the road now, could he?" Ida asked. "The drain pipe under the sink gave way. What a mess. I called around, looking for somebody who could help me. There's a bulletin board at the store, so I called and asked if somebody could look for an advertisement. You know, a plumber looking for extra work. Christopher said he'd ask Eugenie if her husband could help me out. A while later, George showed up with a box of tools and a new piece of pipe. It took him a while. I think he was learning as he went, but he did a fine job. We had a cup of coffee, and his ride came back for him. Just in time, too. I don't usually stay up past nine, and it had to be after ten."

"He fixed your pipe so it worked, and he was drunk?" Katie had a problem with that idea.

"He wasn't drunk." Ida pulled her indignation and her sweater around herself. "I wouldn't have let him in the house drunk, mess or no. He told me he had just come from home, missed most of his supper. I fixed him a plate, and he ate while he worked. He even mopped up under the cupboard when he was through. I offered him a couple of dollars, was all I had. He said no, the guy that brought him was going to pay, and he had been specifically told not to take my money. There are still decent folks out there, don't you think?"

Katie and Marlie got suited up to leave. At the door, Marlie asked Ida who had dropped George off, but the septuagenarian said she had never known.

* * *

"What do you think?" Marlie asked Katie. They had driven up the road in silence. Now, they were parked across the street from the little house where Ruth and George had lived, watching the Cardinals visiting the feeder.

"I think the person who gave George a ride, and that hired him to fix Ida's leak, is the same person that picked him up at ten o'clock to take him home.

And that would possibly be the last person to see him alive."

"What's the other possibility?" Marlie asked.

"If he went to the Wagon Wheel or any other tavern, his final conversation could have been with anybody."

"How are you going to know?" asked Marlie.

Katie shrugged, then started the truck. "I just know it wasn't Ruth because she said she took a sleeping pill right after he left and didn't even wake up when he got home."

Looking in the side-view mirror of the truck, Katie could see the mailbox for Philip's garage behind them. She thought about asking him, but he wouldn't have been there late on a Sunday night. She shifted into drive, and the old pickup truck rolled ahead. At the stop sign for US Route 15, Marlie asked her to pull into the parking lot at the creamery.

"Do you need to use the payphone, Marlie?" Katie asked. "You could use the house phone."

"No." Marlie was pressed against the passenger's door, shoulders hunched. Katie had seen her like that one other time when she had been distressed and unsure. "I want to talk to you. Can you park away from the entrance?"

Katie pulled all the way to the back of the lot where the tankers were stored. Knocking the truck into neutral, she set the emergency brake before sitting back. Marlie was looking off, out the side window. Katie did the thing hardest for her in the world, wait.

"Katie." Marlie turned to her, voice soft and eyes sorrowful.

She's breaking up with me, Katie thought, jaw going tight.

"I want to tell you what I found out about the sheriff's job. I just didn't want to talk in front of Ruth and Rick because I'm not ready to answer a lot of questions."

"Okay," said Katie, jaw relaxing.

Marlie took her time, exhaling, getting her thoughts together, before she said. "After I walked out on the deputy job here in Parentville so Geoffrey Ash wouldn't tell Sheriff Lewis about me being a lesbian, I knew my dreams were gone. When you proved he killed his nephew and that poor girl, things shifted a little, at least for me. I was out of the picture, so there wasn't any finger-pointing. I took a chance and met with a representative of the Union of Police Associations. He's from a good size city. I figured he'd be more open-minded than some. I explained to him exactly why I had left and told him that if there was any way possible, I wanted to go back to being a deputy sheriff."

"And?" Katie asked hopefully.

"Mr. Reynolds, the representative, told me that he'd present my case to the regional commissioner. Katie, that was exactly not what I wanted. If he outed me, I'd never stand a chance. So, I told him no, and why I didn't want him to. We went on talking for a while. Finally, he said he was still going to represent me. As a lawyer, my sexuality could not be an issue for him taking the case, and it shouldn't be one for me getting the job. We both knew that the system doesn't work that way. He said he would go to the commission and explain that I had left due to the severe mental anguish and fear that Ash brought into my life. But he made it perfectly clear he would not divulge what I said unless the commissioner demanded it, and then only behind closed doors. I took the chance and let Mr. Reynolds go."

Katie realized her hand was creeping up to her neck and forced it back into her lap.

"The commission came back and said if I could find a sheriff that would take me on, I could have my job back, but I would be starting from square one. I would not be reinstated in my original job, nor would I receive any preferential treatment."

"That's good. Right?" Katie asked, happiness creeping into her voice.

"While this was all happening, a new class of deputy recruits graduated from Norwich University. Twenty-three young men to fill seventeen slots." Marlie looked away again. "I thought it was going to be hopeless. Every one of those guys would be interviewed before I was. I knew it, and Mr. Reynolds knew it."

"You're wrong, Marlie," said Katie, reaching out to turn Marlie back to her. "As soon as a sheriff met you, they'd know you were their best choice."

"That's not the way it works, Katie. Deputies select three first-choice districts. The top five candidates get interviewed. There are going to be a couple of poor saps who never get that call, and I come after them. That's my punishment for running away from the job."

Katie didn't know what to say.

"Okay. Now listen before I dissolve into tears and you start crying after me. There's this. Mr. Reynolds called me about an open deputy slot which is specifically looking for a woman. It's at a woman's correctional installation. He wanted permission to send my resume and see if he could cut off the rest of the list. You know, I was already trained, save money, all that junk."

"You said yes?"

"That's right, I did. Ten days ago, I got an acceptance letter. I had to respond immediately as the first shift would start at midnight, New Year's morning. I told them I would be there," said Marlie.

"That's why you're going to your grandmother's house for Christmas?"

"I'm going because she asked me to. She's old, and failing a little." Marlie wet her lips. "Katie, the job is in Pennsylvania. I have to move."

"What? No! What?" Katie leaned away, her head on the ice-cold window glass.

It was Marlie's turn to reach out, but Katie waved her away.

"I don't understand. Why would you go to Pennsylvania?"

"Mr. Reynolds pointed out that after six months on the job, I would be eligible to transfer if I can find a slot. That's the same six months this new group of deputies is going to be testing their endurance. A lot will fail. Historically, sixty percent of the class will not last a year. I'm going to take this job, and the day I can legally do so, I am going to be applying for the slot one of those guys leaves. I don't care where it is. I'll take it. The longer I'm not working in the field, the harder it will be for me to find a job. I'll be considered, I don't know, stale. Like I would need retraining."

It was Katie's turn to stare out the window.

"Katie?" Marlie whispered.

"I'll go with you. We can find a place. I'm sure there are jobs I could do." Katie realized she was babbling and pressed her lips shut.

"What about the farm? Ruth and Rick?"

"Ha. A year ago, they didn't know me. It won't matter. They can have everything here." Katie shifted the truck into reverse. "I don't have much to pack." Her thoughts were like fleas jumping off a wet dog. Every one going in a different direction, and none of them connected to the others. *I'll just leave a note on the table and be gone in the night.*

Marlie laid her hand on Katie's, holding the shift still. "No. I won't let you do that. We are us, a couple, you and I. If I have to be down there for six months, or maybe a little longer, we'll figure it out."

"You don't know that, Marlie," Katie whispered. "You have no way of knowing what is going to happen six months from now."

Sliding across the seat, Marlie put her arms around her love. "No. I don't know anything. If I did, I wouldn't be in this mess. But you are really good at shoveling manure out until you get right down to bedrock. Together we can move this heap and build on top of something solid, that bedrock. Look at what you're doing now. Most people would look away, many did. Not you. Ruth is your friend, your family. You love her. I want you to love me the same way, and I don't want to hurt you while you do. Katie, this is my decision. I will not allow you to follow me to Pennsylvania. I will not be standing there with open arms." Then she took a deep breath and said through the blur of tears, "But if you're a good girl and promise to eat all your supper, I'll be back."

Katie looked away from the frozen glass toward Marlie. Her round, beautiful face held a smile that trembled a little at the edges. And her big, brown eyes were filled with tears, sparkling like stars in the cold winter sky.

"I promise," whispered Katie. It was all the words she could say past the fistful of choke in her throat.

They sat there in silence, leaning on each other, cold hand in cold hand, until a vehicle further up in the lot fired to life. After that, it was a slow and quiet ride back to the farmhouse.

Chapter Seventeen

The next morning, all four left the house together and in one way or another, all headed toward work. Ruth would be working at the thrift store all day with Dorothea. They were putting together Christmas boxes for some of the more needy folks and getting ready for the coat and boot sale. Rick would drop Ruth off, and then Katie would pick her up, as he had things to do after work.

It was only to be expected that when Katie arrived, the ladies were still not quite finished with their project.

"Katie." Dorothea waved her over. "I need some Scotch tape. Will you go up to the store?" At Katie's nod, the elderly custodian of the cash pulled two dollars out of the metal cash box. Holding it out to Katie, she said, "Make sure you get a receipt," before relinquishing the money.

Walking to the store, past the doctor's building and other older village residential structures, Katie admired quaint gingerbread touches in the eaves and the trimming on front porches. Even the red brick two-story with its upper porch had at one time been similarly adorned. It was the one building on the street set back with a half-circle drive. Pausing for a moment to consider the impossibly narrow curve of the drive and the fact it was said to be a house of the night, or ill-repute, she shook her head and continued on.

At the store, a man of about her own age was pushing slush away from the entrance walk. For a moment, seeing his wide shoulders and longish brown curls, she thought it might be Arlo, Eugenie's husband. However, lifting his face to mop his brow, he presented features that were definitely younger.

Checking out, Katie accepted her change and receipt before asking, "That guy that's out front shoveling? That's not Arlo, right?"

The cashier looked out the window for only a second. "No, that's Jonathon. Do you need to talk to him?"

"No, I'm good," said Katie. But once outside, she stopped beside the shoveler. "Jonathon? I'm Katelyn Took. Do you have a few minutes to answer some questions about George Beauregard, Junior?"

Jonathan leaned on the handle of his shovel. Though his breathing was accelerated, he was by no means out of breath. "Are you another one of his grandchildren?" he asked with contempt.

The question startled Katie. It had never occurred to her that anyone, for any reason, would think that.

"No," she blurted out, "my grandfather was Fred Moore."

Nodding in acceptance of her declaration, Jonathon asked, "Would you mind telling me why you want to know?"

"Ruth Beauregard was a friend of my grandmother," Katie explained. "When Gram passed, Ruth and I started sharing space." Taking care of her made it sound like Ruth was in her dotage. The last time Katie heard herself say that to someone, she had decided to correct other people's image of her friend, but this time it might work for her. "Lately, she's been trying to talk about the time of his passing. I wasn't here, so it's hard to understand. I thought perhaps as a member of the family; you might have some insight."

Jonathon continued to lean on the shovel handle, silently looking up the street. Finally, he hefted it onto his shoulder. "Follow me," he said. He led Katie around the back of the building, up the steps to the dock area, and through the swinging loading doors. When she realized where they were going and that Christopher might be there, Katie slowed down.

Realizing she was falling behind, Jonathon said, "It's okay. I'm the manager today. Normally we frown on people using this entrance, but you're with me, so you're good."

In the office, Jonathon motioned her to a seat before sitting behind the desk. "I'm assuming you aren't from here, so I'll give you a little commonly known history. My great-grandfather started the mercantile from the back of a horse-drawn wagon. He was a traveling peddler, that's what they were called in those days. Eventually, he bought a small building that stood where the parking lot is today. My grandfather, George Beauregard, Senior, had this building erected when he was in his early twenties. So, basically, we are a fourth-generation mercantile. My grandfather was a gregarious, controlling man." Jonathon looked down at the desk, obviously considering what he was going to say next. "He demanded we love and honor him, but to be honest, as far as I'm concerned, he didn't earn that right. George Junior was already a layabout and a drunk at my first memory of him. And yet, his father and his mother adored him."

"He didn't want to work in the store. It was beneath him to sell food, supplies, and whatever. My father loved it. Granddad would tell my father how to do everything. If dad had an idea, it was no good. Then suddenly, a few months later, Granddad would spring that same idea, and it would be the answer to all the world's evil. He drove my father nuts." Jonathon gave a hard sigh. "You might not understand the strain this created. My parents had some bad fights. Mom said Dad could go anywhere and work for one of the big names in the grocery business. Dad wouldn't leave town."

"But your grandfather left the store to your dad?" asked Katie.

"Actually, my grandfather left forty percent of the store to George and thirty percent to both my grandmother and dad. My grandmother died only a few months after her husband. That was when we, or at least I, learned she was George's stepmother." Jonathon stood up, retrieved some papers from the top of the file cabinet, then sat back down in his seat, ignoring them. "I'm only telling you this because I know Ruth believes she's guilty, and I don't think she is. My grandmother's will left her thirty percent of the store to Dad, giving him control. George had been living largely off the business for a while and owed a large amount of money."

"You mean he had an open account?" asked Katie.

"He wasn't the only one, but the three biggest ones were all related. There was George, a woman named Mildred Hooper who lived here in town, and another woman named Edna Barrett who lived over the line in Monkton. My father got a lawyer. They came to an agreement that Dad would pay off George, Hooper, and Barrette's accounts, and that amount of money would be transferred to store percentage and then to Dad."

"So, your father acquired a larger percentage of the company?"

"It was all legal and above board. Dad even made Uncle George sober up so he would know what was going on."

"What did Ruth say about all this?" asked Katie.

"I don't know how much she knew," said Jonathon. "Her name was never mentioned, and I don't believe she was part of the negotiations. But here's the thing, after this was a done deal, my folks were having a really bad row. My dad was slamming around, and even though he never raised a hand to my mother, I was concerned enough to sneak down the stairs and listen. It seems that for a long while, my father had been making George's house payments. George decided he was going to leave town, and he wanted Dad to buy the house. Dad turned the receipts for what he had paid over to the lawyer. George was offered the remainder of the value, and he took it. My mother was furious. She hadn't known this. Well, George never left town, so renting the place wasn't an option because he wouldn't move out, and he did not bother to work.

"On top of all that, word leaked out about Dad buying George out. People George had borrowed or stolen from started coming out of the woodwork. According to the lawyer, if they had a receipt or it could be positively verified, it was legal; the bills needed to be paid out of what George got for the house. According to my father, George pissed away most of what he got. People came to dad threatening a lean on the store unless they were paid. Dad started paying off those debts. In return, each dollar out put another credit into Dad's ownership of the business. In time, he owned all the rights to the store. Immediately, my mother had him post a legal notice in the newspaper that they, and the store, were no longer responsible for George's debts. It mortified her, but it had to be done."

"So, then George stopped coming around?"

"No, that's exactly when it got worse." Jonathon shuffled the papers again, then tucked them into a desk drawer. "Not only did that not stop George from coming in here demanding money whenever he wanted, but there was another man George owed an enormous amount of money to. This guy hadn't been paid off because he had a lawyer as well and wanted an extraordinarily high rate of interest. The little guys just wanted what was due, and they got it. This guy wanted way more. He knew that only a specific amount of money would be paid out, but he kept pushing, never settling. The day came when the value of the store was reached. That's when the notice went in the paper, and Dad stopped paying out. This guy took Dad to court. The judge sided with us. The man was left cold."

"You said it was a lot of money. Did this guy live locally?" Katie asked.

Jonathon nodded.

"Who was it?" Katie croaked, tongue sticking to the roof of her mouth.

"Kenneth Sampson," said Jonathon.

Chapter Eighteen

While Katie and Ruth made supper, with Katie doing the directing, Rick sat in the living room trying to tune the old radio so there was less squelch and more music. The last snowstorm had knocked over the antenna on the roof, leaving the single television channel they received with more shaky fuzz running across the screen than a discernible picture. It also meant that any time the wind blew, radio reception came and went. The scratch and interference were putting everyone's nerves on end.

Ruth went out to talk to Rick. Katie, with her own thoughts still centered on what Marlie had told her the day before, didn't pay any attention. Shortly after, Ruth returned to mashing potatoes, while Rick's boots went thumping up the stairs to the second floor. He was back quickly.

"Can you help me lug the stereo down from the storage room, Katie?" Rick asked.

"It doesn't work," Katie said. She had already checked out Irma's chest-style stereo. It, and most of the other household furnishings, had been moved up to a never used room on the second floor. Katie had questioned Ruth as to why, but the older woman wasn't really sure, other than it would be less to keep free of cat hair. "I plugged it in, but it won't play a record."

"You're such a girl." Rick laughed. "It wouldn't play a record because the needle assembly is missing. I spent a while myself trying to figure it out. When I realized the whole casing unit was gone, I went down to Sears and Roebucks, where Irma got it. They don't have parts. But one of the guys told me to take the model number off the back and drive over to the RadioShack store. It took longer to drive there than it did to install the casing unit. I just went upstairs and put it together. It's playing now. All we have to do is get it downstairs and level. I was going to wait until one of the guys was here to help lug it, but the static on the radio is making me want to grind my teeth."

Together, they made two trips. One for the heavy stereo and another for the two faux leather cases of 33 1/3 albums.

"Why," Katie grunted. "Is it that every time I hauled something with either you or Poppa, I am on the bottom side going down or the upside going up?"

"Just lucky, I guess. Watch yourself. Don't step on that cat."

Ruth had kept the supper warm while they trooped up and down. With the stereo in place near one of the two living room outlets, Rick put on a Perry Como album, and they sat down to eat before more than the potatoes were scorched. Rick declared the stereo would save his ears because the static had made him want to rip them off.

Chapter Nineteen

"Library is closing in fifteen minutes," said the head librarian. Charlene reminded Katie of a Chick-a-Dee with her pixie haircut and quick movements. "Oh, it's you, Katie. Can I help?"

"If you've got some gossip," said Katie.

Charlene quirked an eye.

As she unbuttoned her coat, Katie explained about her concerns for Ruth. "I'm having a problem trying to help her because, basically, I don't know what happened."

"That's the gossip part, right?" asked Charlene, settling back into her seat in front of the old roll-top desk.

"Whatever you've got," said Katie.

Charlene pulled the telephone across the desk and dialed a five-digit in-town number. "Hi," she said into the receiver. "Got a minute?" After relating what Katie had said moments earlier, she passed the receiver across the desk. "This is my sister Rose. She was working on the rescue the morning they found George." Leaving Katie so she'd have a little privacy. The librarian went to the front and locked the doors. One quick walk-by to pick up a pile of books, and she disappeared into the stacks.

"I hope Ruth is okay," said Rose. When Katie answered, she was. The EMT continued. "Let's see if I can clear up some of your questions. The sheriff's department forwarded the call to us. We received notice of a death under suspicious circumstances early in the morning. There's no undertaker here in town, so it's not unusual for us to get that type of call. It was still dark. I would say it was like six, maybe. We went out, but there was nothing we could do. George was already cold. He'd been dead for a long time. While we were waiting for the sheriff and the doctor to finish up, we were notified an undertaker was on route."

"Had George been dead overnight? Or since midnight?"

"I don't know. Longer than six hours anyway. We didn't get really close. Sheriff Lewis was already there. Doctor Darlpin arrived around the same time we did. It was a single stab wound in the chest, piercing the fourth and fifth ribs, left side. It was a perfect shot."

"And it was a big hunting knife? The paper said it was thirteen inches long," said Katie.

"The knife was in a big plastic bag on the table," said Rose. "I only saw it from a distance. I didn't know it was a hunting knife. George's brother showed up. Also, Ruth was there. At first, she was pretty lucid. Calm, even considering what had happened. She was trying to tell Sheriff Lewis something. Christopher was all wound up. He was right in her face, telling her to be quiet and demanding to know why she had killed his brother. The next thing we knew, Doctor Darlpin had a needle shoved in Ruth's arm, and she was sliding to the floor. Neither he nor Christopher made any effort to catch her."

"Are you sure?" Katie asked. That didn't seem right, for the doctor to let her fall to the floor with a needle in her arm.

"Katie. I watched Sheriff Lewis push Christopher out of the way so that he could catch Ruth before she hit the ground. We actually hauled her off right after that and left George to wait for the guys from the funeral home."

"Crap," said Katie. "Which funeral home?"

"Richmond. I rode in the back of the ambulance with Ruth. Usually, I drive, but she was so far under that the other EMT, who had only been with us for a short time, bowed out. He probably thought we were going to lose her. She never came to, all the way to the Mary Fletcher hospital in Burlington."

Katie was silent, listening to the hum of the telephone line and for the telltale clicks that would indicate somebody in another house on the party line had picked up their receiver.

"As long as we're talking about this, Katie, there's something about the whole thing that has always bothered me."

"What's that?" Katie asked, drawn back from the worry of an eavesdropper to the other woman.

"Ruth isn't a big woman. That knife was buried deep. Maybe possible, I guess, an act of passion and all that. But she didn't have any fresh marks on her, you know, from a beating. There was a lot of older bruising, and there had been rumors for a long while. And she also didn't have any blood spray on her, and given her size, she would have had to be standing close. There wasn't a lot on George either, because the knife wasn't removed for hours. But she should have had some backsplash on her face or chest. Her hands and the front of her nightgown were all bloody. She kept saying she tried to help him."

There was a heavy pause while Katie thought of what she wanted to ask, and Rose wondered if she'd said too much.

"You're pretty brave to be out asking these questions, raising memories people don't want to have," Rose said.

"It wasn't all that long ago," said Katie.

"No, but it's a bad memory. Over the years, the Beauregards have touched a lot of lives. I think it's like the ripple coming off a stone thrown into a pond. It goes for a long way. Like I said, you're brave."

Katie laughed mirthlessly. "I'm not brave at all. If I had any courage, I'd be asking these same questions about Ruth."

The truth was, she didn't want to. She had known Ruth for only a short time, but the person she knew was the one she wanted to continue to know. Gram had brought Ruth into her home. That took more than faith. It was trust, and that was good enough for Katie.

"What about in the house? Was there a mess?" asked Katie.

"Not in the little I saw of it." Rose paused. "You should ask Dorothea. I believe she and one of the other church ladies went in and cleaned up later on. The house was sealed. Nothing happened there until Christopher decided to sell it."

"Christopher? Wouldn't the house have gone to Ruth?"

"No. The house belonged to Christopher. Why would Ruth have gotten it?"

Because, thought Katie as she said goodbye and hung up, *she believed it belonged to George.*

To the left of the church, across the street, was the doctor's office. When the old doctor, Matthew Darlpin, had lost his license for culpability in the death of Irma Moser Moore, the new doctor, a woman by the name of Ann Gillian, bought the building and the practice. Gossip around town was that Darlpin had left a mess and, if his nurse could be believed, there were some questionable dealings.

Even as Katie watched, the lights on the first floor went out. The office was closed. A lone car, probably the nurse's, pulled out onto Main Street. There were lights on upstairs, but Katie wasn't sure if it was an apartment, and if so, was it where Dr. Gillian was living?

"Time enough tomorrow," she said to the passing wind, which rocked the pickup, and somehow snuck cold fingers in to chill her arms and legs.

Chapter Twenty

Friday night, Katie walked into the front door of the Wagon Wheel Tavern. Standing beside the bouncer was a sixty-year-old, six-foot-tall lecher sucking on a cold pipe. The man's faded blue eyes lit up slightly. Striking a kitchen match against the edge of the counter, he sucked to draw into the pipe. Hovering over the bowl, the yellow-edged blue flame dipped, quickly returning with a plume of smoke following. The match dropped to the floor, heedless of what it would find there. The man didn't care. Neither did Katie.

She offered the till keeper her five-dollar cover charge, but the lecher waved her through. The till keeper didn't appear fazed. The bouncer never turned. Nodding slightly without adding a smile, Katie advanced into the long, low area. This part of the tavern served as the dining room, where meals were available from 11:00 A.M. until the music started. The short leg of the L offered space for the band, a dance floor, and a row of vertically lined eight-seater picnic tables against the back wall. The entire place smelled of smoke and sweat, a stink that had permeated the barnwood walls. She had heard the food was actually good here, but this was her first time through the doors since high school.

The bar had been added to the area in the crux of the L, long on one side, short on the other, like its mother. Half archways on either side offered access. Midway up the bar, a long place was left cleared of bar stools. Like the waitress station at the end, this was where the clientele could walk up and order their own. Katie looked over the offerings on the shelves behind the bartenders. Any one of the three of them, including the woman, could have been bouncers.

"Schlitz," Katie said.

"Draft or bottle?"

"Bottle."

The beer was ice cold. Dew was already forming on the outside when she picked it up. She handed the barman four dollars for a three-dollar beer. No glass accompanied the long neck.

"I'm looking for Ginny Wilder," said Katie. "Have you seen her here tonight?"

The man snorted. "Lady, any night there's booze, Ginny is here."

At Katie's quirked eyebrow, he added. "Red dress on the dance floor. You can't miss her."

Katie turned, ready to go out of the archway she'd come in. Across the floor, over the heads of the seated patrons, the lecher was watching. She opted to exit directly onto the dance floor via the second archway. The hardwood floor started right at the edge of the entrance from the bar, but the first six feet were packed with humanity that hadn't arrived in time to get a seat. There were a few women, but most of the group were studs, or so they thought, hooting, hollering, and cussing. One pair facing the wall, back to the crowd, were discretely toking up. Even though outside it was barely zero, a number of the studs were shirtless, boasting cheap imitation leather vests or faux cowhide with plenty of silver hardware. Bill caps outnumbered the cowboy hats Katie had gotten used to seeing in Illinois. Most of the caps carried familiar logos; John Deere, McColloch, Stihl. Freebies passed out by dealers and distributors when the product was purchased.

Squeezing through, continuing to move ahead like she had a place to be besides standing there, Katie edged down the line of picnic tables. There was a spot at the end of a bench. Katie parked her butt there. Behind her, a tiny man was bopping along to the music, cigarette in one hand, glass of beer in the other. Across the table, a woman of the same advanced age glared at Katie over an empty beer pitcher.

"Private party," the woman yelled over the band.

Katie nodded, with her head toward where the bouncer and the lecher

111

were dragging the doping pair out. She rubbed her upper arm and winced. The woman followed the men with her eyes, then nodded. Squeezing over, bumping the next woman with her butt, she made room, and Katie switched sides.

"Priscilla," the woman said, then nodded toward the man across from her and the woman beside her. "Bumpie. Florence."

"Kate," said Katie. At Priscilla's meaningful look at the back end of the doper, as he flew out the door, she added. "I thought he was going to be a prom date, not a reason to go to jail."

"Lotta that these days," shouted Priscilla. "You gotta be more careful."

Bumpie was standing on the bench, waving the waitress over. Besides catching her attention, he caught the lecher's eye. Both headed toward the table.

"Oh, crap," said Katie, but Priscilla was on it.

Jumping up, she circled Katie and hip-bumped the girl toward Florence, who did the same, sending Katie toward a guy that had to be with Flo. He was as surprised when Katie showed up as she was. The lecher stopped for only a moment, still sucking on his cold pipe, watching Katie with glittering blue eyes that were more nasty than nice. She ducked her head to avoid eye contact, fingers nervously tearing the label off the long neck. It was still frosty cold in her fingers and full. Even though her throat was dry, Katie was afraid to take a single sip. She had fallen down that slippery slope too many times. The lecher had a few minutes of conversation with Bumpie before moving on. When he was gone, Florence changed places with Katie again.

The band stopped between songs to suck down some suds, and Priscilla said, "That tall geezer with a pipe is Ken Sampson. I'm telling you this because you're new here. Stay away from him. He's like acid. You'll smoke, burn, and disappear."

"He seems to like you people," said Katie.

"We live in the house next door," said Priscilla. Katie had seen the house. It was very close. "This used to be our property. Right after we bought the farm, the barn burned. Ken bought the land and the old chicken barn and put in the tavern. We're regular guests here every Friday and Saturday night."

The band was tuning up for their next set. As soon as the first cords were played, a woman in a slinky and very short halter dress hit the floor. There didn't appear to be a man with her.

I'll bet that's Ginny Wilder, thought Katie.

The view of Ginny gyrating and shaking it all loose was lost as a crowd of studs encircled her. Now the mane-tossing, dark-haired beauty had half the available single guys trying to get close enough to score points. The rest of the dancing crowd, including Priscilla and Bumpie, hit the floor. Other than a few possessive women, nobody paid Ginny a lot of attention. She swung herself around the floor, offering a great view of her shimmying breasts and bottom while avoiding being snared in the clutches of any male.

Katie stayed in her seat until the next break. The music stopped, and Ginny was gone before most people ambled off the hardwood. Katie stood up and caught the swirl of red as the other woman ducked out of the emergency entrance. Katie had traveled halfway across the floor before she saw the bouncer stop a lusting swain from following the dancer. Hopefully, as a woman herself, she would make it past. The guy guarding the door even hit the panic bar for her, springing the heavy wooden panel wide open. Outside, Ginny was leaning against the untreated barn board, fanning herself and dragging deep on a Salem cigarette.

"Hey, Ginny," said Katie.

It was winter. The other woman was scantily clothed and sweaty, yet not shivering.

"Hey," she said, giving Katie barely a glance.

"Look, I know you're probably busy tonight," Katie began.

Ginny cut her off. "What is that supposed to mean?"

Realizing she might have stepped on thin ice, Katie held up her hand, offering a truce. "Just that it's Friday night, the place is packed, you're here to enjoy yourself." Katie sighed. "You don't know me from Adam, Ginny. The truth is, I'm trying to find your mother."

Ginny moved off the wall, crushing the cigarette with one red shod toe. "The heck you are."

"No, please. If you would give me a few minutes. Either here or maybe on a different day. I'm searching for the person that killed George Beauregard. I'm not interested in anything to do with your family except figure out who killed him. I think that person is still here in the area." She paused when Ginny didn't react, and then added. "He could be out for other family members, and I'm related to one I don't want to lose."

Ginny's eyes grew wider.

"I was hoping your mother or grandmother could offer some insight."

"The only insight my grandmother can offer is how it feels to be six feet under." Ginny pushed past to the door. Rapping hard on the wood, she waited a heartbeat before the bouncer pushed it open. "Days, I work at the Cup and Spoon Diner in Bristol, Sunday through Thursday, breakfast to lunch." She swung through the door and was gone.

Katie opted not to return to the tavern. Instead, she walked around the parking lot where she had left her truck. Outside the front door, Ken Sampson was talking to a group of farmer boys in cowboy hats. She made a wide circle to her truck, but was sure he had seen her.

"I'm going to need a shower to get rid of the smoke stink and the eyeball lice," she told herself.

Chapter Twenty-One

Sunday morning, right after Rick and Ruth left for church, Katie headed to The Cup and Spoon. Her line of travel followed Rick's truck through the village. She tried to stay far enough back so he wouldn't notice her. He might not, because Ruth was eager to meet up with her church lady and knitting group friends. Since she had become clear-headed and involved in the Feral Cat Rescue Society, old friends were coming back. Rick's truck turned into the church parking lot, and moments later, Katie sped past.

Half an hour later, she walked into the diner and found out that a lot of people this way weren't churchgoers. While she waited for a seat, she watched Ginny Wilder and identified her seating section. The other woman held sway over the last five counter seats, as well as some primo booth space real estate. A seat opened at the counter, and cutting the line, Katie hustled over and sat down.

Ginny set down a mug of coffee when she went by, never asking if it was what Katie wanted. The place was busy. Katie wondered if she would have a chance to ask questions. A short wait later, a plate of bacon and eggs appeared in front of her. Dutifully, Katie lifted a fork. A plate with a rasher of bacon arrived. Somebody yelled a goodbye, and Ginny appeared before her, waving at the group that headed out.

"It'll be slow for a couple of minutes until the church folk start showing up," said Ginny. She took a piece of bacon off the plate, folded it in fourths, and put it in her mouth. "What is it you want, exactly?"

Katie gave Ginny an abbreviated version of what she was doing. "I'm

115

trying to find some of Mildred Hooper's children."

"Mildred was my grandmother." Ginny looked over her tables and picked up another slice of bacon. "Most of her kids are dead. There's my mom, and I've got an uncle. He's not local, though."

"Is your mom? Local, that is?" asked Katie.

For the first time, Ginny looked at Katie. Slowly chewing on the piece of bacon, she seemed to be considering what she would say.

"What exactly do you want from my mother?" Ginny asked.

"There are a lot of different versions of George," said Katie. "I figured family would know best."

"The man was slime." Ginny folded another bacon slice.

"Okay. So, where can I find your mother?"

Ginny tucked the last square of bacon in her mouth, ripped a check off her order pad, and laid it on the counter. "I'll tell her you're looking." The waitress slid around the counter to a new group of people and got into a conversation that Katie knew would last until she left. At the cash register, Katie realized the rasher of bacon was in her check.

* * *

There were two ways to drive back to Parentville from Bristol. One was the quicker route she had taken to get there. The other would loop around and come in through Monkton. Katie elected to take the scenic route. She hadn't been to Monkton in a while.

It was clear and cold. The closer she got to the Parentville line, the slower she drove. Janice had given her directions to the house where her niece lived. Hoping she could work backwards and still find the place, Katie traveled down US Route 15, pulling over when more aggressive drivers came up behind her. She spied the small red house on the other side of the road and slowed to a crawl. The house looked like thousands of others huddling down for the winter. The snow sheet on the front lawn was smooth, no signs of lawn ornaments or mowers creating uneven humps in the expanse down to the drainage ditch. There was nothing that said there were children in

116

residence. From the road, Katie could see the two front windows, but no glitter of Christmas tree tinsel caught the light. A scraggly wire of outdoor lights edged the front door. The attempt at holiday spirit had not included boughs or a wreath. It reminded Katie it was time to decorate and urged herself not to be so stingy.

She drove up to the next house and turned around back. At the edge of the drive, she stopped to look over the property one last time. No small boot tracks in the snow, no evidence of a dog. A path across the stoop was barely shoveled off. Once dark red, now faded to the same shade as tinted lips at the end of the day, with a white door whose expanse was chipped and stained around the knob, the house and tilted garage sat thinking sad thoughts and offering no hope. In lieu of a porch, the over-wide stoop had a handrail on one side, offering a resting place for a tin ashtray half-filled with crushed-out Winston's. Katie stood on the ground, level with the ashtray, trying to decide if she should advance.

A woman stepped outside wearing a floor-length maroon and pink plush robe. Long tendrils of brown and gray hair escaped from her topknot. The woman silently watched Katie as she cupped her hands around a kitchen match and with a deep inhale, sucked smoke into her lungs while flares of red burned and blackened on the edge of her cigarette.

"Miss. Kline?" Katie asked.

"Sittoyou?" slurred the woman, taking another deep drag. "And it's Kline."

"My grandmother was Irma Moore," said Katie, hoping to deflect questions about why she was standing on the steps of this woman's house. "I believe she may have known your parents."

"Yeah?" This drag was followed by a gagging, coughing fit. After spitting a wad of green to the side, Pam Kline sucked from the cigarette again. Great white curls of smoke edged with yellow snaked out of her nostrils. "Which one?"

"Both."

The woman straightened a little and waited. They stood there long enough for the cigarette to be half burned. It was evident she wasn't going to be easy to talk to.

"I'm trying to uncover some information that may help me care for my, eh, aunt. Can you tell me a little about your parents?" Katie leaned against the railing, trying to relax and invite a confidence. "You know what they were like?"

"I know who you are. That old woman? She ain't your aunt." There was one drag left on the cigarette. Katie knew that was all the time she had left. Pam spit again. "My mother was a victim. The man who sired me was never a father, but he was a pervert."

"Oh-kay," Katie said slowly. She didn't move.

The woman pulled a pack of Winston's from her pocket, slapping it against her opposite palm; she knocked a smoke half out, then plucked it with her lips, and used the dying filter of her first cigarette to ignite the four-inch white paper rod hanging from her mouth. From where Katie was standing, she was looking up at Pam. She could see the heavy cleft from tier upon tier of wrinkles. Crumbling layers of old makeup clogged, distorted pores. Pam looked off over Katie's head, giving a view of yesterday's smeared mascara mixed with sleep-heavy lashes. Katie wanted to offer to return later, but knew Pam wouldn't respond differently then. If she opened the door at all.

Bringing up her parents had shut the other woman down. The cigarette in her hand was forgotten, except by the wind. Each gust glowed the ash and shortened the Winston's life.

"Everybody knows everybody here," Pam said at last. "They know all the secrets, all the dirty little gossip told behind closed doors. They act like they don't. So prim and proper. So eager to help, but only until there's no more dirt to dig. Yeah, I'm talking to all of you!" she yelled.

Katie took a step back. She was on the ground.

"You wanta know about my parents? Well, little girl, it's like this, if your daddy is a rich man, he can rape and beat and ignore what he leaves behind." Pam looked hard at Katie, who fought the urge to retreat another step. "That was my father. My mother was fourteen years old and greener than summer grass when she got married and barely fifteen when divorced. She was still a green kid. Then this grown man walks into her life. He took her, then paid my grandparents to keep their mouths shut and not make a stink. He was long gone before she learned she was carrying his bastard. Her folks turned her out. Six years later, she blew her brains out and left a mess for me to find when I got home from school. Her parents drove down south and brought the bastard back up with them. They raised her under their name, but there wasn't any love. They're gone now too. All four of them gone from this earth, and only the bastard, only I remain. I still hear the whispers. I know what others say."

Pam took a hard drag of the cigarette. It was almost down to the filter. Katie figured any moment, the other woman would be yelping and throwing the butt away, fingers red from a burn. But Pam held onto that last burning ember. Her other hand, fingernails chewed down to the bloody quick, rubbed across her face. After a few moments, she spoke again. The hard edge had given way to a little girl lost wistfulness.

"My mother's husband used to visit a few times a year," she said.

"Your father?" asked Katie, unsure who she meant.

"No. Weren't you listening? My father was a different man. He was George Beauregard, Junior." Pam used a chipped fingernail on her right hand to press back the cuticles on her left. "My mother had married this guy in high school. She knew after a couple of months he wasn't a keeper, so she left."

So, her ex still wanted her to come back, but she wanted what? Adventure, the chance to be some old guy's fancy piece. Or was she too proud to admit she'd made a mistake? Katie thought.

Pam stopped picking at her nails and looked up. Katie felt the other woman's eyes pierce through her face. Her thoughts were an open book.

"My mother was dead and gone by then. Yet, this guy kept coming around. He would come and stand on the front steps. Not even on the porch. After fifteen or twenty minutes, he would leave. I knew he was someone from mom's past, but it wasn't until my grandparents died, I knew who. He brought me a doll in a red dress once. My grandmother told him not to come back."

Unsure what to do with this information, Katie nodded without speaking. Finally, she found her tongue. "What was his name? Your mother's husband?"

"Jim Nattress. That's what it said in Mom's obituary. I found it in my grandmother's jewelry box." Pam crushed out her cigarette and went into the house, leaving Katie alone in the driveway.

She had found the right house and talked to the woman Janice wanted her to. All she had gained was the knowledge that Jim Nattress had to be added to her list of suspects.

Chapter Twenty-Two

Katie was standing in front of the open cupboard door. There was a small selection of can goods. She wanted to make something different for supper, though she had no idea what. Her foray to Bristol and Monkton, and the conversations she'd had with Ginny Wilder and Pam Kline, had left her feeling sullied. Cooking always helped fight depression. Right now, she needed to concoct some violently wild meal that would shake her senses and make her feel like forging ahead again. She became aware the cats were all nose and ears pointed toward the door at the same moment the knock came.

"Hi, Davey," she said, pulling the heavy kitchen door open. "Come on in."

"Nope," said the boy. "Dad says to get your gear on. He's getting the cleat track tractor out. We're going to go bobsledding in the duck meadow." With that, the boy, with a grin splitting the cherry-red cheeks of his face, spun around and ran off.

Katie was instantly interested. She ran into the living room and, through the windows, followed Davey's skidding and sliding descent down the rise until he was out of sight.

"Ruth," she called out, "do you have ski pants?"

"Not hardly," Ruth answered. "Why would I need them?"

"Raymond Dean has a bobsled. They just invited us to take a run over the duck meadow."

Ruth ran over to look out the same window as Katie. There was nothing to see. At the same moment, both women moved away.

"I've got two pairs of old wide-wale corduroy britches," said Ruth. "I'll put

121

on both of them."

Rick wasn't interested in the bobsledding, but he helped the women get ready, providing heavy wool hunting socks to be worn over thinner cotton ones and putting his heavy ear flap hat on Ruth's head again.

"Try not to break any bones," he said as Katie and Ruth hurried outside.

Raymond owned an antiquated yellow and mostly rusted Wain-Roy tractor. It had a bucket used for moving manure on one end and a claw digger for scooping on the other. The tractor also boasted cleat tracks, a solid running chain of metal plates that went from front to back on the sides where tires should be. Each metal plate had a three-inch cleat standing out of the middle. It would dig in and go where rubber tires couldn't. Today he was towing an equally aged bobsled. The four ten-foot-long planks that made up the oak sled were still solid. On either end was a short pair of skis, the ones in the back were rigid, and on either side was a hand-operated brake. A brakeman would yank back on the handles, the staves would come down, dig into the snow, and, theoretically, stop the bobsled.

"You get to be the brakeman," Grace called to Katie. "Ruth, you're right behind me."

Grace was seated in the front. Between her knees was the big round steering wheel confiscated from a defunct tractor. The steering wheel would control the front skis, which had just enough play to give the long sled some control. Everyone sat with their legs wrapped around and in the lap of the person in front of them. Ruth and the boys would ride, leaning with the turns and holding on to the slightly raised handle running the full length. If they all worked together, they would be able to control the sled. But if one person failed and fell off, chances were several would. There was no stopping to collect any lost riders.

"Last chance," Raymond yelled to Rick, who was standing on the door stoop.

But Rick waved them on and backed inside.

Raymond towed the bobsled and riding party to the top of the Took duck meadow. It was a hillside hay field with a natural duck pond in the middle. Below it was the heifer pasture, the fencing long gone, and the orchard off to the right. Once they had the bobsled in position and everyone was seated and ready, Raymond placed a large tire against the back edge of the bobsled behind Katie, and, using the rolled-up bucket of the Wain-Roy, shoved them off. This being the first run on virgin snow, the bobsled was slow to pick up speed, but once it had some momentum, they streamed along. Their line of descent would take them directly over the duck pond, adding a solid bump as it ran over the retaining ridge on either side.

"Hang on," Grace yelled as they approached the first ridge.

Please let the pond be frozen solid, Katie prayed.

They were over, across, and over again without losing any riders.

"Lean left," yelled Grace, spotting a rounded lump in the snowpack and turning the steering wheel to avoid it.

It could have been a forgotten bale of hay or a fence post. They slid around to one side, then all together, leaned right to avoid another obstacle. Once in the heifer pasture, Grace angled the bobsled toward the edge of the orchard. When they finally came to a stop, everyone was laughing and whooping with glee. Katie was also covered with a sheen of snow dust. It was a badge of recognition every brakeman earned. After a short wait, they saw the Wain-Roy chugging through the orchard. Raymond hooked onto the bobsled. Using a circuitous route through his own tractor tracks, he dragged them back around and to the top for another run.

After the second ride, Ruth left the sled for the warmth of the cook stove. But Katie, Grace, and the boys went for two more runs. When they were finished, and the Wain-Roy stopped for Katie to get off at her own front door, Rick came running out.

"We've got hot chocolate and cookies ready for everybody," he said, waving them into the house.

The stomping and melting snow had the cats all scuttling away. While they warmed up and shared conversation, the boys admired the puppies.

"Don't get any ideas," Raymond said to the boys. "We've got two dogs. That's enough."

Grace sipped chocolate and listened as Katie told them about the lost terrier and the abandoned babies.

"You know," she said. "Right before Thanksgiving, I was down at Beauregard's, dropping off butter and cheese. While I was waiting for Christopher to pay me, I saw a notice on the bulletin board about a lost wire-haired terrier. These puppies have that same kind of kinky fur. Maybe, Katie, you should check and see if that notice is still there. You might find the person who owns these cuties."

"That's a great idea, Grace. Thanks." Katie smiled at their guest and turned to Ruth and Rick. Her smile faded because, though Ruth seemed to think it was a good idea, Rick looked stricken.

Oh, Katie thought. *Solomon.*

Chapter Twenty-Three

There were a number of notices on the bulletin board. Hay and all manner of other items for sale. Some thumbtacks held three or four pieces of paper in place. Katie read the top layer, then began flipping scraps of paper over until she found one for a lost dog. The notice described a four-year-old female wire-haired terrier that had gone missing not far from where she had picked up the puppies. Pulling the notice free, she tucked it into her pocket before checking the other notices on the board. She had never considered finding local information here, and there was a lot of it. Deep underneath, she found a notice about a lost cat. It wasn't a feline that she had picked up, and the paper was dry and brittle.

"I hope you found your way home," she said to herself. She was tempted to pull the notice down, but was too superstitious to do so. If the lost kitty was still out there, this could be its lifeline.

"Can I help you?" asked the young male clerk.

"No, thanks. I found what I was looking for." Katie eyed the young man for a minute. He was looking over the board.

"I guess this got kind of filled up, didn't it?" he asked. "Every month or so, we take down the older notices. It's pretty slow today, so I guess this will be a good time." He pulled the first thumbtack and flipped to the furthest back notice.

"Are you Christopher's son?" Katie asked. There wasn't a lot of resemblance, with the exception of height and bearing.

"Yeah. I'm Karl." He looked more closely at Katie. "Do I know you?"

She smiled. "I've been gone for a while. You might not remember me,

Katelyn Took?"

"Sorry," he said. "I really don't."

"Do you mind telling me if you remember George Beauregard? He would have been your father's brother."

Karl took a half step back. Now he was giving Katie a wary look. "Why would you be asking about Uncle George?"

Katie decided this young man, who must have been around twenty, was educated enough not to make a snap judgment on what she had to say.

"I'm not trying to rattle any cages here," she explained. "My friend Ruth, you may know her, was married to George. She's having a crisis of faith. I'm just trying to help her work through it."

Karl relaxed. "I know Ruth. She's pretty quiet. There's a rumor she had some kind of breakdown a while ago and is missing a couple of screws, but every time I've waited on her, she's been fine."

"Yes," Katie nodded. "She did have a bad time. She's pretty well past it, but I wasn't here then. It's hard to know what to do for her because I don't really know what happened."

"Somebody killed my uncle." Karl continued checking notices, taking some down and stacking them on the edge of the counter. "My dad believes it was Ruth. He's adamant about it. But I get around, you know? Other people have different ideas. Uncle George never bothered me. He was a drunk, and I heard he had a bad temper when he was drinking, but the only time I ever saw it was when he would come in and demand my father give him alcohol. Dad always said no, said he wouldn't help George kill himself. I remember once, George got all loud and nasty. He was telling Dad the store belonged to him, and he'd have what he wanted. That was the only time I have never seen my father lose control. He grabbed hold of my uncle and dragged him out the back door."

"Did they come to blows?" asked Katie.

"No, Dad just left Uncle George lying out there on the dock. It took my father a long time to calm down. He stayed in his office. When he came out, he went out to the dock to check on George, but he was gone." Karl grinned and whispered. "George had pissed all over the back door. Dad flipped out again."

"That's disgusting," said Katie, unable to keep a straight face. "What about your grandfather?"

"I didn't really know him," said Karl. "I was just a kid when he died." Picking up the stack of notices, he circled to the back of the counter, throwing them in the trash as he greeted a customer.

Katie went back outside. The pay phone was right there. The notice had a phone number. Dropping a dime in the slot, she waited until a woman answered.

"Hi," said Katie, "I'm the animal control officer for Parentville. I'd like to talk to you about some puppies."

* * *

"So," Katie said, stirring her cream of carrot soup. "The woman said yes. They had a female terrier who disappeared in front of the first big snowstorm, and that she was pregnant when she went missing. She said when the dog came back, the puppies had been born, but they didn't know where."

"And the dog didn't go back to her babies?" Ruth asked.

"They probably kept her restrained so she couldn't," said Rick.

"That's what I think," said Katie. "They don't want the puppies. She specifically told me not to bring them to her."

There was a white line around Rick's mouth. "What does the law say?"

Katie looked at him questioningly.

"Katie. That woman has a responsibility. You need to call Sheriff Lewis and find out what it is."

Suddenly Katie was uncomfortable.

"I know the two of you don't get along," said Rick. "But your job is to pick up strays and take them home. That's what these little guys are: strays. Call Lewis."

Sheriff Lewis pulled into the dooryard an hour and a half later. Ruth had just gotten done feeding the two female puppies. Rick had taken to feeding Solomon whenever he was home.

127

"Are you taking the puppies?" Ruth asked as soon as Lewis was in the house.

Sheriff Lewis held his campaign hat in his hands, a scowl on his face.

"Both the man and the woman claimed the puppies weren't theirs. I said it was no problem. I would take the female. A vet would check them all and make a determination. If they were wrong, they'd get the fine, the veterinarian's bill and all related sheriffs and court costs would have to be paid."

Katie's jaw dropped.

"They relented, said it was pretty possible. Therefore, they would take the puppies," said Lewis.

"You can't do that," Ruth cut in. "These puppies are bottle babies. That female won't have milk for them after all this time. Not only that, if those people don't want the puppies, they'll just, just get rid of them." Katie heard the horror rising in Ruth's words.

"Hold on, Ruth," she said, laying a hand on her friend's arm. "Maybe there's a different solution."

"Don't you think I thought about that?" Lewis asked Ruth. "What I told them was that I'd have you bring the puppies out, but I'd better find them there every time I came to check. Or I'd hold the puppies back, but there were conditions. First, they had to get their dog spayed. They had ten days, and I had to see a record of it. If the dog disappeared, I'd be fining them heavy. I wouldn't accept any excuses. When they showed up with the notice, I wanted a check for twenty dollars to cover puppy food. I know it's not a lot of money, but from what I saw, it's going to hurt them. I also told them that if new owners weren't found for the puppies by the time they were six weeks old, I'd be back looking for room and board money."

"I'm keeping one of the puppies," said Rick.

Katie rolled her eyes. She had known that was coming.

"Well, then that leaves two. Is that good for you, Katie? Basically, as the animal control officer, this is your call."

"I don't have to check with the town?"

"You can if you want, but other than to verify the female dog has a license.

I think we've got this all handled. I'll be typing up a report and will have a deputy hand deliver a copy to the owners. That way, they can't say they didn't know any of this." There was a twinkle in Sheriff Lewis' eye.

He's enjoying this, thought Katie. "I guess I'm good with it. I'll check on the license. Will you keep me informed?"

"I'll make sure you get a copy of the report and the follow-up."

After Lewis left, Rick laid a hand on her shoulder. "Looks like you're going to need to start keeping a file."

"See, I told you before that Sheriff Lewis would come around," said Ruth. "You're practically buddies."

"Until the next time I step on his toes," Katie said.

Chapter Twenty-Four

Katie left the feed store after arranging to take the late lunch break, telling Stan she needed to go home to make a couple of telephone calls and might be late returning.

"I'm sorry, Stan," she said. "But these places are only open during the week, and I can't wait a lot longer to make the calls."

Even though Stan knew Katie had Tuesdays off with Cindy there to help out, he could be flexible. "Go ahead; you can stay after to make up the time. I'll be able to get out of here quicker if you do the final mop-up, and I only have to close the books."

"It's a deal," she said.

Cleaning the heavy mud and gravel out of the aisles after the store closed was a back-breaking job. But she'd trade the time needed to contact the judge who had handled the George Beauregard murder case for a little hard work.

With Ruth down at the Dean farm helping Grace, Katie could make her call in private. The only other telephone on their party line was the Dean farm. No one there would intrude.

"I know I'm going to get stuck on hold, so I'll peel while I wait," she told the cats after gathering what she'd need for supper prep.

"Good afternoon, this is Katelyn Took. I would like to speak with Judge Abelle, or maybe his assistant." She told the switchboard operator.

She had been right in assuming she would be placed on hold. There was plenty of time to peel the potatoes and carrots she had gathered on the table, as well as twiddle her thumbs. Eventually, she was forwarded to the secretary of the judge's assistant.

In as few words as possible, she explained who she was, and that she was trying to get information regarding the murder case of George Beauregard. The secretary sounded skeptical about being able to help Katie, but asked for her address, working address, and phone number. "I'll see what I can do," was the only promise Katie got from the woman.

Katie rinsed the vegetables, sliced them, and threw them in the pot on the back of the wood stove where she had left meat simmering that morning. Driving back to the feed store, she wondered if she had provided enough information to the woman at the courthouse.

"You did what?" Cindy gasped, eyes wide and mouth opened.

"Do you think I should have gone there in person?" Katie asked.

"Myself, personally, I don't think you should have approached those people at all," said Cindy, natural curls swishing back and forth as she shook her head emphatically.

Katie was still suffering some self-doubt when the entrance door for the feed store, which was right beside where she was working, opened, and Corporal Derrick of the Vermont State Police and Sheriff Martin Lewis entered.

"Crap," both Katie and Cindy said at the same time.

Lewis nodded in the direction of Katie. Cindy pointed toward the office and gave Katie a shove in that direction. The interview with the two officers was short. They both told Katie that law enforcement and the research associated with it were better left to the professionals.

"If you hear something that you believe is of value," said Corporal Derrick, "please feel free to forward the information to me or Sheriff Lewis."

Katie nodded in agreement. Lewis stood beside Derrick, and though he did not have much to say, there was a sparkle in his eye that brought a flush to Katie's cheeks.

"Those guys just fry my bacon." Katie hissed after the men left.

"If you keep pissing Lewis off, you aren't going to have to worry about frying anything," said Cindy. "Because he's going to make sure you get three square meals a day and a roof over your head."

Stan, who had appeared while his office was in use, agreed. "Maybe you had better step back on this one, Katie. I don't know if Lewis really cares about the people concerned or not, but you're barking up his family tree."

Katie went back to work. There was a dark lump in her chest. No longer would she be able to ask her friends for help or even talk about what she was doing. Both Cindy and Stan had made it clear she needed to stop.

How can I do that? She wondered.

Later, she wrote a letter to Marlie. In it, she wrote, *It's not just the murder of George Beauregard and how it affects Ruth, but I keep hearing people tell me that this type of stuff is swept under the rug, ignored by neighbors and even family. Maybe if one, just one time, the worse is exposed, other people will speak out. I don't know. I don't trust my own thoughts any more right now. It just makes me so angry. What else is slithering around in the dark? How could I have been so blind? How long is it going to be before people like us can walk around unmolested in public?*

The writing made her feel better. It didn't solve the problem, but when she laid her pen down, she knew she was not done looking. *I just need to be less of a public spectacle*, she thought.

* * *

While Ruth and Rick sorted record albums, Katie headed down to Dean's farm for butter and milk and to make payment for any amount due on their week's purchases after Ruth's work.

"Grace," said Katie, holding the envelope with the remainder of Ruth's wages, "has Ruth said anything to you about George lately?"

Grace raised her head slowly from her account book. "Ruth has never talked about George. What's going on?"

Before Katie could get started, Grace sent her young boys off to do their homework. She and Raymond sat across from Katie, listening while she explained what she was trying to find out.

"Basically, you're just collecting facts?" Raymond asked. At Katie's nod, he continued, "Both Grace and I grew up right here in town. George's the-other-side-of-the-sheet kids went to school with us. I know for some families, the Hoopers were a blight. Parents would tell their kids to avoid the Hooper children. Those kids would react by being cruel. My father told me the sins of the father should not be visited upon the children. And if he caught one of us boys, or even heard a whisper that one of us was involved in bullying, we were in for a public whipping on Main Street."

At Katie's raised brows, Raymond nodded, perfectly serious.

"I had no doubt he would do it," he said. "For him, it was the same as thieving. Grace's family lived further out of town. She didn't see as much as we did. By the time she was in high school where we went, only Geneva was still around."

"Did you know them?" Katie asked.

"Darlene was the oldest, the same age as my brother, Shane. There was another girl, two boys, then Geneva. I was the same age as Rudy; my brother Todd was younger, like Grace. Darlene married a boy from Essex. They had a couple of kids, and the last I heard divorced. I don't know the whereabouts of either of the other girls or the oldest boy. Rudy overdosed over in Charlotte a few years ago."

"I don't know anything other than that," said Grace. "Geneva was terribly shy. Other than the fact they didn't have a daddy at home, I don't think they were all that different."

"So, mostly all that's a dead end," said Katie, despair evident in the slump of her shoulders.

"I'm not sure where Darlene is, but her two girls are around here somewhere. One lives in the village. She rents the mother-in-law apartment on the back of Julbert's house. I think her name is Virginia. If she hasn't gotten married, she'd still be a Wilder."

Katie thanked her friends, left an envelope for Davey, who was helping take care of Bonnie and, with her dairy groceries in hand, headed back to the house. She had hoped to be able to talk to a few of Mildred Hooper's offspring, but it looked like Virginia Wilder was the best she'd be able to do.

At least now I know where Ginny Wilder lives, and where she works, Katie thought.

Chapter Twenty-Five

The tension Katie felt during the drive home evaporated when she came over the rise and Marlie's car was already parked in the dooryard.

"You're early!" Katie blushed. "Nothing like stating the obvious."

Ruth had already put Marlie to work feeding the puppies.

"Are they adorable? The bigger they get, the cuter they are. I bet you want to keep them all."

Katie elected to not say she wasn't interested in any. Instead, she started talking about the people she had been speaking with about George Beauregard, and her visit to the Wagon Wheel and the Cup and Spoon Diner. When she mentioned Ginny Wilder's name, Marlie put the puppy she was holding back in the box. Ruth had gone upstairs. After making sure the elderly woman wasn't returning, Marlie turned to Katie.

"You actually talked to Ginny?" Marlie asked.

Hearing a nervous edge, Katie looked more closely at the other woman. "Yes. Why? Is she not to be trusted?"

"No, that's not it, Katie." Marlie rubbed her palms over her knees. "Ginny is pretty forthright. I don't think she would lie to you."

"You know her?" Katie asked, surprised. Marlie rarely talked about other people she knew in town, but this woman could possibly have been a friend.

"Yeah." Marlie checked the staircase again. "It's like this, Katie. Virginia Wilder and I used to be friends, you know, close friends."

Katie sat back on her heels. "Oh?"

"We, I don't know. To be honest, we were together for a while. Then

Virginia said I was too intense, and that was it."

"You were a couple?" asked Katie. "And Virginia broke it off?"

Above them, Ruth's footsteps clattered in the hall.

"That's right. She broke it off because I was so serious about being a deputy, and she wanted to have fun. She's the one that took me to the Red Dog Bar in Burlington where I saw Geoffrey Ash."

Ruth was coming down the stairs.

"Are you still friends?"

"Well, we aren't enemies," said Marlie. She paused as Ruth collected empty milk bottles and headed to the kitchen. "But we haven't hung around together for a very long time."

"Good to know." Katie got to her feet.

Marlie also rose. "I don't want to have secrets. I wanted to tell you myself. You never know who will say what. But it's over, Katie, between Virginia and me."

Even though she wasn't sure how she felt, Katie smiled. "Like I said, good to know." Kissing her fingertips, she touched Marlie's cheek. "I've got a little investigating to do, and I need a posse. Want to go"

With Marlie riding shotgun, Katie drove over to Richmond.

Wrinkling her nose, Marlie said. "You have to do this today? Funeral homes are not my favorite day off field trip."

"Relax," said Katie, flicking on her directional light and slowing for a stop sign. "It's a nice day for a ride. You don't have to go inside, and besides, they're probably closed on Sunday or by the time I get out of work. Tuesdays are pretty much my only choice."

On the short main street, she looked back and forth for Richmond Funeral Home. What she saw was Hutton's Funeral Home and Mortuary. Deciding that this half-a-horse town wouldn't boast two such enterprises, she pulled into the rutted dirt lot.

"Are you coming in?" she asked, trying to sound mildly interested, and not vocalizing the need she had for someone to walk through that front door with her.

Marlie shook her head and turned away.

Crap, Katie said to herself, walking up the two steps to the small front porch. A bell tinkled as she opened the door. *Shouldn't that be a gong with a raven, like a castle bell tower? Or maybe a creaking coffin lid?*

A woman in her mid-forties came out from the back end of the building, discreetly wiping around her mouth. It was, after all, lunchtime.

"May I help you?" she asked, crossing her hands in front of her lower abdomen. She had a practiced smile that hovered between welcome to our business and sorry for your loss.

After wetting her lips, Katie offered a small smile in return and said, "My name is Katelyn Took. I'm looking for some information regarding a gentleman that passed away a little over five years ago. I believe this is the, ah, business that collected his remains."

"Are you with the police?"

Jeez, why does everyone think that first thing? "No, actually, family." Katie changed to a more forlorn smile.

The woman didn't offer for them to adjourn and have a seat in her office, but the building seemed to be empty anyway, so Katie kept talking.

"The gentleman was George Beauregard, Junior, from Parentville. And the question is in regards to the cause of his demise." This wasn't the time to beat around the bush, and she could see another casket waiting for the family in the adjoining room. The heebie-jeebies ran up her shins, causing her socks to crawl downward.

"Both of the Mr. George Beauregards were guests here," the woman said without inflection. The set of her shoulders indicated she wasn't going to be very helpful. "There really is a limited amount of information we can give out."

A man came through the same doorway the woman had. He was pulling on his suit jacket. And, like the woman, he had a slight bit of grease on his lip.

Definitely lunch, Katie thought.

"Perhaps I can be of more help," he said. "I'm Edward Hutton."

"I understand about your inability to share information," said Katie. "After all, you don't know me from Adam. My questions involve what you found for wounds on George Junior's body. His wife is my aunt, and she's still suffering from the experience. We're trying to get her some help, maybe tie up a few of the loose ends."

"I heard she was questioned in connection." Mrs. Hutton gave an audible sniff.

Her husband laid his hand on her arm. "Why don't you go finish your lunch while it's still hot, dear? It's okay. I'll be right there."

The woman walked away with what Poppa would have called a corn cob stuck-up-her-butt attitude.

Mr. Hutton chewed his lip for a moment. Moving from the entry hall to a viewing room where the closed casket rested among a few floral arraignments, he said. "What I am going to tell you is no more than I told the sheriff and the other gentleman when they arrived here the morning after we collected the remains."

"Okay," said Katie. Her feet shuffled in a wide arc away from the casket, while her mind grabbed onto the word sheriff.

"Even though the family did not ask for an autopsy, I was curious as to his wound. I had heard it was inflicted by his wife, and while I was there, a young deputy was conferring with one of the rescue workers. I got the impression the wife was a woman of slight build."

"Hold on," said Katie. "Do you remember who either the deputy or the rescue person was? Could it have been a woman?"

"Yes, the person from the local rescue unit was a woman, dark hair, I believe. I didn't get either name. Like I said, the deputy was young and still all shiny." Mr. Hutton blushed slightly. "By that, I mean new to the department."

"And tall?" Katie asked. At Mr. Hutton's nod, she knew he meant Deputy Brad and stifled a grimace.

"As I was saying, I examined the wound very closely."

"Like in, you cut him open?" Katie asked.

Mr. Hutton blushed again. "Only slightly more than I would have to prepare a body for viewing and interment."

"Okay, that's fine. What did you find?" It may have been a professional breach, but Katie didn't care what the mortician had done to George Beauregard's earthly remains.

"The wound went all the way back to where the fourth rib came off the spine, actually nicking into it. It was very confusing."

"In what way?" Even though she had no love for a man she'd never met, Katie had to swallow hard to push down her rising gorge.

Mr. Hutton moved all the way across the room to a bay window that fronted on the porch. Katie followed, and when she realized she was hedging him in against the window seat, she took two small steps backward.

"I can absolutely understand why Mrs. Beauregard was unable to remove the knife, but for a woman of small stature to have driven it in so deeply, she would have had to be standing over him and then used a hammer to pound it in."

Katie blinked. The man's statement had been much more blunt than what she had heard before.

Hutton's head cocked, the look on her face confusing him. He asked, "You don't understand why she couldn't withdraw the knife?"

Before he launched into an explanation, Katie held up her hand. "No, I've been told how that works. Thank you. It's the hammer part that came as a surprise." Her hands were restless, and she shoved them into her pockets. "Go on, please."

"Well, let's see," said Mr. Hutton, "without going into information, I can't divulge. I will say Mr. Beauregard did not have a lot of other bruising. No fingerprints like he had been held against his will. There were no defensive marks. Let's see. Oh, his shirt was saturated with alcohol and Wild Cherry. He was wearing a t-shirt and boxer shorts and socks, that was all. Not only could you see the stains, but the smell was quite strong."

"Wild Cherry?" Katie asked, wondering if that was a type of brandy.

"Oh, yes, sorry. That would be Wild Cherry cough syrup. It's commonly used and has a very distinctive odor. As I was telling both the sheriff and the gentleman, used in combination with alcohol, that alone would have been deadly."

Katie took an involuntary step backwards. "Mr. Hutton, is it possible that

CHAPTER TWENTY-FIVE

Mr. Beauregard was already expired before he was stabbed?"

Now it was Mr. Hutton's turn to look nervous. "It had crossed my mind. I mentioned it to both men and inquired as to if they would want a fuller autopsy. Both declined. The gentleman went so far as to say, he believed it was Mrs. Beauregard who was using the cough syrup. That the deceased deplored the taste."

Katie was silent for a moment. On the back of her retina was a view of her own medicine cabinet, with the brown medicinal bottle and its black and white label clearly identifying it as Wild Cherry cough syrup. The wind battered the window, and she remembered what she was doing.

"What did you do with Mr. Beauregard's clothing?" she asked.

"The gentleman took them when he brought in Mr. Beauregard's outfit for the viewing."

"The sheriff, you mean?"

"No." Mr. Hutton looked right at Katie. She knew then he had considered this event before and found his reactions at the time to be lacking. "About an hour before the sheriff arrived, the other gentleman came in. As I said, he brought the clothing for the viewing. As I was busy, I spoke with him for only a few minutes before returning to what I was doing. My wife handled the paperwork and the details. When he asked, she gave him the parcel with the stained clothing. Though I would have held them for the sheriff, there wasn't anything I could say because that is generally how this works."

Katie exhaled. A question came to her lips, but Mr. Hutton was ahead of her. "It was," he said, "Mr. Beauregard's younger brother."

* * *

"Are you hungry?" Katie asked when she returned to the car. "There's a greasy spoon up the road on the way to Waterbury. Rick says they serve a hot roast beef sandwich to die for."

"I'm thinking from the nervous twitch in your face, you heard something in there that's making your brain boil over," said Marlie.

The distance was short, and by the time they had arrived at the diner,

Katie had given back all she heard. Once they were seated and their order was placed, she pulled out her little notebook. Marlie waited patiently while Katie wrote down the conversation she'd had with Mr. Hutton. The waitress put down the heavy China just as she finished. The plates were platters stacked high with hand-cut French fries sitting beside slabs of rare roast beef on toast, all smothered with thick gravy.

While they ate, Marlie asked her questions. Then both women worked to tie knots between what Katie had heard in the past and what she had just learned.

After refusing dessert, they finished their coffee.

"Ruth will be up from her nap by now," said Katie. "Maybe I should have gotten a piece of that peach pie for her."

"Maybe, Katie, instead, you should sit down and tell her what you've found out and what you think it means."

"I don't know what it means," Katie said, opening the door to the pickup. "Like I said, did Hutton mean George could have already been dead from an accidental mixing of alcohol and medication? Or behind door number two, somebody administered a lethal cocktail, or three, he was just unconscious, presenting the perfect opportunity."

"If Ruth was going to kill George, she would have needed that opportunity." Marlie didn't look very happy to be making that point.

"Do you think Ruth killed her husband?" Katie asked.

"Honestly, no. But I saw weirder things working as a sheriff."

Chapter Twenty-Six

Stan left his office carrying an ordering tear sheet. He was headed across the store towards the area where the winter-weight hunting jackets and vests had been decimated by the recent deer and bear season.

"Message for you," he said to Katie as he walked past.

The memo note he handed her relayed that Robin Pierce, manager of the Vermont County Coop Creamery, had seen a full-grown black cat and four kittens hanging around the area where farm trucks backed in to unload the heavy milk cans every day.

"Five cats," Katie told Ruth when she called home on her break. "More than I have live traps for. If Rick stops by on his run, have him bring both of the cat traps and the smaller one we use for squirrels. Give him two cans of mackerel and a can opener, as well."

"How about a carrier?" asked Ruth. "If you catch a kitten, you can transfer and reuse a trap."

"Good idea," said Katie. "If you don't see him, I'll pick up the traps and come back to town later this evening."

Ruth took down the names of Rick's last three stops. She'd try to pin him down. Twenty minutes before closing, Rick's delivery truck pulled into the feed store parking lot. Braking in front of Katie's window, Rick blew the horn, waving to show he had received the message and had her gear on board. When she left the store, he was placing the last of the traps in the rear bed of her truck.

"This bag," he said, handing her a paper sack, "is mackerel and a jar of milk.

141

This one is sandwiches for you. Ruth says this old thermos won't hold heat long, so drink the tea before it gets cold." He waited until she had placed both bags, plus her snare rod and the big, long-handled fish net, in the cab of her truck. "Do you need me to go along?"

At her negative reply, he started his own truck and drove away. Katie followed, continuing straight through the village until she came to the creamery. The building was buttoned up for the night, but Katie knew where she was going. At the deserted concrete deck where farmers unloaded their full and reloaded their empty milk cans, she pulled all three traps from the back of her truck. The cold metal smelled slightly gamey, but she was hoping if the cats were hungry, they wouldn't pay too much attention.

From a sack full of lids saved from mayonnaise and pickle jars, she removed six, filling them with mackerel and milk before baiting the live traps. She spaced the traps away from each other and set the spring action doors. Each trap was draped with a piece of old canvas, making it a dark cavern. Parked across the lot, with the engine off, she ate her cold supper and watched the small portion of the parking lot illuminated by a light mounted on the exterior of the building.

The tea was tepid, but she sipped from the cup, keeping her eyes on the square of light. Suddenly, one kitten, then another, then two more ran across the lit space. They were running away from the building. Katie waited. Within a few minutes, the kittens ran back the way they had come. She continued to wait. The illuminated Roman numerals on her Timex said fifteen minutes had passed since the return trip of the kittens. Katie walked over to check the traps. All three had been sprung. In one trap was a large black cat. Snarling and hissing, she let Katie know she wanted nothing to do with her. In each of the other traps, huddled in the furthest corner, were smaller, quieter forms.

Katie took the two traps containing kittens back to the truck. In the security of the cab, she fished the spitting, clawing babies out one at a time, placing them in a carrier together. Katie reset and baited the traps back where they had been. For the next half an hour, she sat in the truck, starting it only once to heat the cab. No more kittens crossed her path, but from her parking spot, she could see the road and watched traffic move back and forth. Though unable to make out any vehicle as belonging to someone specific, she played a useless identifying game. Whispering aloud, so the kittens could hear her, she guessed at the model of a moving car seen only as a black space between white headlights and red taillights.

"Car. Pickup. Car. Car. Pickup. Tractor-trailer. Guy is either running late or lost. Car."

Thirty minutes passed before she checked the traps again. One was empty. The other held another disgruntled kitten. Katie considered her options. She hadn't seen the other kitten crossing the light, and in the dark, she'd never be able to figure out where it was holed up. After placing the third baby with its litter-mates, she loaded the trap into the truck bed. Outside the loading dock, she emptied the last of the mackerel into a couple of can lids. While Katie knelt on the ground, dishing out the mackerel, she talked to the mother cat, who had settled down to only the occasional snarl.

"You've done pretty good so far," Katie said. "Four babies in the middle of winter. They've got nice thick coats, and they don't appear all that thin."

She looked around the deserted lot. At the far end were the tankers, ready to haul out the next day. The crackle of ice shifting in the banks of shoveled snow, and the stink of ozone released and hovering over those same banks, didn't make Katie shiver the way a cry from a far-off coyote did.

"I'm going to let you lose, mama," she crooned. "If I don't, your last baby probably won't last the night. I'm not seeing it anywhere, and I'm hoping it's gone back to its bed. Don't get me wrong. I'll be back. I know you will be harder to catch because you'll remember this, but I'll try. Enjoy the mackerel." Releasing the door, Katie moved away until the female darted out, slinking, low-belied away. Taking her traps, Katie drove toward home.

* * *

"Did you get them?" Ruth asked.

"Three of the babies." Katie warmed her frozen fingers over the wood stove. "Rick, leave two of the traps in the truck. I'll try again tomorrow.

I threw a tarp over both of them so if it snows tonight, the latches won't freeze."

"Next vehicle you get has a top on the truck bed," he said.

She nodded, but a different vehicle wasn't on her horizon. Rick had already brought in one of the large dog crates they had found while yard sailing. It was set up with a small litter box and a warm bed, as well as food and water tins attached to a piece of 2"x4" board to prevent the kittens from spilling. While Ruth transferred Katie's catch. Sasha watched with worried eyes.

"No, Sasha," Ruth said gently. "Not tonight. Maybe tomorrow Katie will catch their mama. We don't want her to reject the babies because you stepped in. Go see your puppies. Go on."

Sasha moved a few steps away. The puppies were playing on the floor at Rick's feet. With the new arrivals tucked away, already hiding among the blankets of the nesting box, Ruth slid the wood box frame used to contain the puppies closer.

"How's that, Sasha," she asked. "Does that make you feel better?"

"Oops," said Rick. "Somebody piddled on the floor."

The collection of cats, all at a level where the playful young dogs could not reach them, turned a jaundiced eye.

Katie stood in the kitchen door, watching. The warm cup of tea clasped in her fingers caused just enough pain in her frozen digits for her to flick them one at a time off and back.

"Between all eight, the meager funds in the cat account available for vetting is going to be sucked dry," she said. "There won't be enough unless Sheriff Lewis can get the owner of the puppies' mother to pay up. But I'm willing to bet that even with Sheriff Lewis' assistance, that guy isn't going to throw in a dime."

"If it's okay with you," Rick had said. "I'd like to keep Solomon. I'll pay his vet bill separately."

"Sure," said Katie. "It's inevitable some of these cats will go to houses where there are dogs. Having one here will make the transition easier." Ruth smiled broadly. "One, Ruth. We are keeping only one. Can you check with Lewis tomorrow and see if the female had been spayed?"

Rick raised an eyebrow.

Katie sighed. "I'm just curious as to the worth of Sheriff Lewis' power in a situation like this. And, you know, he's not going to want to talk to me."

* * *

The working day at the dairy started at four. Katie knew that she'd be able to find Mr. Pierce by five. When she reported her limited success, he agreed to keep an eye open for the rest of the cats.

"She may move to a new spot," said Katie. "Then again, if she's been successful here finding food, she may not. For a day or so, she'll be looking for the other kittens. I can come down and try trapping them again, but I'd like to know they're still here first."

"I'll tell my guys to keep on the lookout," he said. "Releasing her is going to make her harder to catch."

Katie nodded, but it was her job. If the female was actually totally feral, reconditioning her to live with people might be out of the question. If she had just been turned out of somebody's home, it was possible. Regardless, once Katie caught her, Doctor Veronica would spay and provide shots. If feral, the female would be released from where she was caught. The kittens would be tamed and moved to their new homes. That was Ruth's part of the job. Before noon, Katie's elderly partner would have contacted Doctor Veronica, letting her know what would be coming. In another three weeks, the puppies would be making their trip to the vet.

Chapter Twenty-Seven

It was early as Katie drove through town, but Jonathon Beauregard was already pushing slush across the back of the parking lot, so she pulled in. The day had gotten slightly warmer than seasonal, and the hard pack had softened up. Churning car tires created ruts and ponds that would freeze solidly during the night. Once frozen again, the rough parking area and walkways would be a hazard.

"Hey, Jonathon," Katie called out.

The young man looked up, hesitating the forward momentum of the wide wooden snow scoop. Recognizing Katie, he waved in a go-away manner and went back to work.

What crawled up his butt? She wondered at the snub. Resolutely, she headed toward his retreating back. "Why is it every time I see you, there's a shovel in your hands?"

Jonathon hadn't heard her getting closer until she spoke. She was right behind him, and startled; he swung around. Katie got a good look at the bruise on the side of his face and the black eye before he turned away.

"What happened?" she blurted out.

"Wet snow, slippery ice, hence the shovel," Jonathan grunted and got the scoop filled with wet slush moving again.

Katie wasn't deterred. She circled around him. Laying her hand on his arm, she asked, "Did you see the doctor? That looks pretty ugly."

Jonathon smirked. "You city people. Out here, you don't run to the doctor every time you trip over your own feet and fall."

While he was talking, Katie was taking a good look. There was a small place at the top of Jonathon's cheek that looked like the skin had split.

"If you hadn't told me," she said, "I would have thought someone punched you."

Jonathon's head jerked up. He went slightly pale around the eyes, but his cheeks instantly bloomed a deep red. "Don't be foolish. I have to finish up, so goodbye." He maneuvered around her and pushed toward the banking.

Katie headed toward the front entrance of the store. Both Jonathon's manner and the strained way he had pushed her off felt wrong. He had been so friendly before.

Standing on the loading dock against the heavy swinging doors, Christopher watched the exchange, eyes narrowed. Jonathon had always been an obedient son, accepting his father's word and learning the business. Then, Christopher had come in and heard the boy questioning his mother about George's death.

"What are you talking about?" Christopher had demanded. "That's nothing to be upsetting your mother about. It's done and past."

"People are talking," said Jonathon. "They're coming into the store and asking questions. I just wanted to know."

"Ignore them," Christopher said.

"I can't ignore them! They're standing right in front of me at the cash register, with others in hearing distance. I'm not looking to have a long story to tell them. I just don't want to sound like some ignorant shop boy every time I open my mouth."

In his frustration, Jonathon's voice had risen. He was standing close to his father, irritation plain on his face. For the first time in the boy's life, Christopher swung out and backhanded him. The slap was hard enough to rocket Jonathon's head back on his shoulders, sending him spiraling around. He slammed into the edge of the table before falling to the floor.

Christopher's hand hurt. His heart ached. Tracey ran to her son, and Christopher left the house. He was ashamed and angry. Late in the evening, when he came back, the house was dark. Tracey sat at the kitchen table.

"Your father was a mean man, so was your brother. They both got what they deserved," said Tracey. "If you ever lay a hand on either one of my boys again, I'll see you run out of this town without a cent in your pocket. Do you understand?"

"I'm sorry." Christopher hung his head.

"Tell the boy." Tracey got up and went to bed.

Behind where she was sitting was a blanket and a pillow. The solid closing of the door upstairs let Christopher know he would not be sleeping there. In his room, Jonathon listened. He heard his father creep up the stairs and the whispered apology, but he didn't open his eyes.

* * *

"I have to tell you," Katie told Cindy the next day, "it sure looked to me like Jonathon had been on the losing end of a fistfight."

"I've never heard of Christopher being a violent man," said Cindy. "And I don't believe that type of behavior comes in the blood."

"No," Katie said, "but it can be learned."

Chapter Twenty-Eight

It was two days before Mr. Pierce called back saying the female cat and kitten were back. It was during the daylight hours, Katie and one of the employees of the dairy caught the kitten using the broad net. A feat she did not believe they would accomplish. The mother cat escaped them, but Katie saw her crouched under one of the tankers, fifty feet away, watching. On her return, Katie took the carrier inside the feed store while she finished her shift. There was a great amount of oohing and aahing around the cat carrier. Stan okayed Katie to hang up a notice that she had two puppies and four kittens looking for adoption between Christmas and New Year's.

"Yes," she said to an interested party, "all will have had their first shots and will be either spayed or neutered."

Here in farm country, both events were an oddity. People had dogs and cats, all of which lived outside and in, yet few ever traveled to the veterinarian. Even fewer were licensed.

"You didn't catch the mother cat?" Stan asked.

"No, the kittens are big enough to eat on their own if provided," she said. "Mr. Pierce said he would put the trap out the next time he sees the female. As long as she's not caught and left outside overnight, I'm okay with it."

Katie had left the piece of blanket the kittens had slept on in the trap for Mr. Pierce to use, hoping their scent would draw the mother.

* * *

Katie sauntered into the Wagon Wheel at nine, just as the supper hour was ending. She had stopped into the Saint Jude's thrift store earlier. For the first time in months, she was out of jeans or duc work pants. Courtesy of somebody else's donation, she was wearing hip-hugging pants with a vertical pattern that added to her height, leather buccaneer platform heels, and a long-sleeved midi-top with two-inch fringe. They were a little out of date for Illinois, but around here, they'd do. She felt like a circus freak, but from the ogling glances she got from guys she passed, not everyone had the same thoughts. Marlie had taught her to do the eye makeup, but the heightened color was her own.

Across the dining room, through the archway, she could see Ken Sampson leaning on the bar. Katie wove her way among the tables, hoping not to topple on the heels. She stood behind Sampson, one elbow on the bar.

"Mr. Sampson? What are the chances you're looking for a waitress?"

Sampson turned until he was standing with both elbows on the bar. His cold pipe hung from his lips. They were thin and wet. Katie's skin crawled as he looked her up and down, a slow smile growing. The same cruel glitter she had seen before lighting his eyes.

"I knew your grandfather," said Sampson. His hand shoved deep into his trouser pocket to pull out a pipe lighter, one click and a flame shot out; his slimy lips tightened around the pipe stem and drew it into the bowl.

"Yeah, how's that?" Katie's stomach roiled. Inhaling through her teeth, she looked over the liquor menu pinned up on the wall.

"For a while there, he was one of my best customers."

She knew he meant George Beauregard. Why was it people thought she was his granddaughter? Was it her tall, thin frame or thick, brown hair? Maybe it was just her attitude. She didn't know, but this time she wasn't going to correct him.

"So, you got a job opening or not?" She shot him an insolent look, thinking how she'd like to use the bar stool to mop the floor with him.

"Nothing in the dining room," he said. "Ever done any cocktail waitress-ing?"

"Some." She let her eyes roam over the crowd, ignoring his leer.

"How about you come with me and fill out an application?"

Katie slid her butt up onto the empty stool behind her. "How about if I wait here until you get back?" She smiled, letting him know she wouldn't be an easy conquest.

His grin brightened; he liked a challenge.

Forty-five minutes later, Katie was signed up, given a bank, and working her first shift.

"Five different prices," said Irene, the bar-back. The bartender working the main section had turned Katie over to his subordinate. "Draft, bottle, wine, alcohol with water or soda, and trash drinks. Try to avoid those. Gloria is the head waitress; she'll tell you what area is yours."

"Works for me," she said, writing the prices on a napkin and stuffing it in her waistband. "Which one is Gloria?"

"The hard looking broad all snuggled up to Sampson," said Irene. "Word to the wise. Watch yourself."

Katie would be working three nights, Friday, Saturday, and Sunday, until ten. Two hours into the shift, she knew all the prices, had already had her first run-in with Gloria, and her feet hurt.

"What is Gloria's problem? All I did was tell some guy I wasn't his type. It's not like I punched him out." Kate asked the bar-back while waiting for her drink order.

"You never came in here much, did you?" said Irene, adding water to a glass of ice and Johnny Walker. "She wants to be the new Mrs. Sampson. Been chasing that man for twenty years. Problem is, he's not ready to ditch the old Mrs. Sampson."

"Why is that?" Katie asked, lining up the drinks on her tray.

"Because she's the one holding all the money cards for this place."

Katie walked back out onto the floor, wondering which one of the women in the room was the old Mrs. Sampson. *Or maybe he and Gloria are so loose in front of all these folks, because she's not here.* That made more sense.

She had been assigned the area furthest from the dance floor, just outside the kitchen doors. It was okay for tonight, but if she was going to get information fast, she needed to be out where the action was. Deviating from the path she should have followed back to her tables, Katie headed toward the table where Priscilla and Bumpie would be.

She barely got there when Gloria was at her elbow.

"This isn't your area," the older woman yelled over the band noise.

"Just saying hello," Katie shouted back. With a smile, she wound her way back to her section. On the dance floor, Ginny Wilder was gyrating to the beat.

Around twelve, Katie's area started to thin out. Ken walked over, looming above her, and said she was done for the night.

"Turn in your bank and punch out. First drink is on me," he said.

She smiled, sorted her bank from her tips, and settled up with the bar-back. The time clock was in the kitchen. Katie punched out, but instead of heading back into the bar, she slid out the kitchen door and left for the evening.

Rick was waiting up.

"You stink," he said.

"I was out for a little while at the Wagon Wheel."

"Where did you get that outfit?"

"At the thrift store. It's my working at the Wagon Wheel clothes." She explained what she was doing while the bathtub filled. "Go to bed," she said before closing the door. "We both have to work tomorrow morning."

* * *

Saturday was a long day at the feed store. Katie had gotten barely four hours of sleep. The weather had turned cold again, which dragged down more of her flagging energy.

"How long are you going to do this?" Rick asked while Nate reloaded the truck out in the feed shed."

"Only until I find out what the deal was between Sampson and George Beauregard," said Katie.

"I hate to tell you, Katie. But Sampson is a snake. He's way smarter than a lot of people give him credit for. He's going to see through you in a heartbeat. Not only that, but he's got this woman working for him that's cut from the same piece of cloth."

CHAPTER TWENTY-EIGHT

"You mean his wife?" asked Katie.

"Heck no. Sampson's wife is the assistant to some hotshot in Washington, DC. That's where they're from. She only comes up here every now and again. I don't think she spends a lot of time at the Wagon Wheel. That's his territory."

"Well, she can't be too smart then, can she?" Katie asked.

"Dora Sampson is incredibly well-educated. I've met her. Her problem is that she's a southern Baptist and one of the homeliest women I've ever encountered. To her, being married is number one. Staying married is everything. Don't discredit her because her upbringing isn't what you understand. Ken Sampson knew what he was doing when he took her for a wife. Dora's a good woman. Just in a bad place."

Katie didn't think she could dislike Ken Sampson any more than she had the night before. She was wrong. Through the rest of the afternoon, sneaking thoughts of his undoing crowded her mind.

Stop, she thought. *Don't get distracted. He is not your problem.*

Ruth handed Katie a plate as soon as the younger woman hung her jacket on the peg.

"What's this?" Katie asked.

"Grilled cheese sandwich and a date nut bar. When you get done that, you have time for a nap before you put on your party clothes," said Ruth, disapproval in every syllable. "I washed the stink out of them as well."

Exhausted but believing she was too wired to sleep, Katie grudgingly went upstairs.

"Just for a minute," she yawned, turning back the covers.

Two and a half hours later, Ruth shook her awake. There was another grilled cheese, followed by a chilling ride through the village and down the Bristol Road.

"I should have worn a thermal underwear shirt." The chattering of her teeth sped up with each touch of the jacket's cold lining on her bare midriff.

Spying Ken Sampson standing under the big lights outside the front door, she parked in the area set aside for the kitchen help and slid in the door on that end. At the bar, Irene gave Katie her bank. While she was looking through the stack of small cocktail trays, trying to find one that wasn't severally scratched and pitted, Katie spied Sampson out of the corner of her eye. He was watching her. She refused to give him the satisfaction of acknowledging him.

"You're in section five again tonight, Kate," Irene said.

"Where all the cheapsters sit." Julie, one of the waitresses, snickered. Julie worked the switchover, dinner, and then the bar. Katie was the only strictly cocktail waitress working that night.

One of Katie's booths was taken by the kitchen staff, all men. Part of their wages was a meal after the dinner hour and before final clean up. Several of her other tables were empty.

She leaned on the side of the booth seat. "Slow night."

Guys, dish boys, back staff, and the like hurried through their meals, anxious to be done and on their way home. Ultimately, only the fry cook, Matt, and the chief, John, were still seated. Talk was, John had a coke habit. A common problem in Illinois, but not so much around here. From the lax look on his face, as he beat out the rhythm of the music on his knees, Katie figured out he was already imbibing.

"You guys have been working here for a while, haven't you?" she asked.

"Ten years," said Matt. His teeth were black and rotted.

"Do you remember a guy who used to hang out here? George Beauregard?"

"I remember him," said Matt, lighting two cigarettes and handing one to John. "What's he to you?"

"Family," said Katie. *Sort of.*

"Why are you asking?" Matt asked.

Other than the drumming on his knees, or the occasional toke off the cigarette that hung from his lips, John never moved.

Katie shifted, eyes on the crowd, trying to locate Sampson.

"Fear, actually. I heard he was one of Ken's heavies. I'd like to be prepared if some red-neck with a grudge is coming looking to settle up."

Matt spat out a great braying guffaw. "You're kidding, right? The only time Beauregard worked for Ken was when the toilets backed up and the septic tank needed to be shoveled out. And Ken always said he was easy to pay off because he'd drink the rot-gut liquor no one in their right mind wanted." Matt slid out of the booth, still chuckling, as he went through the swinging doors into the kitchen.

Katie shoved off the side of the booth to check on her table when John spoke up.

"If you start asking questions about Beauregard, Ken's going to know in less than five minutes. And if you mention the slob's name to him, he'll break you in two."

Surprised John would say anything to her, Katie's eyebrows shot up. "Why?"

"Beauregard stole a lot of money from Ken. Then the SOB died before Ken could get it back. He sued the estate, and they told him to piss up a rope." Stubbing out his cigarette, he followed Matt.

Katie looked at the door that still wobbled on its hinges. John had said George was a thief, and Sampson had gone after the family for his money. If Christopher had blown him off, and everybody thought Ruth wasn't mentally strong enough to know what was going on, what were the chances Sampson would be looking to dig his filthy talons into other family members? Like Ginny Wilder? Or even somebody that wasn't, but he thought was related?

Pasting a smile on her face as she walked up to a new table, Katie thought, *I don't care how good the food is; I don't like this place.*

For most of the evening, Ken stayed beside the woman collecting the cover charge. That kept him right at the end of Katie's area. He watched her. She ignored him. When he walked through to the kitchen, she'd head off into the bar as though she were on an errand. On one such trip, she saw Irene grab a pack of smokes and duck out the emergency exit. Stashing her tray under the bar, Katie followed.

"Irene?" she called when the door closed behind her.

"Over here."

Irene was squatting out of the wind in front of the keg shed. An area abandoned except when empty kegs were rolled out.

"What's up?" she asked, offering the pack.

"No thanks," said Katie.

The wind tore through her thin garments, and she could feel herself losing body heat. She told Irene the same story she had fed the guys.

"Listen," Irene said. "Ken is my boss, and this is a good job. I'm not going to say a word about him. George was a jerk around here. Comic relief, you know? Hanging around, bumming drinks. About four months before he got wiped out, something really bad went down between him and Ken. I mean, they came to blows. I don't know what it was, and I'm not looking to."

She took a long drag, immediately coughing out a stream of smoke.

"You can ask anyone here, but I bet other than John, no one knows. Be careful what you say to him. He's tight in Ken's back pocket."

Leaving Irene, Katie went back inside. Ken was coming out of the kitchen. His eyes caught Katie and gutted her like a fish on the riverbank. She knew what had happened. Just as Irene had predicted, John had relayed Katie's questions to Sampson. Leaving her bank on the bar, Katie made a beeline across the dining room and out the door. Double timing it to her car, she kept moving even when Ken stepped out and called her name.

"I'll just send Rick back for my jacket," she said aloud as her teeth chattered and she tried to keep her partially naked back off the cold vinyl seat. "If I don't freeze to death before I get home, that is."

Chapter Twenty-Nine

"I bet you thought you were real smart dropping that bomb about Mildred Hooper's grandson the other day and then leaving before I had a chance to ask who he was," Katie said.

"Oh, did you want to know?" asked Cindy slyly.

"Give it up," said Katie.

"Hmm, let's see if I can remember," said Cindy. "It's so hard to recall. I mean, I have so much on my mind. Christmas is coming. I have two bicycles to assemble."

"Aargh," groaned Katie. "Drop them off at my house. I'll even let you leave them there until Christmas Eve."

"Perfect," said Cindy. "It's Nate."

Katie's head whipped around in the direction of the feed shed. "What? Nate? I got caught driving drunk, Nate?"

Cindy's head bobbled up and down. "Yup, one and the same."

In the middle of the morning, Nate, whose new job was lifting and loading heavy feed bags for customers, came inside for a break and a warm-up. Katie had been keeping an eye open for him, and when a space between customers allowed, she darted out to the break area. Nate was sitting with his back to the door, hands held out toward the furnace.

"Can I ask you a quick question, Nate?" she said.

"You can, but lately, I'm not fast on the uptake," he said. "Unless this is the one you're asking everyone in town about. You know, who wanted to kill George Beauregard?"

Katie stood there, stunned.

157

"I can't help you, Katie." Nate turned to look at her. "He was related to me, but my folks split when I was a little kid, and my mother flat out wouldn't talk about him. Everything I know is gossip you've already heard by this time. I'm sorry. I really am. I could use doing something good for a change." The young man recapped his thermos and went out the door.

It was a day of surprises for Katie.

Later, Mr. Pierce called. He had taken to putting the trap out in the morning after the last milk truck had left and coming back to check on it an hour later. Using cut up chunks of warm steak, he had lured the mother in. With the spitting female trapped, he offered to meet Katie at the corner by the post office to drop her off. Katie ran out on her lunchtime to collect the live trap.

"She's pretty wild," he said. "I don't think she's going to make much of a pet."

"Sometimes they don't," said Katie. She went on to explain the plan for a feral release.

"What about the kittens?" Mr. Pierce asked.

"Three solidly black short hairs. Two males. The other one is also a male, but with longer dark gray and white fur."

"I'd like that one," said Mr. Pierce, blushing slightly. "The kitten is for my granddaughter, Marah. They live next door, and her mother said she could have one. My wife says to tell you, we'll reimburse you for the vet bills."

At Katie's raised eyebrows, he added, "She's a member of the knitting group. Ruth is very verbal about how this works."

"I'll make sure Ruth knows," Katie said.

"I'm willing to bet she already does."

Katie was to find out later he was right.

Once again, Katie took the trap into the feed store, storing it in Stan's office.

"I'm glad you're not bringing her back," said Stan when Katie collected the trap.

"Why is that?" Katie asked.

"All she's done all afternoon is growl at me," said her boss.

"What a good kitty," Katie cooed.

Laughing, Stan ordered her to get out.

* * *

The drive up Fire Lane 61 was another slippery, teeth-clenching experience. This time, Katie met Rick and Raymond hand shoveling sand out of the Wain-Roy bucket. The cleat tracks held the tractor in place. Katie knew, as her wheels slid slightly, that if she couldn't make the grade, the Wain-Roy would be towing her home.

* * *

"Hello," said Katie, telephone receiver to ear, but eyes on a boiling pot on the stove.

"Leave my son out of your wicked work." Christopher Beauregard hissed into the phone.

Katie turned slightly. Now the rough plaster wall filled her sight.

"He's an adult. It was just a casual conversation," she said coolly. The image of Jonathon's battered face popped up in her mind. She felt there was no doubt Christopher could be as ugly as both of the Georges.

"I said, leave my family alone, or you'll have more trouble on your hands than that batty old broad."

"You know, don't you, Mr. Beauregard, this is a two-party line, and the phone rang in somebody else's house? I bet right at this moment, gossiping ears are listening."

On the other end of the line, the telephone receiver crashed into the phone cradle. Katie hung up, and, turning, found Rick coming through the kitchen door right behind her.

"Who are you pissing off now?" he asked.

Though she didn't want to, over supper, Katie explained what she had learned and that Christopher Beauregard and Ken Sampson weren't taking it well.

159

"I'm thinking," she said. "I should give those two some space and let them calm down."

"Katie." Ruth laid her knife and fork on the table. "I want you to stop. I don't want you in this mess. It's okay. I'm a grown woman and I can either buck up or back out."

"Do it, Katie," Rick said.

Nodding in agreement, Katie concentrated on chewing and not choking.

Chapter Thirty

Stan backed slowly up the wide center aisle of the feed store, pulling the hydraulic hand jack loaded with a pallet of red and white bags of rock salt. "Katie, when you have a minute, could you call my house? Cindy is looking for you."

With one eye on the cash register counter where Davidson was ringing out a short line of customers, his long ponytail waving as his head kept time with the piped-in music, Katie dialed Cindy.

"S'up?" she asked.

"I'm leaving town at six to drive over to Gaynes Shoppers World for some Christmas shopping. Would you like to go?"

"That would be great," said Katie. "Do you want to catch a burger at that new place on the Williston Road?"

"McDonald's? Yes!"

They made arrangements for Katie to leave her car in the creamery parking lot and for Cindy to pick her up there.

* * *

The burger and fries were hot, juicy, and delicious. Both women agreed McDonald's might last for a while longer.

"It's like The Lure, only better," Cindy giggled. "Don't tell my kids we were here!"

Gaynes, the anchor store in a small strip mall, was further up the road, but still close to downtown Burlington. The parking lot was full to overflowing.

161

The women had to park all the way to the far end and behind RadioShack.

"We're going to be hours just trying to check out of here," groaned Cindy. "And this is going to be my last available shopping time."

"That's okay," said Katie. "We have all evening. I don't have to be in bed until nine-thirty."

Cindy gave her a playful shove. "You idiot."

After agreeing on where to meet when they were finished, they separated inside the store. Cindy headed to toys, and Katie went looking for a nice pair of lady's trousers for Ruth, and lined gloves and heavy socks for Rick. Knowing what she wanted made her fast. Finished, she headed toward the big toy area. The aisles were solidly filled with adults and shopping carts. Unable to see Cindy, and unwilling to wade through the throng of scowling shoppers, Katie got in line at the registers. When she had her purchases in hand, she wandered outside, still unsure what to get Marlie. Nothing caught her eye, but while she stood on the sidewalk next to a group of cigar-puffing men waiting for their shopping womenfolk, she noticed the small jewelry store. In the window was a display of double woven silver charm bracelets and themed charms.

"Hi," Katie said to the gentleman behind the counter. "If I get one of those State of Vermont charms, can you engrave a zip code on the back? Then put a bigger loop on the charm so a silver neck chain could thread through?"

Twenty minutes later, Katie left the jewelry store with a four-inch square pasteboard box lined with pink tissue paper and the perfect gift. Cindy was just leaving Gaynes Shoppers World with a shopping cart filled to overflowing with yellow bags with the store logo on the side and sharp-cornered boxes already poking through. Her purchases included a build-at-home doll house.

"Stan is going to kill you." Katie declared.

"Just stand here and guard the cart while I get the car. There is no way I am pushing this monster through the slush."

The ride back to Parentville was filled with laughing recollections of other harried shoppers. Katie sat in her truck for about ten minutes after Cindy drove away, giving the old girl time to warm up. The engine was running, but the headlights were still off. From where she sat, Katie could watch what was happening on Route 15, the state name for Main Street. She could have counted the number of cars that drove by on one hand, and it was not even ten o'clock.

"Well, here's another reason I was gone from here for so long," Katie said out loud. "For six and a half months, I've been back, and practically nothing happens during daylight except work. And absolutely nothing after dark." She depressed the clutch and shifted into drive. No one answered her, but that didn't stop her from talking. "You go to work in the dark; you drive home in the dark. Heck, I even chase stray animals in the dark. It's like living in a cave."

She flipped on the turn signal for a right turn onto the Parentville/Charlotte Road. Then, giggling, flipped it right back off. After all, there was nobody out there to see what she was doing. Riding down the slight incline, passing the dark post office, she slowed going over the double culvert put in to allow the LaPlatte Brook tributary to cross under the road. The road surface wasn't slippery. She wanted a quick look at the open water rushing into the culvert. It was so black; it appeared like solid glass. Only the reflection of star shine indicated there was any movement. Behind her at the corner, another vehicle had pulled out from beside the general store and began the descent.

From the culvert, the road began a soft rise, barely noticeable unless you were on foot. The last house on the left was Meadowbrook Farm, merely a homestead now. On the other side, the entire space was open, hay and cornfields, and graze. Katie moved smoothly along, humming to herself and considering the gifts she had purchased. Even though her fingers and toes were chilly, there was a warm glow in her chest that kept her comfortable.

She was almost to the turnoff for Fire Lane 61, when the headlights of a vehicle that was running dark behind her were switched on. Startled, she touched the brakes. Instantly she felt a little tap as though she were being passed, and the other driver misjudged where her rear left corner was. Katie pulled further right. She was running on the edge of the ditch. Before she had time to consider the ramifications of where the passenger side of her vehicle was, the other, taller truck hit her again. It's right front fender, making contact with her left rear fender right in front of the tire. The force was enough to push Katie aside. The two right tires on her vehicle were under the edge of the ditch. Speeding up, the other truck circled wide and sped off. The road swung left, and it was gone.

Katie fought to hold the truck from wallowing into the ditch. All of her warm thoughts were gone, with the realization that up ahead was another smaller culvert. If she hit the edge of that culvert, the corrugated steel would slice into her vehicle. She might walk away, but not without injuries, and her truck would be a total. The only fairly wide place before that culvert was where the road curved left. Bracing herself for the worst, she pressed back into the seat and twisted the steering wheel. The truck fought against her, the tires not wanting to jump the frozen rim of the ditch. Then suddenly, she hit a spot where the snowplow had clipped the rim, leaving a lower rut. The pickup jumped the short embankment. Katie immediately tromped down on the clutch and the brake. When the truck started to spin, she lifted off the brake while turning the truck into the spin. The vehicle shook left, then right, then left again. She pumped the brakes. The truck stopped, stalled in the road, and was facing the way it had been coming. Katie didn't even want to know how close she was to the five-foot bank on the passenger side of her truck. Swallowing hard, she restarted the engine and drove straight ahead, right up Fire Lane 61.

Chapter Thirty-One

"This morning at church, we got our list of names for helping out folks for Christmas and New Year's dinner," Rick said.

"Yeah, how many did we get?" Katie asked.

"Just two, Charlie and Ida Jarvis."

"Seriously? Charlie was coming anyway, along with Chet, Dorothea, and Ellen." Katie greased a second cookie sheet for Ruth.

"Chet's name showed up on somebody else's list, but Ruthie got her nose right in there, and told them he was coming here."

"Don't say it like that, Rick." Ruth shook her head. "It was the polite thing to do, so somebody else wouldn't plan on him. There are more folks than him that might need a hand."

"What do you call all those platefuls of food you send over to Chet?" Rick snapped.

Katie started to say at least the plates came back, but she decided it wasn't worth the effort.

"I'm thinking we're going to need forty or fifty golf ball size meatballs for seven people." Katie finished stirring the minced onions and spices in the roaster pan of ground beef and venison.

"How are you going to keep them from mushing back together in the freezer?" Rick moved the hand grinder aside, replacing it with an empty one, and started re-grinding the last batch of meat.

Ruth scooped a bit of meatball mash out of the roaster, patted it together solidly, removing air bubbles, and then rolled it between her palms.

"This piece of string walks into a bar," she said.

165

Both Katie and Rick stopped what they were doing to look at her.

"The string climbed up on a bar stool and said to the bartender, give me a beer."

Rick's eyebrows rose.

"The bartender pointed to a sign on the wall that said, NO STRING SERVED HERE."

Ruth placed the perfectly round meatball on the cookie sheet and pinched free another lump.

"The string got down and left. Once outside, he threw himself down on the ground and rolled around until he was a dirty, tangled mess. Then he went back into the bar."

Another meatball was placed gently beside its brother. Katie opened her mouth, but Ruth wasn't done.

"The string said to the bartender, I'll have a beer. The bartender pointed to the sign and said, I told you we don't serve your kind. The string smiled. The bartender said, you're a piece of string, aren't you?"

"Nope, said the string. Frayed knot."

Another meatball settled on the cookie sheet. After a questioning look at each other, Katie and Rick went back to work.

An uncomfortable silence settled over the kitchen. At least for Katie, and possibly Rick, it was uncomfortable. Ruth kept rolling out meatballs, humming to herself in a contented manner. Finally, Katie couldn't stand it anymore. Both Cindy and Marlie had told her to be upfront with Ruth and ask her questions. Doctor Gillian had said Ruth was progressing well, but she hadn't come right out and said the elderly woman was one hundred percent straight in her mind. There had been a few nights where Katie had lain awake trying to use other older people, Dorothea and Father Metevier, as a gauge for discerning how well Ruth was doing. They were both at least ten years older, and, as far as Katie could tell, smart as they had been in their youth. That would be with the exception of Father Metevier's treatment of Boots, but then, this was his first cat.

"Ruth," Katie said, "what was with the, you know, string joke?"

Rick made a move toward the cellar door, but Katie pinned him with a look and pointed back to the chair he had just evacuated. Like a chastised little boy, he returned, but kept focused on the lamp he was rewiring.

"It was a joke," said Ruth. "Didn't you get it?"

"As a matter of fact, I did," said Katie. "It's only that it seemed to pop out of thin air and caught me by surprise."

"Well." The color in Ruth's full cheeks rose. "If you have to know, it's the only joke I can remember. You and Rick seemed so tense. I mean, even the cats are staying away. I thought a joke would help you relax." She pressed her lips together, intent on making the meatball exactly round.

Katie took a step sideways and, squatting slightly, hip bumped her friend. "And here I told Rick you would never notice."

"Notice what?" Ruth's head came up, beetle-brown eyes locked on Rick.

"That he gave up eating the apple butter and is working his way through the pear jam you and Grace put up," Katie said with a shrug.

"What? Rick!" Ruth's jaw snapped up tight, in contrast to Rick's, which fell to the table.

"Katie," he said, "I never…"

"I'm sorry, Rick. I truly am, but between that and all the cookies you've been filching out of the big freezer, you're going to go into sugar shock."

Ruth gave out a gasp and ran to the sink, where she rinsed her hands. With the dish towel still in her grasp, she yanked open the cellar door. Katie and Rick could hear her clattering steps downward.

"What now?" He asked, wide eyes on Katie.

"If I were you, I would run because she's going to find an empty jar and a big space in the oatmeal and raisin container."

Rick grabbed his coat and fled. From below, Ruth's Christian-tainted cussing could be heard preceding her up the stairs.

"Where is he?" she demanded, headed toward the living room.

"He's gone, but that's okay. I wanted to talk to you. Woman to woman. Oh, and Marlie ate the pear jam, and took the cookies. I told her you wouldn't mind."

"Oh, Katie." Ruth tried to look stern, but it wasn't natural for her. Scooping more meat mix, she asked. "What is it you need to know now?"

"I don't need to know anything. But I have some questions, and they have to do with you and George Beauregard, and the morning he died."

"Go ahead. I've been waiting." Though she sounded resigned, Ruth didn't lose a step in what she was doing.

Katie put the full cookie sheet of meatballs in the oven and set the timer for ten minutes.

"Ruth, did you purchase Wild Cherry cough syrup just before George died? Were you sick?"

"No, I wasn't sick, and I didn't have two cents to rub together. If we got anything like that, I would have had Christopher put it on our tab at the store."

"You had a tab at the store? Would George have asked for cough syrup?"

"No, he wouldn't. I know it has alcohol in it, but the stuff made him gag. We had a tab so we could get what we needed. Unfortunately, George abused it so often to get booze, Christopher laid down the law. He was the only one we could get supplies from."

"So, Christopher knew exactly what you were taking all the time?"

Ruth nodded. The blush was gone.

"The night before George died, Christopher picked him up and took him over to Ida Jarvis' house to fix her plumbing, right?"

Ruth shook her head slowly. Katie saw a salty tear fall onto the table. "This is bad, Katie. I wish you hadn't asked."

Katie went into the bathroom for a wash-up and to give Ruth time to compose herself. When she came out, Ruth was sitting out on the porch. It was cold, but she was out of the wind, and the early afternoon sun shone down on her. Exactly where she was would be the warmest spot in the yard all afternoon.

"What are you doing, Ruth?" Katie asked.

She had brought two mugs of tea out with her, as well as three or four cats. She passed Ruth a mug. One of the cats was already whining to go back in the house.

"I told you; your feet were going to be cold," Katie told the noisy feline. "Buck up and take it like a dog."

The cat narrowed its eyes and tried one more plaintive meow. When Katie made no move to open the door, the cat wandered over to the sunny edge where all the furry ladies were perched.

"You know, Katie," said Ruth, breaking the silence between the two women. "A while ago, you were asking me about what happened the night George was murdered."

"That was days ago, Ruth."

"I know. It's just, well, I try not to think about it. Or maybe, more precisely, I used to try not to think so much about it."

"My fault, huh?" asked Katie.

Ruth smiled. "Anyway, since we had our little talk, I've been thinking about what I said."

"What part?"

"The ones that don't make sense, even to me." Ruth lifted the mug out of her lap, allowing room for one of the cats, the crybaby, to move in. "You asked when I called the sheriff. That's one of those really baffling things. I couldn't have, and yet they showed up. I don't know how they knew."

"Sheriff Lewis said your neighbor called him. Lewis said George was supposed to go with Christopher that morning to sort through some of Senior's stuff left at the farmhouse. According to Lewis, Christopher banged on the door, and it swung open. He walked in, and he could hear you wailing. He ran next door to Schmidt's. They called Lewis."

"Christopher," Ruth said slowly.

"Yeah." Katie, who had been watching the sunbathing cats, looked up. Ruth was staring right into the sun.

"Everything seems so disjointed, kind of twisted around, about that morning," said Ruth. "I remember having this dream where I was sitting in the kitchen drinking coffee with George. Then suddenly, it was Christopher. But it couldn't have been because I was wearing my nightgown. I would never have done that."

Katie leaned on the railing. "What else do you remember?"

"Of the dream? The coffee was bitter, had a bad taste, like it had been re-heated on the stove. I think it was the evening, which is equally not right.

George would drink coffee day or night. I never drink coffee after noontime. That's it. I don't remember anything else about the dream. I mean, I woke up in my bed."

"And when you woke up, you were all fuzzy in your head, right?" asked Katie.

"Yes. That was weird. Maybe I took my sleeping medicine too late. Then there was the bit you asked me about the cough syrup."

"Where was the cough syrup?"

"I don't know. I never saw it. But it must have been somewhere I could bump into it because it was spilled down the front of my nightgown. My fingers were sticky. Or maybe it was blood. Yes, I think so. It was blood." Rising from the chair, Ruth took her mug into the house. When the door opened, all the cats snoozing in the sun made a bee-line back into the living room.

Katie wandered down to where Rick and some of his cronies, who had arrived hoping a supper invitation would be forthcoming, were tinkering with the Massey-Ferguson tractor.

"What's up?" Rick asked.

"How much alcohol is there in cough syrup?" Katie asked.

Chapter Thirty-Two

The kitchen table was stacked with neat piles of bills. Paper clips held the stacks together like silver metal stanchions, keeping the herd in check. The top invoice on each stack was the current request for funds or notice of payment due for that stack. It wasn't much of a filing system, but it was the way it worked for Katie. There was also a thin ledger Cindy helped Katie put together when they had contacted every person or company Irma had owed money to. Working together with the debtors, they set up payment plans and created a budget Katie tried to adhere to. There were a lot of debtors. The needs of the many made sure Katie did not live extravagantly, not that a feed store employee could.

Before ripping the check from her checkbook, a commodity she hadn't believed less than a year ago she would ever need, Katie made an entry on a ledger page. Having depleted the funds available, this was the last check she would write for this month. It was also the only payment that gave her any satisfaction. The Moore farm, now referred to by Katie as the Took-Moore farm, straddled the border of Parentville, where the Moore homestead was, and Charlotte, where until it had burned, the Moser house was located. Her grandparents had been Moores, her parents, who had both passed away when she was three, Tooks. Both towns held liens against the property. Charlotte, where the gravel pit was located, had received the lion's share of the money paid by L&F Construction to excavate there. Two more payments, and she could mark that ledger page as being paid in full. It was the one tunnel she could see a light at the end of.

Her feeling of elation was dashed down as deep as the gravel, when a

171

shimmering image of Marlie appeared in the seat across the table. Every organ, from the pit of her stomach upward, rushed to fill Katie's throat.

I'm sorry, Katie, Marlie had said. *I can't see any other way.*

Katie wanted to believe her. No. She did believe. There was no doubt in her mind that Marlie was making the right choice, moving to Pennsylvania following her career. Since the day Katie had run away from home on the eve of her eighteenth birthday, she had gone where the wind would take her. Suddenly, when there was a solid reason for her to pack up and go, a responsibility she had been fighting since her return was holding her down. Looking through the doorway, she could see the little pile of presents Ruth had left waiting for a Christmas tree to put them under. There was one for each of them, and one for Marlie, as well.

Teardrops fell on the table, marring the envelope lying there. Katie swiped her eyes with her sleeve, trembling fingers worked the check into the envelope. Behind her, the kitchen door opened, and she ducked her head, licking the stamp and carefully affixing it.

"Katie, have you seen Ruth?" Rick asked.

"Not in a little while. Why?" She remained focused on the stack of payments ready to be sent out.

"She was kind of, I don't know, weird there earlier. I was wondering what she might be up to." His voice was heavy with concern.

"If she isn't in here, then she must have walked down to the Dean farm," Katie said.

Rick moved past to stand in the easternmost window, watching down the road. Katie picked up everything except the envelopes to be put out in the mailbox. Placing the paperwork in a shoe box on top of the refrigerator, she grabbed her coat and left the same way Rick had arrived. She had to get out before the uncontrollable sobbing she experienced for the last three nights started again.

The rush of cold air against her stressed, sweaty skin braced her up. She turned into the wind, freezing the tears on her lashes. The path led to the chicken coop, then out to the driveway where the Massey-Ferguson tractor hid under a canvas tarp waiting for the next snow. Rick had been outside tinkering and left one corner unsecured. The same wind lifted the corner of the canvas, creating a pointy, flapping wave towards the barn. Her eyes traveled that way, and in the snow, she saw fresh tracks cutting across the narrow stretch of lawn and over the short slope to the milk house door. She followed.

The door was open. Once inside, Katie paused until the sounds of movement told her what direction Ruth had moved in. Beyond where she and Rick had removed the stanchions selling the metal to a scrapyard, Ruth worked in a small open area. To Katie's eye, it appeared the older woman, wrapped in coat, scarves, and mittens, was arbitrarily lifting boxes and stacking them elsewhere.

"What are you doing out here, Ruth?" Katie asked.

Ruth jerked around, falling back on a box she had just put down.

"Oh, my goodness," she squeaked. "You scared me to death, Katie."

"It's freezing out here. What are you doing?" Katie repeated.

Ruth went back to moving boxes and bags of Irma's collected roadside loot. "Once the holidays are gone by, it's going to be a long winter. Grace won't need me every day for helping with the butter and goat cheese business until it's time to put the gardens in. I thought I'd take some boxes in the house and get stuff sorted and ready for the yard sale. If we move it down to the old schoolhouse, there will be room for lots more."

Throughout the previous summer and fall, Ruth had run a perpetual yard sale out of the milk house. Irma had left plenty to sell. It gave Ruth pleasure to clean up and hawk her old friend's saleable items. That had been Irma's intent to run her own little thrift store. At the corner of the Took property where Fire Lane 61 joined the Parentville-Charlotte Road was an abandoned one-room schoolhouse. Fred Moore had been educated there. Over the years, he had kept it intact. With his passing, weeds, and saplings had all but hid it from view. But Irma had applied for a historical grant just prior to her death. When it came through, there was enough money to allow for a new roof and to replace the broken windowpanes. Ruth, Rick, and his friends had cleared the place out, tightening it up for the winter.

"That's true," said Katie. "Where are you going to put these boxes?"

173

"I'm only going as far as the milk house right now. After New Year's, when the puppies are gone, I'll lug a few up to the house at a time."

Katie knew that meant Rick would lug them up to the house. For the next thirty minutes, she helped move the boxes Ruth thought appropriate to the milk house. With no clean path through and over the stacks and heaps, it was not a fast project.

"Don't mix these boxes in with the stuff packed from last fall." Ruth admonished.

Katie had to stop and rearrange what she was doing. Finally, Ruth was chilled enough to call it quits.

"You know," Katie said as she helped Ruth climb up the bank to the back lawn, "we could just haul all that junk back to the dump and be rid of it." Now that she was not concentrating on saving her neck while lugging the heavy boxes, hoping the bottoms didn't fall out, her depression returned.

"What are you saying, Katie? Your grandmother would wash your mouth out with soap."

"Give it a rest, Ruth." Katie was tired of the elderly woman touting how far along they had come in saving the farm and fostering the cats.

"There's a big difference between you and me, Katie." Ruth yanked her arm free, tromping across the last bit of snow unaided. "You need some kind of continual instant gratification. I'm in it for the long haul."

Katie's face burned. A scathing retort burned on the tip of her tongue. Before she could spit it out, Ruth stepped out onto the shoveled path and turned.

"I'm not trying to be nasty," she said, though her tone was sharp. "Something happened during all those years you were growing up before I knew you. It was like acid burning inside, making you bitter. You do a good job of keeping it in check, but I can see when it's boiling to the surface. It's the holidays. Everybody is super sensitive. Even Rick, even me. Get past yourself and move on. If this is about Marlie, celebrate the fact she is doing something positive, even if it hurts you. Grow up, Katie." With that, Ruth turned her back on her best friend's granddaughter and went through the kitchen door, slamming it behind her.

"And you think I've got a hair across my butt, you crazy old lady!" Katie shouted at the door.

Instead of going inside, she followed the path down and around the backside of the tractor. In the snowbank, she dug out a seat and sat down. The sun, still high in the western sky, lit up clouds from behind, tinting their edges the same pinkish color Katie had seen when she and Poppa candled eggs.

"Where are you, Poppa?" she asked aloud, tears streaming down her face and her voice choking deep in her throat. "Why am I always alone? Why am I still here when I want to be with you?"

"Isn't your butt cold buried in that snowbank?" Rick asked.

Katie looked away, sure he had seen her tears and probably heard what she had said. She didn't care. All she wanted was the one person who had loved her unconditionally to wrap his arms around her and hold on.

Instead, his best buddy dug out a seat three feet away and settled in. When he spoke, his voice mirrored Katie's, sad and reminiscent.

"I was about twenty years old and hunting with my dad. We were leaving the woods at the end of the last day. Dad handed me his rifle and stepped off the trail for nature's call. I waited for him in the clear cut, admiring the beauty that belongs to Vermont only. When Dad reentered, he was sixty yards south of where I sat with both rifles. He said later he hadn't seen me. I started walking toward him.

"A black bear broke cover about mid-way between me and Dad. It didn't look all that large, but a bear is a bear. It was moving across the open area quickly. I assumed it had seen my father and was sneaking along behind him. For no apparent reason, the bear turned slightly, veering in Dad's direction. The sight of the bear moving towards my unarmed father caused my tongue to lodge in the back of my throat. Standing, I whistled, hoping to attract Dad's attention. He didn't hear me, but the bear did. It went from a walk to a lope, and it turned further toward the nearest forested area. The side where Dad was.

"I could no longer see Dad's hat. I dropped my rifle and raised Dad's. It was a bigger, more powerful weapon. There was every chance the bear would move past my father, but I couldn't allow myself to take that chance. My brain was crowded with everything I had been taught about hunting. Wind, height, angling for the grade, right up to snug it up and exhale. I fired once, snapped the bolt, and fired again. The bear dropped. So did Dad, though I didn't see him.

"Dropping the rifle, I ran down the hill screaming at the top of my lungs. I got snagged on brambles, tripped and fell, lost my hat. Nothing mattered except making sure my father was safe. By the time I got to where the bear was, my father was getting up. He hadn't been in my line of fire, but had reacted to the sound of the rifle shot. He was cussing profusely and covered in leaves and dirt from his head-first dive to the ground. I was drenched in sweat. I gotta tell you, until the day he died, I took a heck of a ribbing for shooting a one-hundred-and-thirty-pound black. But every time I think of that day, I choke up."

Katie wondered what the heck that had to do with sitting in the snow.

"I'm telling you this because, just like Ruth, you and I have specific memories we carry when all others fade. Every time I think about Dad, that's the moment I remember. Think about it, do you have fewer real memories and sharper specific ones? Don't lie to yourself, I bet you do. Ruth has the same. The only difference is mine is a good one. I'm hoping yours is too, but for Ruth, it's a raised fist coming at her, and she has nowhere to go.

"I left here when George and Ruth got married. I was a sawyer and had a better job at the furniture factory than George. Had a more secure future to offer, and I never would have raised a hand to her. But she chose him. So, I got up one morning, packed my stuff, and drove away." Katie heard him sucking his teeth while he was thinking. "Katie, there were a lot of people right here in the village that knew he was bad to her. She's not the only one, there are others. For none of them, no one stepped forward. The law says a formal complaint needs to be made. I'm thinking if you represent the law, and you know that bad is happening, even if it's family, you should be intervening.

"I came back here a couple of years before George died. Ruth wouldn't have anything to do with me, and by that time, she pretty much never left the house. I'd see Christopher dropping off groceries periodically, or the Ladies' Auxiliary leaving a basket. She might be out in the yard hanging laundry. That was about all.

"Phfft," Katie snorted. "How did you see all that?"

"I was doing pick-up work here and there, had plenty of time. Six or eight times a day, I'd drive by the house, trying to work up the courage to approach her again. Hell, the night George was killed, I drove right past. I saw him and her sitting at the kitchen table. It was real late, and the room was all lit up. With it being dark outside, they didn't see me stop to watch. Then I drove on. The next time I was there, in the morning, the ambulance was pulling out. I knew it was for Ruth. I thought George had finally hurt her horribly. If the sheriff's cruiser hadn't been there, I'd a gone in looking for him. Instead, I followed the ambulance to Burlington. I spent three days sitting in the hospital lobby before somebody would talk to me. Even then, it was a security officer who told me to leave. When I explained why I was there, he went off and came back with enough information so I could go home knowing she wasn't at death's door."

The sun was almost on the horizon. The pretty pink clouds had gone dark. Katie started to heft herself out of her snow seat, then paused.

"Rick," she asked, "what time did you go by and see George and Ruth at the kitchen table?"

Rick stood up and offered his hand. "Hmm, I was at the store when it closed, so a few minutes after nine. Why?"

Katie shook her head. But she was thinking something different. *It couldn't have been George Beauregard sitting there with Ruth. Ida Jarvis said he didn't leave her house till after ten.*

Chapter Thirty-Three

Katie walked through the front door of Beauregard's General Store and Mercantile. She stayed near the front. Christopher was nowhere in sight. He could have actually not been there at all, but she wouldn't know. The person she wanted to talk to was Eugenie. A different woman was manning the cash register, so Katie walked along, looking down each aisle. Almost to the far side, she spotted Eugenie, clipboard in hand, taking inventory of the pharmaceutical collection. Eugenie didn't even look up when Katie approached. Standing beside the other woman, trying to remember the questions she had practiced saying, Katie's eyes landed on the Wild Cherry Cough Syrup box.

Taking a box down, flipping it over to read the back, Katie said, "Hey Eugenie, how's it going?" There was a squeak in her voice. She had to cough.

Eugenie flickered a quick peek at Katie, then went back to counting inventory. "Good. You know, same old same old."

"Hmm, yeah." Katie replaced the box and picked up another. "Is this a regular part of your job, counting boxes of aspirin? I would have thought you'd assign that to a flunky."

Eugenie guffawed. "You're kidding, right? Get one of those airheads to get the order ready? For heaven's sake, we'd have an overload of coca cola and chocolate bars and nothing else." She continued to chuckle as Katie reached for a third box.

"Just saying, when I have to count flannel shirts from the store and the stockroom, I start dreaming of plaids."

"Well, lucky for me, we don't keep any of this stuff out back. It's all out here and pretty basic. I've been doing it for so many years. I've got my fingers on the pulse all the time."

"Yeah." It was Katie's turn to laugh. The dry spot in the back of her throat made it difficult. "How can you keep it all straight, the groceries, the liquor?" Unbidden came the memory of her palming a pint of whiskey right after she'd come back. Maybe she could send Eugenie the money anonymously.

Eugenie actually stopped to stare at Katie. "Boy, have you got that wrong. I'm not a manager, just a small fish. Gladys LaPointe keeps track of dry goods. Christopher does all the rest."

"Like the meat counter?"

"The meat counter, fresh produce, frozen foods, and, of course, the beer and liquor. You want to talk about a pain in the butt job. That's it. Stuff goes missing, and he's crawling all over us."

Katie stopped picking up boxes. It was time to jump on the hard question. Either she was going to get an answer or run like crazy when Eugenie screamed for Christopher.

"Eugenie." She rasped out the other woman's name. "If liquor disappears, Christopher knows. But if he took any of the booze, no one else would be the wiser, right?"

Eugenie's face got a pinched look. "Are you asking if Christopher has a drinking problem?"

"No." Katie watched Eugenie closely, watching for a sign it was time to get out of Dodge. "What I'm saying is, if he took a pint or so and gave it to someone else, you wouldn't know."

"Does this have anything to do with all the questions you're asking around town?"

Katie was stunned. With one look at her face, Eugenie grabbed her upper arm in a pinching grip and dragged her to the door. "Stepping outside for a cigarette," she told the cashier, slamming her clipboard down.

Once down the ramp, Eugenie circled the front of the building, still towing Katie until they were on the far side, where a narrow space separated the store from the old rooming house. It took Katie all of five seconds to realize that neither building had any windows in the alley. She tried to pull away, but years of lifting heavy boxes of merchandise gave Eugenie a strong grip.

"I know you've got a question. If you're going to ask me, spit it out. Then don't come back. Christopher took out his pissy temper on Jonathon, but the boy still has a job. I won't. His father won't give a fiddler's fart if he lets me go."

"The day before George Beauregard, Junior, died, Christopher took a bottle of Wild Cherry cough syrup. That morning, he took another one. You would be the only person who realized it. Did you?"

Eugenie let go, quickly stepping back. "I saw Christopher take the one bottle. I pointed out to him that a couple of bottles had been stolen. I didn't know who took them. Understand? I did not know Christopher Beauregard took more than that one bottle of cough syrup."

Her hands were shaking when she pulled a crushed pack of smokes and a lighter out of her back pocket. Katie nodded her thanks, then walked away, leaving the coatless woman to fight the wind for custody of a flame.

Chapter Thirty-Four

Katie expected to see Marlie's car backed into her spot in front of the farmhouse when she crested the ridge. That had been the way for each of the last few weeks. Today she was disappointed. It was frightening how close that one small fact brought her to tears.

"For crying out loud!" she shouted before she backed in. "Get a grip, stupid."

The night before, she had thawed out some of the meatballs she and Ruth had made and frozen for New Year's. Using canned tomatoes, Ruth's dried herbs, and store-bought tomato paste, Katie had made a big pot of spaghetti sauce. The vote for spaghetti or noodles had ended in a dead tie.

"Marlie called this afternoon," said Ruth as Katie knocked snow off her boots and slipped them off.

Katie's heart fell even further.

"She said to tell you she's bringing tortellini pasta and lemon crème cake, whatever that is." Ruth looked at the black cat clock hanging on the wall, its dangling tail sweeping back and forth. "She should be here any time."

As if in answer, a vehicle was heard outside. But when Katie looked, it was Rick's truck. Then, when it was in place, a second set of lights swept through the windows. Katie was hard-pressed to hide her elation. Marlie had arrived.

While Marlie cooed over the puppies and patted cats, Katie put their supper on the table. All the time she stirred and spooned, she listened to the sound of Marlie's voice, forcing herself to memorize the cadence, her lover's laugh. Rick was kept busy hauling firewood in, chicken water out, stoking the big furnace, and cleaning the fireplaces out for the next morning. It was the normal way of their early evening, made better by one more in their midst.

"Do you know where you're going to be living?" Ruth asked Marlie, passing cold bean salad across the table.

Katie's teeth grabbed her bottom lip. She, too, wanted to know. It just wasn't a question she felt strong enough to ask.

Marcie laid her fork aside, exhaling deeply as if she had been waiting and now could speak freely. "I did find a place. Actually, a rep down there did. It's a rent-by-the-week efficiency apartment. You know, like a converted motel? Anyway, that's good, but it created a different problem."

"How's that?" Rick asked. His plate was wiped clean by his attentive use of a dinner roll. However, he was scooping more tortellini onto his plate.

"I don't own a lot of stuff, but I have some."

Katie remembered on her visits to Marlie's apartment in Rutland, the furnishings had been sparse.

"The rental comes furnished, and my grandmother lives in senior housing. She has no room to store my furniture or household stuff."

"Say no more," said Rick. "Do you have an extra key to your apartment? After you leave on the twenty-sixth, Phil or Charlie, and I will go over and pick up what's there. You leave it packed, ready to go, and we'll move it. There's room here, right, Katie?"

All three sets of eyes turned to Katie. She had her mouth full and suddenly was having a problem swallowing.

"Is that okay?" Marlie asked in a small voice.

Gulping, then reaching for her water glass to dislodge the clog of pasta stuck in her throat, Katie could barely whisper yes. Her eyes filled. Though those around the table expressed concern that she might be choking, Katie was thinking with Marlie's possessions here; she would have to come back.

When she could finally speak, she said, "We'll move it all into the parlor. The room is basically empty and safer than the barn."

"Yeah," Rick said. "No raccoons there. Where did you get the tortellini?"

Marlie smiled her thanks, receiving a watery grin in response. "There's a place in Charlotte."

Rick hooted with laughter. "I know exactly the place. I bet you got the lemon crème cake there as well."

* * *

It was a quiet evening. They cleaned up, then bundled up like arctic snow babies and went for a walk in the dark. Staying on the plowed surface meant walking down Fire Lane 61. The hill was an icy ramp. Even holding on to each other, the women couldn't retain their footing. Part of their descent was on the seat of their pants. A dog barked in response to their laughter, but Katie called out to the Dean's old hound, Thunder, that it was okay. With one last warning woof, the dog made his way back to the kitchen door, scratching to be let into the warmth his people shared.

"If we're going down the hill this way," Marlie said, slipping and grasping Katie's arm again. "How are we going to get back up?"

"Two choices. We can walk in the crusty stuff on the edges, or crawl on our hands and knees."

"So, we have a choice of Band-Aids or patches?" Marlie asked.

Where the road curved, there was an old hay baler a short distance from the plowed road. Floundering through the snow together, Katie and Marlie made it to the piece of machinery and in the lee of its bulk, sat side by side. Katie wrapped her arms around Marlie. An unexpected sadness rushed her. The thick place that had settled in her chest stopped her from saying the things she wanted to.

"I didn't expect this to be so hard," Marlie said softly. "When the chance came up, I thought, oh, it's just for a short time. Everything will work out. Now, I'm afraid."

"Don't be." Katie's voice was husky. "You're doing the right thing. We both know it, even if we don't like it. You can write, so can I. Then when you find a spot, I'll be right here waiting for you." The silence was compounded by the moonless night. "Remember, this is Vermont, not Oklahoma. No matter where you are here, you're only a few hours away." Try as she might, Katie

183

couldn't think of another comforting thing to say.

Something skittered across the crusty snow, a branch or leaves. Far away, they could hear yipping.

"Listen to that dog," said Marlie. "I know how it feels. I would feel safer if Solomon was all grown up and out here with us."

Katie didn't have the heart to tell her sweet friend that the yipping was a young coyote, born the previous spring, celebrating because its mama had brought home dinner.

* * *

This was the last time Katie would see Marlie before her lover moved to Pennsylvania. She wanted it to be special enough so that when Marlie remembered, she would want to come back.

"Are you sure this is the way to spring this on, Marlie? Shouldn't we ease her into the morning first?" Ruth asked. She had a rucksack open on the table, into which she was shoving extra mittens, a thermos of coffee, and sandwiches that consisted of scrambled eggs, bacon, and cheese inside baking powder biscuits left from the night before.

Katie tromped upstairs, making as much noise as possible. Cats that had started following her darted away when the stomping began. At the door to her bedroom where Marlie was still sleeping, Katie pounded until a shocked voice yelled, "What?!"

"Up an at 'em, girlie," Katie yelled. "Put on your woolies. We're going for a walk in the woods."

The door yanked open, revealing Marlie covered neck to toes in a lavender flannel nightgown edged with lace at the neck and cuffs. She was also wearing a confused frown.

She yawned before asking. "What are you talking about?"

"This is the morning I go and get the Christmas tree," Katie said, as if this were a yearly ritual instead of the first time. "If you want to come, bundle up and get downstairs." Turning on her heel, she stomped away.

"Okay," said Rick, laying the handsaw on the table before picking up his coffee cup. "I understand the stomping up the stairs, but the return trip was over the top."

"Yes," said Ruth, "even the puppies are hiding under Sasha." She pulled the ties on the rucksack firmly together. Somehow, a package of brownies had fallen in, and she didn't want Katie to take them out.

Moments later, Marlie went charging through the kitchen into the bathroom. Her hands were busy catching all of her hair in a scrunchie, and a sweatshirt hung from her mouth. When she came back out ten minutes later, she was all put together and, with the exception of her outerwear, ready to go.

"Are we going to have coffee?" she asked as Katie handed her a bright orange knit hat.

"It's in the bag," Katie said.

"And dry mittens and breakfast," smiled Ruth.

Katie reached for the ties on the top of the bag. "How about rope?"

Ruth yanked the bag away. "That too!" Before Katie could say anything, she turned on Rick. "You're going to be late for work if you don't get to it."

The elderly man, however, was leaning on the edge of the table, watching Marlie get ready for the outdoor trek. There was an amused look on his face as each layer made her rounder. Eventually, only her eyes showed.

"How are you going to put on your snowshoes?" Crinkle lines around his eyes showed over the rim of his mug.

Marlie spun around to Katie. "I have to wear snowshoes?"

"No," Katie glared at Rick. "To save time, we picked out the tree before the snow fell, and yesterday, Rick plowed out to it. We're going to walk up the lane to the bottom of the ledges, cut the tree, eat breakfast, and then pull it home. It'll be fun."

Marlie didn't look convinced. "Shouldn't I be wearing a hunting vest?"

"If you want," said Katie, pressing her lips together in a smile. Marlie was no hunter or woodsman. Hunting season was finished, but obviously, she was nervous that some gun-toting poacher would still be out there.

At Marlie's nod, she helped her friend into the reflective vest and, with only a small amount of squeezing, got it snapped. When Katie picked up the saw and the rucksack, Marlie and Ruth's eyes traveled to the second vest hanging on the wall. Cussing under her breath, Katie yanked it down and pulled the kitchen door open. As the two women headed out, Katie could hear Rick's roaring laughter following.

It was crisp and cold. To the east, a line of yellow and white flowed away from the sun, still hovering on the horizon. On the westward side, the last vestiges of night hung by its fingernails. A few light puffs of clouds moved across the sky, pushed by a wind that didn't reach ground level. Snow crunched beneath the boots. Not far away, a blue jay sent out his jarring call, welcoming them to his winter wonderland.

Marlie's voice was muffled by her scarf. "For crying out loud, Katie. It's barely daylight. What makes you think this is a good time to be walking all the way to the ridge?"

"It's only a little over a mile. The tree isn't far up the side."

Marlie stopped. "Wait, a minute! We're not going to hike up the ridge, are we?"

Katie kept walking, though she did slow down. "Not far, only a couple hundred feet." When she still could hear only her steps, she added, "I tell you what, why don't you go back, and I'll just get the tree. Okay?" It was a hard thing to say. She wanted this to be an experience they shared. Suddenly, behind her, she heard quick, rushing steps as Marlie ran to catch up.

"Oh, no," she said. "I'm not letting you go alone. Heaven only knows what kind of trouble you'll find up there."

The pale sun continued to rise as they moved along. A fox darted across their path, but other than that, their only company was the chickadees and the noisy jay.

As promised, there was a plowed path to within a hundred yards of the tree. Katie shook the snow off the evergreen and then with her mittened hands, pulled snow away from the base until she could lie on her belly beneath the boughs.

"My job is cutting," she said. "Your job is to stand on the other side and hold the tree. As you feel it develop some give, pull it towards you slowly, but don't snap it."

Marlie looked dubiously at the eight-foot spruce. "Aren't you supposed to use an ax?"

"Swinging an ax under here is frustrating," Katie explained. "Besides, the trunk of this tree isn't all that big."

Marlie moved around to the far side of the tree, and Katie pressed the teeth of the blade into the soft wood. With fairly little effort, the tree began to drift toward Marlie. Katie moved slightly to be out of kickback range.

"Get ready to get out of the way," Katie said.

Marlie's answer was lost as the last splinters of the trunk gave, and the tree toppled. Brushing the snow off as she got to her feet, Katie smiled in Marlie's direction. Unfortunately, other than the felled tree, all she could see was the bright orange cap and a couple of waving arms!

"Oh crap," Katie rushed over and yanked the tree off her friend. Marlie lay in the depression of her body and the tree, snow on her lashes, and hooting with laughter. "I wasn't ready!"

They pulled the tree back to the plowed track and left it with the butt facing home. Nearby, they found a wide rock to sit on while sharing the meal packed in the rucksack.

"You're supposed to eat the biscuit," said Katie.

"Look at the birds!" Marlie crumbled another piece and tossed it to the ground in front of them. Chickadees and Titmice greedily snapped up the crumbs. A crow cawed its dismay at not being invited to dine while the jay in his bright blue jacket landed, grabbed, and flew off.

Katie fought the urge to bring up Marlie's imminent departure, instead, she pointed out the bright red winter berries the birds would eat, a deer trail that crossed their track, and said, "We'll put on dry mittens, that will keep us warmer. We can tie a rope to the tree and pull it, or just grab the bottom couple of boughs, one on each side."

"That will be easier, right?" asked Marlie. "I mean, so the trunk doesn't keep getting caught on the ground."

"Very good," Katie laughed.

"I bow to you, Professor," said Marlie. "Get it? Bough, like a tree?" Then, before Katie could say a word, pressed her lips against Katie's.

They sat quietly together until Marlie pointed out that her butt was freezing to the rock.

* * *

By the time they got back to the farmhouse, both were panting, and an array of outerwear was draped across the top of the tree. Katie trimmed the bottom of the tree off straight and between the girls and Ruth, got it through the door. Getting the tree to stand up straight required one of them to lie on the floor, releasing and tightening the screws of the red and green metal Christmas tree stand, while the other reached into the center and steadied the trunk.

"A little to the left," Ruth directed from six feet away. "A little more, oops, back a quarter of an inch. Perfect."

Immediately, one of the cats jumped into the branches, and the tree toppled over.

"Okay. Now," said Katie, teeth clenched. "We're going to stand it up and tie it in the corner over there, away from the heat."

Marlie held the tree in place while Katie ran for a hammer, nails, and baling twine. There was a short conversation with her telling Ruth they were not going to go through the maneuver of straightening it again. After the tree was secure, Katie untangled the old electric lights. Marlie put tree hooks into the assortment of miniature hats, mittens, and scarfs Ruth had knitted.

"I made hot chocolate," Ruth said. "And these are for the babies." From a shoe box hidden in the cat room, she pulled out knitted catnip balls and by the handfuls, sent them rolling across the room. "Merry Christmas, darlings."

With the cats occupied and Katie switching out bad light bulbs, Marlie was left to hang the string of greeting card garland and ornaments left from Gram, as well as the ones made by Ruth.

"What about the star?" she asked. "And the tinsel?"

"We're leaving the star for Rick," Ruth said. "Everyone should have a hand in this. And tinsel is bad for the cats. They play with it and eat it. It gets in their guts and can get all twisted up. They could die."

She was sitting on the sofa with a mug of hot chocolate in one hand and a frosted cookie in the other. All around her, cats in various stages of catnip overdose snoozed.

Marlie turned, ornament in hand. "That's awful." Looking at Old Tom passed out at her feet, she said. "No more tinsel. Ever."

Ruth had come up with an old Brownie camera. They took turns taking pictures of each other.

"I can't wait for it to get dark," said Marlie. "We can go outside and look at the tree through the windows."

Though she heartily agreed, Katie didn't want to see the day end. In the morning, Marlie would drive away, headed back to Rutland to pack her belongings, and on December twenty-sixth, drive south.

"How about I make stuffed meatloaf for supper?" she asked.

"With mushroom gravy?" asked Ruth.

"Well, I'll have to use mushroom soup, but okay."

"Stuffed with what?" Marlie asked.

"Mashed potatoes, and today, green beans and a little of the leftover canned tomatoes," Katie explained. "I make it so it's not real tall, bake it slow and slice it so when you pour the gravy on, it looks like just meatloaf."

"But it is so good," Ruth said with a happy sigh. "What would you like for dessert, Marlie?"

"Well," the young woman said shyly. "I'd like to try making a pie."

Rick came home at the end of the day to find a fire blazing in the fireplace, the Christmas tree star waiting for him to reach up and put it into place, and Marlie dusted with flour and pleased as punch.

* * *

In the morning, when Marlie and Katie were ready to leave, the four of them stood in front of the tree. Tears ran down Ruth and Marlie's cheeks. Only sheer determination kept Katie from crying with them. Both she and Rick swallowed hard, endured the hugs and the goodbyes. Beneath the tree, three packages wrapped in red and white paper and sporting pretty bows had appeared out of the trunk of Marlie's car. In exchange, the young woman was taking with her gifts that had been both handmade and purchased specifically with her in mind.

Chapter Thirty-Five

A few days after Marlie's departure, Katie came downstairs to find Ruth in the kitchen lining up small cardboard boxes on the farmer's table. Each box was lined with wax paper, and waited for Katie and Ruth to sort the goodies they had baked to place inside. Tucked under the front and addressed in neat cursive was a Christmas card envelope with the name of the recipient of that box. There was one for the Deans, Father Metevier, Dorothea and Ellen, the Baldwins, the ladies from the knitting club, and Charlene, their librarian hostess. There was also a box, as well as a filled dinner plate, for Chet and Charlie.

"Are you ready?" Ruth asked. "I've got one here that we can send to Marlie. She'll get it before New Year's, and it'll be a nice surprise."

Besides the cookies that had been baked and frozen in advance, she had laid out a platter of brownies and date bars. Together they filled the boxes, tucking individually wrapped Hersey kisses and red and green ribbon candy into any open spaces. When all the treats were in place, with the exception of a few they had left for Rick, who would be playing the part of a reindeer to Ruth's Santa Claus, the boxes were closed. Katie donned her outdoor gear while Ruth sealed each box in the brown paper wrap she had made. Finally, when her hay bale hemp bows were in place, Ruth summoned Rick. Together, they stacked the boxes in the middle of the bench seat of his pickup. They were ready to go, deliveries awaited.

The day was clear with no wind. The temperature hovered just below zero. Katie let the chickens and the pair of geese, who had been abandoned in the front yard during the fall, into the outside enclosure while she hoed and shoveled their area clean. Rick had dropped three grain bags of sawdust by the door. Once Katie had the floor and nesting boxes refilled, she let the fowl back inside. Clucking happily, the small brood gathered beneath the heat lamp until curiosity drove them to scratch and peck at their fresh décor.

There was no getting the wheelbarrow and its soiled contents to the spot where Ruth declared their own garden space would be the next year. Katie emptied the wheelbarrow near the corner of the cattle holding yard and put her tools away in the shed. Her old snowshoes hung on the wall. With them in hand, she tackled the next chore on her list.

Using six empty cardboard milk cartons, Ruth had strung baling twine through the top, making a hanging loop, and then cut windows on each side three inches from the bottom. A pair of long sticks were shoved through the cardboard below the windows, creating roosts, and the well was filled with a mixture of birdseed, cranberries, and peanut butter. From inside the house, Katie brought out a wire clothes hanger. Straightening all but the hooked end gave her a tool that would allow her to pull appropriate branches down to grabbing level. Strapping on her snowshoes, Katie moved around the yard, hanging five of the feeders on the handy branches. As she worked, she was mindful of finding places near the windows where the cats would be able to sit and watch the feathered wild birds feed.

With her snowshoes under her arm and carrying the last bird feeder, she walked down the short rise to the barn. Entering through the milk house, she traversed the width of the crowded barn and opened the pig door on the far side. Across from the long unused sty space and beyond the corner of the orchard was the family burying place. Katie donned her snowshoes again and trekked across the virgin snow.

A handy fir bough bent with a pull of her hook, and Katie was able to hang the last feeder above the resting place of her grandparents. The burying place was ringed with four-foot granite markers. Long pipes ran between the pillars of stone. One had been bent in the middle by a fallen tree long before Katie had first come here. The crooked spot provided a place for Katie to perch when she was finished. From her seat, she could look across the meadows and the LaPlatte Brook. On the far side, a last remaining corridor of firs hid the encroaching housing development. Soon a bright red male cardinal found the container of treats. He sang out, and chickadees followed his directions, swooping in for a bite, then fluttering away.

Katie watched silently, before finally saying aloud. "So, there you go. Ruth made those up, but you have to know I will be the one keeping them filled. Hopefully, some mischievous squirrel won't be pulling all of them down." She watched silently for several minutes before speaking again. "I was just thinking about how when I first came here, we slept in the kitchen when the power went out. Then there was the time you explained about stringing the rope between the garage and the barn. Remember? You told me that when the deep snow came, and the storms blew, you would tie a rope around your waist and use the metal bull ring to stay attached to the long rope. That way, even if the storm blew hard, you would be able to get down to feed the cows." She laughed. "That was when the garage was for cars, not cats, and there actually were cows here. I didn't get it, you know? About the rope and the snow. Even when you explained that the weather could be so bad that you wouldn't be able to see one building from another. That you could be lost in that four-hundred-yard space. I was too young. It took years for me to realize that when you said lost, you meant forever. I don't think I honestly thought either one of you would ever be gone." Katie's voice choked. "Okay, let's not get all maudlin here."

"We didn't find a lot of Christmas decorations, but you should see all Ruth pulled together. Wrapping paper, Christmas card garland, and an absolute ton of teeny-tiny, knitted hats and mittens for the tree. The cats are having a great time pulling them down. And we've got a dog, well, three. But only one is staying."

"I'm sure you're aware of what I've been at. I appreciate any bone you have thrown me for direction." The sun twinkled across the snow crystals. It was not unlike the shine she had seen before in her grandfather's eyes. Once again, her throat filled. "I have to go. My butt is freezing to this pipe. I'll be back, you know that. And, if you do see fit, feel free to drop a bit of inspiration into my pocket. I love you terribly. Tell my folks Merry Christmas."

She blew air kisses and headed back up toward the barn. Above her, a red coat stood framed by the pig door, waiting. Katie followed Ruth's crooked path through the piles of Irma's collection. Once outside, with the milk house door firmly pulled closed, they linked arms for the final leg to tea and cookies. Two women, two ghosts, one overpowering love among all.

Chapter Thirty-Six

"Hello?" said Katie.

On the other end of the telephone line, a woman spoke. Her voice was thick and choked, as though she had been weeping. Given the time of year, she could have been suffering from a head cold. Katie didn't think so.

"This is Eugenie, Katie." The woman paused to blow her nose. "Arlo and I, well, we've been talking about when you was at the store the other day."

There was a pause. Katie waited. She could feel the planes of her face hardening. Just before her teeth clenched, Eugenie spoke again. This time, her voice was lower, barely more than a whisper. Behind her, Arlo said something, but she shushed him.

"Me and Arlo, well, Arlo mostly, has had this bad thing sitting on our chests for a while, and with all that's been going on, you know, you stirring up about the time around when young George died."

Katie almost laughed. Young George would have been older than Eugenie.

"Go ahead, Eugenie," said Katie. "If you've got something to say, get it off your chest. Don't worry; I'm not going to jump on you."

"I wasn't worried about that, Katie. Though that's good of you to say." The woman speaking from across the village, along the twisted copper wire, sighed. The man spoke again. "This is the thing, Katie. After the whole mess was pretty much passed, that being when Ruth was cleared and moved up there with Irma, Christopher decided to sell the house. He got Dorothea and her friends in there to clean and pack it up." Katie didn't correct Eugenie's memory about it only being Dorothea. "When it was all ready to go, Christopher had Arlo and this guy that used to live here, named Leo Clark, load it up and haul it away. Arlo thought they were going to take the bunch of it up to the farm, but Christopher said no. There were two loads taken out and put in the old tumble-down garage behind the store."

Katie tried to picture a garage beyond the back loading dock, but nothing came to mind.

"Katie," Eugenie said slowly. "Ruth's things are still there. They don't belong to Christopher, but that's where he left 'em. I, we, just kind of thought you should know. Arlo has tried several times over the years to bring it up to Christopher, but I don't know, the words didn't come out."

After she thanked Eugenie and put the telephone receiver back in the cradle, Katie turned to where Rick sat at the far end of the table, sipping tea and reading the paper.

"Do you know a man by the name of Leo Clark?"

Rick smiled. "That's a name I haven't heard in a while. He and I used to work at the furniture factory together. After it closed down, he did odd jobs for a bit. Then he moved to Winooski and went to work for Ethan Allen Furniture. How'd you come up with his name?"

Katie's initial response was not to say anything to Ruth. Instead, she decided the time for working in the shadows was done. She called her friend in from the living room, where the radio was playing Christmas music and puppies wrestled on the rug.

When she finished relating what Eugenie said, she asked, "What would be there, Ruth?"

"The furniture, I guess." Ruth shook her head, suddenly saddened. "I don't know. Dishes, my knickknacks, stuff from my parents. I can't think what else."

Moving to the window, she gazed out into the night, finally turning. "They don't matter. It's okay."

"The hell it is, Ruthie," said Rick.

* * *

Early the next morning, Katie and Rick arrived at the general store before any of the employees had pulled into the lot. They left their cars parked near the street and, with the light from the parking lot and the flashlight Katie carried, they walked across the frozen earth, each crunching step sounding like the advance of the militia.

Snow had been plowed back until the pile was twice the height of their heads.

"I don't remember a building back here," said Katie.

"It was in the weeds and scrub," said Rick. "I'm thinking it was about here."

They were standing where the snow mountain was the tallest and deepest. Angling along sideways, they came to a place where there was a crevice between two of the tall piles. Crowbar in hand, Rick went first, feeling his way, leaving Katie with the flashlight. They ended in a sumac sapling forest and fought their way back toward the site Rick remembered.

In the beam of her flashlight, Katie saw it. An old, single-car garage, maybe twelve feet wide, with a decided list to the north. There was no sheen of paint off the weathered sides, and the snow mountain was pushed up against the swing doors in the front. Facing them was a side entrance. A silver hasp and padlock glinted as she moved the light over it.

Rick wasn't deterred. He jammed the crowbar behind the hasp, braced himself, and heaved. The hasp popped out of the rotten door so easily Rick was thrown backwards, stumbling to catch his footing, colliding with Katie. The angle of the tilt wouldn't allow the bottom of the door to open, but putting his weight behind it, Rick was able to push the top open enough to squeeze through. When Katie went to follow him, he told her to stay out. He took the flashlight, leaving Katie standing in the dark. She didn't notice, being more intent on the moving glow that showed through the dirty six-pane window.

A few minutes passed. A small cardboard box came through the opening. Katie jumped to take it. The feel of the damp pressed paper already disintegrating in her arms spoke of its time left deserted and alone in the ramshackle building. They made their way back over the mountain of dirty white across the drive, and Rick laid the box on the floor of his truck. Just as they pulled out onto the street, the first employee of Beauregard's General Store and Mercantile arrived. The young woman didn't give them so much as a second look.

Katie wanted to look in the box, but she knew that was for Ruth. Opening the back door to the feed store, Katie turned around in time to see Rick carry the box to his delivery truck. Taking a few minutes before punching in, Katie called Grace Dean.

"Rick's going to drop the box off," she said after explaining what was going on. "I'm not sure if Ruth should be alone."

"Well," said Grace. "I'm pressing butter today. I guess I'll load my works in the car and give Ruth a lesson in it."

* * *

Katie came home that evening to find the contents of the box cleaned and drying at one end of the farmer's table. Ruth was stoic, glad to have these bits, but fine, if that was all. Rick, on the other hand, had a plan.

Even though she got up early for a second day in a row, Rick was up and gone when she came downstairs.

"Where did he go?" she asked Ruth, gulping hot coffee.

"He took the tractor to town," Ruth said. Her face was flushed and there was still the stain of tears on her cheeks. "I tried to tell him no. Katie, there's going to be trouble."

Even though she normally wouldn't be getting up for another hour, her lunch pail and thermos were sitting on the edge of the counter, waiting for her to grab them and run. The pickup caught up with the unlicensed Massey-Ferguson at the small incline before the single stop sign. She got ready to give him a shove, but Rick's yard toy made the grade. In the lot, two pickups waited. Philip Carwell and Stan Baldwin sat in the cab of Stan's truck. Another, bigger vehicle pulled into the lot behind Katie. George was driving the town truck, its big flood lights lit up the snowbank.

"Doesn't this figure? Friday, the busiest day of the week, and the mess of us are out here making snow forts." Stan stood beside the others while Rick worked with the tractor's bucket, moving snow and dumping it right in the middle of the lot.

Katie turned to tell him he could leave. Her estimation of him plummeting. What she found was a grin on his face that mirrored the other men.

"Christopher is going to be so pissed," he said with a laugh.

The doors were wrenched off the garage. The town truck backed in, and furniture was loaded in the big dump body while smaller items went into the pickups. There wasn't all that much, and though Katie thought they could have got it all in the town truck, the four men were having a moment, and she just stood by.

Though they tried to hurry, moving the snow had taken a while. Two vehicles pulled in, headlights illuminating the workers. Katie turned to see Christopher bearing down on her. Behind him, Eugenie was just getting out of her car, a look of shock on her face, and with one hand covering her mouth.

"What the hell do you think you're doing?" Christopher roared.

"Joe Clark called Rick to wish him Merry Christmas. They had a little talk. We're merely out here taking back what rightfully belongs to someone else," Katie said.

"You got a problem with that, Christopher, old buddy?" Stan's hand dropped on her shoulder.

Instead of answering, Christopher hurried into the store.

"Let's pick up the pace," Stan called out.

The four of them were grunting under the weight of a heavy maple dresser when the town cruiser, lights flashing, pulled in. Sheriff Lewis was barely out of the car when Christopher was in his face. Pushing his uncle aside, Lewis walked up to Katie.

"I should have known I'd find you here," he said.

"Did that guy get the female dog fixed?" she asked.

"Whose stuff is this?" He was still straight-arming Christopher away from himself.

"These are Ruth's belongings, taken from her house when Christopher sold it," said Katie. Before she could say anything else, Stan was back.

"Yeah." He blew on his frozen cupped fingers. "Christopher forgot it was all out here. We offered to help him get it back to her. You know, early Christmas present and all that. Ho, ho, ho."

The other men had paused in their efforts.

"You got a registration for that tractor?" Lewis asked.

"I've got a driver's license," said Rick.

Christopher grabbed Lewis's arm, swinging him around. "Arrest them!" he screamed, spittle freezing on his face as soon as it left his lips. "You sorry punk. Arrest them all!"

Lewis leaned into Christopher's face. "Get out of my way." The flashing red lights were extinguished, and the sheriff's cruiser pulled out.

"You should go inside." Stan calmly told Christopher. "And you go to work, Katie. I'll be right along, and we'll get Rick on the road quick as we can."

After he tied down the load on his truck, he drove across the main street to the Parentville-Charlotte Road and was gone. The other two trucks, with the illegal tractor in the middle, followed.

* * *

Throughout the day, Katie went back and forth over her notes. She didn't need to hold them in her hand to know what they said. They were as much a part of her memory at that time as the way to drive home or the sequence for operating the cash register keys.

She'd reached a conclusion. Right, wrong, or indifferent, it was what she believed. How to get others to follow her line of thinking was the issue.

Chapter Thirty-Seven

Sunday morning, with less than a week left until Christmas, Katie declined to go to mass at Saint Jude's with Ruth and Rick.

"People are going to be asking," said Ruth. "This is not the season to skip out."

"Secret stuff to do, Ruth. Get your butt out of here, so I can get done."

Katie was wearing flannel pajamas under her quilted robe. When the door closed on the elderly couple, she added a bulky sweater and a second pair of socks. While she brewed tea, she considered if she might be coming down with a cold. Neither her chest nor her head were congested. There was no sniffling or sneezing, yet her feet were freezing, and inside she felt her bones shuddering.

For crying out loud, she wondered. *What the heck is wrong?*

She couldn't fathom that her symptoms might not be from the weather, but her inner feelings coming to the surface.

Katie was already finished with her own Christmas preparations. What she needed was time to sit in the living room with the scent of Christmas coming off the tree and the puppies bumbling around on the floor. Maybe then, the spirit of Christmas would come back into her soul. Deck the Halls played softly as she built the fire in the fireplace. Oh, Come All Ye Faithful serenaded her while she consumed her coffee and toast. Away in a Manager brought reminiscent tears. But nothing lit her Christmas Candle.

The shaking and chilblains finally subsided. Even though she got to where she could shuck layers and go up to the chilly second floor for day wear, there was no warm fuzzy glow in her heart.

* * *

"Are we going to make raspberry-stuffed shortbread cookies, Katie?" Ruth asked when she and Rick returned.

Katie discretely wiped her eyes and blew her nose.

"We'll need brown sugar, raspberry preserves, and butter," said Katie.

"I've already sent Rick down to Dean's for butter." Ruth went into the pantry and came back with a half-filled cardboard box. "There's about a pound of brown sugar here, and frozen raspberries. We could render our own."

"You mean," Katie said wryly. "*I* could render our own."

"Well, yeah." Ruth left the box on the table and went back into the pantry to fetch the frozen raspberries.

While they sipped tea and the raspberries simmered on the stove, Katie and Ruth sat across the table from each other. Their thoughts ran along similar paths, and the silence was comfortable. It was broken only when Rick returned.

"I come bearing gifts," he said. "Grace sent goat cheese, some beef and vegetable stew for tonight, and real raised dinner rolls."

"Perfect," Katie responded.

Once the dough for the shortbread was mixed and set in the refrigerator to chill for an hour or so, Ruth wandered off to play with the puppies. Katie opened her little notebook and tore the pages she had used out, lining them up on the table. Using the stubs of Ruth's leftover crayons, she bent to the task of color-coding related items with neat crayon circles. Katie's diligence paused only when Ruth re-entered. It was an exercise in second-guessing herself.

"What are you doing there?" Ruth asked.

"Not for you," said Katie.

With a shrug, Ruth took the saucepan of warm puppy formula and went back to the living room. Katie picked up the black crayon. A single stroke through each one eliminated those items that were not related or that she felt were immaterial to her line of research. With that done, she turned to

202

highlight the main character of each conversation. When she had trimmed down as much as she could, she read through everything again. Her findings caused her palms to sweat. She had been right in her earlier conclusion. Collecting the pages, she used the cast iron handle to lift one of the round covers of the chunk wood cook stove. Before she dropped the pages into the burning wood and flames, she paused. Replacing the cover, she went into the cat room, looking for a safe place to hide her notes. Nothing presented itself. Back in the kitchen, she took down her shoebox of bills. Removing them, she laid the notes at the bottom, replaced the bills, and put the whole box back on top of the fridge, pushing it toward the back.

"Okay, Ruth," she stuck her head into the living room. "Time to roll and cut the shortbread."

The cookies cooled on one end of the table while the three people shared stew at the other. Rick's eyes were drawn repeatedly toward the sweets.

"You can have one," said Ruth. "The rest of them are for Christmas day." She watched him closely. "That odd-shaped one on the end is the last bit. The biggest one. I suggest you select that one."

Taking her advice, Rick slid the cookie onto a napkin and with a fresh cup of tea, retreated to the living room.

Later, while Rick and Ruth listened to WJOY on the stereo radio play Christmas carols, Katie quietly pulled on her outdoor clothing and crept out the kitchen door. It wasn't until the headlights of her truck shone through the front windows of the house as she backed out that the two elderly people were aware she was outside.

"Where is she going?" asked Ruth, walking over to pull open the front door.

Rick, who had passed through the kitchen on his way to fill the furnace and glanced over Katie's shoulder while she had been absorbed in what she was doing, bit down on his lip. Going to the kitchen, he looked for the notes, finally finding them when he fished around in the bill box. The yellow crayon highlights caused him to catch his breath. There were people annotated that would not be amicable to Katie's particular brand of criticism.

"For crying out loud," he cussed.

"What?" Ruth demanded, alarm in her voice.

Instead of answering, Rick dialed the phone. "Stan, get dressed. Meet me down in the sheriff's parking lot. We need to find Katie before she gets herself hurt."

"What?" Grabbing Rick's arm, Ruth shook him hard. "What is going on?"

Pulling away, Rick yanked on his boots. "I think she's gone out to challenge the person she suspects killed George."

"No! She wouldn't do that!" Ruth snatched her boots off the mat.

Rick laid a hand on her arm. "Listen to me. You need to stay here. If she comes back before I do, keep her here. I don't care how. Don't let her leave again."

He pulled his jacket off the hook. Ruth jammed the big fur-lined hat on his head. As his truck pulled out, Ruth traveled from window to window, following him down the road until he was out of sight. Cats swarmed around her feet, including Peanut and LG, but the old woman was not comforted by their presence.

Chapter Thirty-Eight

Katie got to Beauregard's General Store just as the lights went off in the parking lot. She pulled around to the loading dock and walked back to the front. At the door, she met the last clerk coming out. It was seven o'clock, and had been dark for several hours.

"Hi," she said. "I'm looking for Mr. Beauregard, Christopher Beauregard. Is he still here?"

"Yeah, he's in the office." The young woman made to go back into the store with Katie when the horn blew from a red Chevy idling in the lot. "Oh, there's my boyfriend. The office is in the back, okay?"

Katie said yes and went through the door. Behind her, she heard the rasp as the key turned and the deadbolt slid into place. Without a second thought, Katie moved up the long, narrow planks of the hardwood floor. The store was like a hundred others she had been in over the years. The smell of cardboard dust, grease, and oil permeated into the floorboards. There was the nauseating undercurrent of over-ripe produce, and as she got closer to the rear, cold, raw meat. Beyond the meat counter, a light shone from Christopher Beauregard's office. Standing in the doorway, she looked around the room. It was neat, with no stacks of papers cluttering the desk and no empty coffee cup at Christopher's elbow. He was bent over his work, leaning in close to a binder filled with mimeographed sheets.

"Mr. Beauregard? Christopher?" Katie spoke in a low voice, hoping not to startle Christopher. It was a hope in vain.

"Cripes!" he yelped, jumping up from his seat. Even though she had been in full view, he hadn't noticed her. "How did you get in here?"

205

"I came in just as the store was closing. I'd like to talk to you for a few minutes." Katie stood with her heels on the doorjamb. "Do you remember me, Katelyn Took?"

"I know who you are. You work up at Baldwin's, for crying out loud." Christopher settled back into his seat. "If you want to fill out a job application, they're right there in the metal file holder by the door. Just take one and bring it back tomorrow." His eyes drifted back to the pages in the folder.

"Oh, I'm not here for a job," said Katie. "I like working at Baldwin's, and for the town. I came in specifically to talk to you about your brother. George Beauregard."

"George has been dead for over five years. Why would you want to talk about him again?"

The desk chair squealed as he leaned back. Katie hadn't realized how big he was before. The only other times she had encountered him, she had been on the other side of the counter. The thought leapt into her mind that they were the only two in the store, and he might not like what she had to say. With studied casualness, she rocked on her heels, moving back a bit with each backward sway.

"Actually, I'm trying to learn a little about him. You know what he was like. Who his enemies might be. Stuff like that." Katie had moved far enough into the hall to be stepping out of the bright lights of the office and into the security lighting in the store.

Christopher rose from his seat. "Not only do I know who you are, Miss. Took, but I know that batty old broad that murdered my brother lives with you. Did you know that? That his wife, sworn to fidelity, murdered my brother in his sleep and then lied her way out of it."

"Ruth has no recollection of the entire evening," said Katie. "I recently spoke with a doctor who said she did not believe with the level of medication Ruth was taking, she could have functioned enough to have dealt a killing blow."

"That's bull crap, and you know it." Christopher came around the desk in the direction of the door.

Backing slightly, Katie could feel the chill coming off the meat case. She walked around the end until she was directly across from Christopher with the wide glass case between them.

"I have a theory," she said.

Christopher had stopped walking. He leaned against the doorjamb to his office. Reaching to his left, he flipped a bank of switches. The interior fluorescent lights, which had been shut down fifteen minutes before, came right back on. Katie blinked in the glare, but quickly cleared her eyesight.

"We've been searching for the truth for a long while," said Christopher, sounding much friendlier. "Being from away, you might have a fresh perspective. What's your theory?"

"Actually." Katie smiled. "I'm from right here. I was born here, grew up, and went to school here."

"But you left. You decided this wasn't the place for you, and you took off without so much as a word. Yeah, I remember. Your grandmother was devastated. You know, I think that's when she fell off the wagon. Got to be sort of nutsy. Collected cats and other weirdos."

"Yes, I did leave." Katie refused to be baited. "I found things considerably changed when I returned. Well, to be exact, some things had changed. The other stuff was just information I didn't know before. You know, like I didn't know Ruth at all. Or that she and my grandmother had been childhood friends. Then she grew up and married an abusive womanizer."

Christopher shifted against the doorjamb. "I told you before that my brother was a good man. That bird-brained lunatic spent years spreading lies about him."

"Uh-huh. You did tell me that. You left out the part where he's your half-brother and that you have another half-brother who lives in Monkton. His name is Al Lewis. Then there's the part where George Beauregard was a Junior, as in your father, also a womanizer, was George Senior. Yeah, how did it feel that day when Junior came home from the army all spiffy and driving a new car? You know, when your dad begged him to come into the family business. Promised to leave it all to him. You were standing right there watching your bit of glory go sailing out the window."

"You don't know what you're talking about," said Christopher.

Katie watched him, his eyes looking over the store. Was he checking to make sure no one else was in there? Trying to figure out the best way to get her out of his face?

"I know a lot more than you think," she said. "I know every time you turned around, another one of Junior's illegitimate children was in here looking for a job or a handout, and the old man was right there smiling and giving it to them. That which should have been for your kids was going to some you didn't want to know anything about. Oh, yeah, he was proud of them all. Didn't matter they were the other side of the blanket. Even Al Lewis' son could have gotten in line for some of the cream, and his mother was real trash. But you probably could overlook Al because his mother never moved right into the center of town. Everyone knew who the kid's daddy was, but she wasn't in your face. And are you ready for this? I know one night, not long ago, you ran me off the road. It was a warning, I think. But let me tell you, there's a state trooper who knows, in the event something like that happens again and I don't make it."

Christopher ignored Katie's reference to the night she had been sideswiped at the bottom of Fire Lane 61, he was too busy focusing on what she had said about Mildred Hooper's kids and Al Lewis' mother.

"They were vermin. Like Ruth, trash."

"Ruth isn't trash. She came from a good family. One of the oldest in town."

Christopher moved up closer to the meat counter. When he spoke, his lips moved, but his teeth stayed locked together. Thin strings of saliva clung to the sides of his mouth.

"Don't give me that crap about old families. This berg wouldn't exist if it weren't for the Beauregards. This store? We're the lynchpin of this community. We give the credit. Keep these morons fed. Support them."

"No. You only think so. The main business here is the creamery. It always has been. Farmers in a fifty-mile radius haul to here. Even Baldwin's has been doing business in Parentville as long as this store. They may not have as many employees, but let's face it, they're just as solid. How long did Beauregard's stay in the feed and seed business? Maybe two years? But I'm not here to talk about your failings as an entrepreneur. I'm here about your brother. The one that was the toast of the town. The party boy. The hellion who was out whoring and raising the census while he was at it. He drank, drugged, slept around. Was he making you look bad? Or maybe you were just jealous. I hear your wife keeps you on a short leash. Then he was found stabbed to death in his own bed. With his wife sleeping right beside him. The woman he beat every chance he got. That was a sad, sad thing. There you were, grieving with the rest of the family. Your father would have been beside himself, lamenting what a good son Junior had been. The best ever. Far above any of the rest of you. And I bet there are a bunch hidden under the rocks that don't know where they came from. Even your mother, not Junior's by birth, but the only one he had ever known, loved him dearly. How did that make you feel? To be set aside by your own mother?"

Katie had been rocking back and forth, running her hands along the cool metal of the meat case. And all the while watching as Christopher inched closer to the edge of the case.

"Stop right there, Chrissy-boy," she said, "or I won't tell you the rest of my theory."

Christopher stopped moving. "I thought all that blather was your theory."

"No, that bit was what I learned by poking around." She would drop the bomb, then, while he was reeling at her disclosure, run for the front door and get away from him. "What I think happened is that you had finally had enough. Your dad had stepped forward and told you that even though Junior had made a wreck of his life, and you had given all of yours to the store, when Senior died, Junior was going to be in control. You were probably livid. You couldn't argue with him. His mind at that time was such; he couldn't be trusted not to make some rash decision that would be the end of all your hopes. Then you legally wrangled around that, because, in the end, your mother was in your pocket. But it never ended, did it? All those folks with their hands out. And Ken Sampson. Even when he lost in court, he stayed mean and on your back. I know he did. Tracy must have been ballistic. Did George laugh at you? Call you a patsy? Tell you how you were going to support him till the day he died?"

Christopher's hands turned to fists, where they rested on the other side

209

of the meat case. Katie could hear him breathe. Moments before, he had worked at looking calm. Now he was beyond putting up a facade.

"You should watch your mouth, girlie," said Christopher. "There are a lot of empty spaces in the woods around here."

Katie ignored him. "While you were working yourself towards a heart attack, you remembered Ruth. Maybe she came into the store, or you saw her around town someplace. Poor pathetic woman. And everybody knew she was missing a couple of screws. You might even have had something to do with that rumor. The night George died, there was evidence the two of them had shared a cup of coffee. But a neighbor said the lights went out in the house at nine, and George was still in Ida Jarvis' house at ten. That's the house which is just up the road. Poor Ruth, lonely and afraid. I bet she would have welcomed someone to keep her company. Then bingo, she passes out from medicine she's been taking for a while. Stuff she knew how to use.

"So, what I'm thinking is, while you were there sipping coffee, you slipped her an extra pill. The bottle was right there on the table. When she started to pass out, maybe you poured a little, or a lot, of cough syrup down her throat, figuring she would overdose. It was a two-fer. Even if she lived through the night, it would be like she junked out or tried to commit suicide. Once she was back in bed, you went over to Ida's and picked up George. You did a really good job at not being close enough to actually be identified. But, nonetheless, it was you. The guys at the Wagon Wheel made it clear George couldn't buy his own booze; he bummed it off of people. Ken Sampson said he had an appetite for rot gut, but you had access to plenty right here in the store. You brought a bottle of the good stuff along with you, knowing he wouldn't be able to turn away. You even rinsed out the bottle and left it in the dish drainer, maybe wiped off your prints. I gotta tell you, Chrissy, no alcoholic rinses the bottle or washes the glasses. Then you dosed him with cough syrup the same way you did Ruth. That just made it look all the more realistic. Right? People would think she'd given it to him and took the same herself. What you didn't plan on is both of them had grown accustomed to their vices. Her, the sleeping pills, him, the liquor. You helped him into bed, even got his clothes off, waited a while, but he just snored away. You lost your temper and buried that knife in his chest. Here's a new question: how did the knife get into George's house? Hmm, makes you wonder.

"Then, coward that you are, you ran." Katie laughed. "You never even thought to check and see if Ruth was still alive, did you? What a surprise you must have had when you got back there in the morning. Idiot."

Christopher moved. Not towards the end of the case, but in the other direction. Two steps, and then he stopped. He had a sneer on his face that scared Katie. It was time to leave.

"Ha, you got it mostly right. That bimbo, she slept right through it! Her breathing was so faint, I didn't think she'd make the hour." Christopher gave a barking laugh that caused Katie to jump.

His arm swung up. He was holding an evil-looking knife where she could see it. The blade was at least twelve inches long, and the clean steel glinted in the fluorescent's glow.

"See this?" He asked. "You might not recognize it, but that perverted brother of mine would. The twin to this one pierced through him like he was soft as butter. Let me tell you. He was soft. The army did nothing for him. He came back, couldn't hold a job. Couldn't refuse a drink if it was watered down with cat piss. That was George. He looked like a saint, but he stank like a pile of fresh cow shit. This beauty, girlie, this one." He waved the knife. "You're going to know the same way he did the other." Even as he spoke the last, Christopher rushed toward the end of the meat case.

Katie forgot all the rest of what she had planned on saying and ran for her life. She was almost at the front counter when she remembered the sound of the deadbolt hitting home. Swerving to the left, she cut in front of Christopher. There was a standing display of brooms and mops on the end of the next aisle. Grabbing it as she went by, she yanked it down. It was heavier than she expected, and the wire framework pulled her to the ground. She rolled away, crashing into the boxes and cans on the shelves, but finally got her footing and ran.

There has to be another exit. Where is it? She was on the verge of hysteria.

For every step she took, a pounding step followed. Katie was almost to the end of the aisle when she realized Christopher's steps weren't behind her.

211

He's coming down the other aisle, she thought.

Grabbing a shelf, she pulled herself around and ran back the way she had just come. At the end of the aisle, she jumped over the snarl of broom handles. Christopher, who was now running up the same aisle and only steps behind her, wasn't as agile. Ahead of her was a row of shopping carts, each one tucked into the other. There was no time to turn. She scrambled over them and, once on the other side, realized her mistake. Instead of finding a path she could follow to escape, Katie was standing in the front window display surrounded by boxes of cornflakes and towers of laundry soap.

Christopher laughed. Using the sheer power of his mass, he yanked the row of carts aside and closed in on her. Katie backed away. She was against the glass. Her arms spread, palms pressed against the pane. She saw him raise his arm, the cold steel shining again and turned her head to the side. Yet, still kept her eyes on her killer.

Suddenly, there was a sharp crack and an aftershock that surrounded her. Glass was falling. She could feel it slide and instinctively pulled her arms away. A rosette was blossoming in the center of Christopher's shoulder. He was pulling away from her. The long butcher knife was still moving. It grazed her shoulder, shearing through the canvas barn coat and flannel shirt, leaving behind a thin scrapping line. Katie's knees gave. She was tumbling backwards. Around her, shiny shards of glass fell like sparkling raindrops. One moment she was in the bright light; the next thing she knew, darkness was circling from all sides, and her feet were at a height even with her eyes. Then, before she could realize she was falling and in four feet would hit the hard, frozen ground, Katie landed as though she'd jumped backwards onto a mattress. But, instead of a nicely padded Simmons Beautyrest, two pairs of arms enveloped her, yanking her out into the cold and then shielding her from the wind's blast.

"What in the name of all that's holy do you think you are doing?" yelled Sheriff Lewis.

But the arms bore her away, her hysteria finally breaking free. She grabbed hold, burying her face and crying. There was running. She felt it jar her, yet her feet weren't on the ground.

"Move, get out of the way." A woman Katie didn't recognize ordered Rick and Stan aside.

When she had recognized who held her, Katie tightened her grip. She didn't want them to go. She was afraid, and the cigarette, harsh voice did not comfort her. The woman pulled her free and into the kitchen, wrapping a heavy hand-stitched quilt around her shoulders before handing over a diner mug of strong black coffee. Then strange fingers went over her, inch by inch, looking for slivers of glass and prodding small cuts.

"Normally, I'd pour a little snort in that," the woman said, "but that tight-butt sheriff is going to be over here in a couple of minutes."

"Who…" Katie began, staring across the table.

"I'm Darlene Wilder," said the woman, her voice softened slightly. "You've talked to my kids. Do you remember?"

"They told me you weren't around here anymore." Katie took a swig of the hot coffee. There was a scalding that brought tears to her eyes.

"Yeah. I didn't want to talk to you," said Darlene. "I lived that life one time already, and I didn't want to do it again."

"How did you get here?"

Darlene gave a tired sigh. "I've been here right along. This is where I live. Though to be honest, I haven't been outside in maybe a couple of years. Well, not while it was daylight and anybody was around. Don't look at me like that. I've got my reasons."

Katie tore her eyes away and looked up at the men. "How did you find me?"

"Now, this," said Stan, "is a funny story. Rick and I were out looking for you because Ruth thought you were about to do something foolish. We had just found your car when Sheriff Lewis pulled up."

"He was looking for me, too?" Katie asked.

Stan laughed, but it was Darlene who spoke. "No, he showed up because I called him." She passed around more mugs of coffee before sitting at the table with hers. "I saw you go sneaking into the store. That Lowery girl and her no-account boyfriend let you in. To be honest, I figured, what with it being two days before Christmas and all the business the store did today, you were in cahoots with them to rob the place. You know, let you in, skedaddle home quick, for an alibi. I didn't know Christopher Beauregard was still in the store."

Both of the men were grinning. Through the kitchen door and across the living room, Katie could see out the front window. She was sitting in the little run-down house on the corner, right across the street from Beauregard's parking lot. Darlene was still talking.

"Normally, I don't give two hoots about what's going on, but that Lowery girl and her cheap attitude remind me of a bad time. Anyway, I called the sheriff's office. I saw your friends over there, too, and had no idea what they were up to. Then suddenly, the store lit up like it was opening for the day. I knew something wasn't right. Lewis and these guys were standing out front jawing when you came slamming up against the glass. Even from where I was across the street, I could see Beauregard coming at you because the lights were behind him."

"When you hit the glass," said Rick, "I thought you were going to come right through it. Then I saw Christopher waving that knife. I yelled out that he was going to kill you and headed for the door, but Lewis was ahead of me. He already had his firearm drawn and took the shot. I almost fell to the ground."

"Good thing you didn't," said Stan. "If we hadn't moved so quick, Katie would have fallen into all that glass. She'd have gotten cut up worse than she is."

Chapter Thirty-Nine

They sat there for a while, silent and sipping coffee. Outside, more flashing lights showed up. Another sheriff's cruiser, the ambulance, a couple of firemen, and finally, the state police pulled in. Darlene wandered off and came back in a house dress instead of her flannel nightgown and robe. Katie had shrugged off the blanket and removed her coat so that Rick could look at where the knife had sliced through. After applying the Mercurochrome that Darlene provided, he pronounced her fit to return to work the next morning.

"It's okay," Stan said. "We'll only be open half a day. You don't need to come in."

"Are you kidding?" Katie asked. "I want to see if Eddie wears the purple and pink scarf and mittens he won in the Christmas party gift raffle."

"He probably wouldn't, but you did dare him to step up and prove he was man enough to take a joke," said Rick.

"Yeah, then Christmas morning, they'll be wrapped up under the tree with his daughter's name on the package."

They were still laughing when Sheriff Lewis crossed the street. Katie saw him coming over Rick's shoulder, and her chest tightened.

"Exactly what were you thinking?" Sheriff Lewis asked. They were alone in the kitchen, each with a cup of Darlene's strong coffee.

I'll never be able to sleep tonight, Katie thought. She looked at the Sheriff, seeing the tired lines on his face, the wilted drooping of his collar.

"Why would you go into that store knowing you were alone with a man that outweighed you by a hundred pounds and throw an accusation of murder into his face?"

"He murdered his brother," she said, sounding as tired as he looked.

"What he's saying is that you broke in and attacked him." Lewis took a big swig and grimaced.

Katie refocused, suddenly much more awake. "I didn't attack him. He was the one swinging a knife. All I did was tell him about my theory."

"Why don't we move down the road to my office? Then you can tell me your theory."

She sat in the back of the sheriff's cruiser, coat buttoned to her chin, for the three-minute ride. She knew Rick and Stan were following close behind, the same way she knew all the residents of the main street were peeking out from behind their front window curtains, watching as she was hauled off.

Christopher Beauregard had been taken away as well, but he was riding in an ambulance. Deputy Brad rode in the ambulance, and the state trooper followed behind.

How long, she wondered, *before the whole town hears I attacked Christopher and he needed to go to the hospital. Before I know it, somebody, maybe Christopher himself, will start a rumor that Lewis was aiming at me and missed. With all those volunteer firemen in there, he probably already started ranting. One person will whisper to another. By breakfast, I'll have been tried and convicted.*

Regardless of what else he had said, the mercantile owner had been right. He was a well-known businessman, well-seeded in the community. Katie, on the other hand, was nothing but a sales clerk and part-time feral cat wrestler.

Katie got out of the cruiser at the sheriff's office, ready to tell Lewis she wanted a lawyer before this went any further. Stan beat her to the punch. When Lewis refused to allow Stan to use the office phone to make calls on Katie's behalf, Stan went across the street to Author Fortin's big green and white house. Rousing the elderly couple didn't seem to bother her boss as much as losing the twenty minutes it would take for him to drive to his own home. He came back a short time later to tell Sheriff Lewis that Attorney Joseph Costello would be representing Katie.

"Costello will be out first thing in the morning," Stan said, his jaw jutted out like a dare toward Lewis.

"Well then, it appears Ms. Took will be spending the night in the Essex Junction tank." Lewis had a self-satisfied smirk on his face. Before Rick, standing behind Katie, could open his mouth, the sheriff held up his hand. "Sorry, but we don't have a cell here in Parentville. We don't even have a bathroom to keep her locked in. This office is offered two choices; Essex Junction or the sheriff compound in Montpelier. I'm doing you all a favor sending Took to Essex."

"It's two days till Christmas." Rick spat.

Katie reached out to tug on his jacket. Because the sheriff had put cuffs on her, a requirement for her to ride in the cruiser, one hand followed the other upward. "It's okay, Rick. Don't worry. I'll be alright."

Rick looked back. It was clear he didn't believe her words. "Are you arresting her?" he asked Lewis.

"No, I'm holding her on suspicion. Until I have a chance to talk to her, she can cool her heels in a cell."

The realization that she had played right into Sheriff Lewis' hands made Katie bite down on her lip. But the damage was done. Lewis contacted the Essex Junction police department, telling them he was transporting.

Rick said he'd follow behind. "You go up to the house and tell Ruth what's going on," he said to Stan. "I don't know if I'll be back tonight or not."

"You can't stay in your truck," Katie said.

"The hell I can't," he answered.

They marched out of the sheriff's office all in a row. It was ten-thirty at night, but when Katie looked up the main street of the sleepy little town, she saw a lot of houses were still lit up.

* * *

A night in jail was more comfortable than some Katie had spent while she was couch surfing her way around the Midwest. The female officer was decent about making sure Katie was comfortable.

"I understand your lawyer won't be available until the morning," she said. "If he's any type of bigwig, he's probably at the governor's Christmas ball.

Can I get you a cup of coffee?"

"I've had enough coffee to keep me awake until New Year's," Katie said with a laugh. Then, surprisingly, she slept.

Joseph Costello, Attorney at Law, was a big deal. Katie could tell by the deference the police officers treated him with. He was a more prominent figure than the attorney, Wilkins, that had read her grandmother's will. He told her upon arrival; he had been at the governor's gathering and had already had a conversation with both Stan Baldwin and Rick.

"Mr. Baldwin speaks quite highly of you, Ms. Took," said Costello. "We're going to have a short meeting here, and then you will be transported to Burlington, where we will stand before Judge Morton. You can expect Sheriff Lewis to be present."

"That's not going to make him happy, Christmas Eve and all," she said.

"That is not my concern. Now, let's talk about how you got involved with this foray into Christopher Beauregard's past."

Their short meeting took over an hour. Katie was getting nervous at the length of time they were spending on how she had come up with her theory that Christopher was responsible for George's death.

"You said earlier that Christopher confessed to killing his brother. And directly after that, he threatened your life as well?"

"Yes. He told me that he had stabbed George with the exact same type of knife he was going to stab me with. He also said it was easy because George was soft like butter."

Katie leaned forward, rubbing her hands over her eyes. When she finally regained her self-control, Costello spoke again. "Rather than have you go through this repeatedly, we're going to have our meeting with the judge."

"Will Christopher Beauregard be there?" Katie asked.

"No. Unlike yourself, Mr. Beauregard was charged with criminal assault. He has already been moved to Windsor State Petitionary. They have a hospital wing there. His wound wasn't life-threatening, but he will need to be monitored. It's more prudent than housing him in the hospital."

Costello stayed with Katie while she was cuffed and seated in a squad car. When they arrived at the court building at the bottom of Church Street in Burlington, he was right with her again. In the corridor on the way to Judge Saul Morton's private office, they passed Rick and Stan. Both men were wearing suits and fell in behind the officers walking with Katie. In the judge's quarters, they were directed to seats by the door. When seated, Katie's back was to them. Though they were no longer in sight, she was comforted by their presence. A female officer stayed beside Katie. Sheriff Lewis was also present, in a fresh uniform, as was an attorney for the state.

There was a large stack of paperwork on the desk in front of Judge Morton. He seemed intent on reading through specific sections that had been tagged ahead of time. A woman, Katie assumed to be his secretary, sat beside him, taking notes on a steno pad as he dictated. She could hear the droning murmur of his voice, but the words were unclear.

Finally, he raised his head. "I've been over the information provided by both Attorney Alderman and Attorney Costello," he said.

Katie was surprised. She hadn't seen Costello pass anything across the desk.

"Currently, Mr. Beauregard is being held for his own safety and because of a charge of assault against you, Miss Took. Normally, the officer in charge at the scene, in this case Sheriff Lewis, would have taken your statement and then, given what we have here, released you on your own reconnaissance until this hearing. Yet, you requested a lawyer right out of the gate, leading the sheriff to believe you were more than an innocent bystander. You also are charging that Mr. Christopher Beauregard is guilty of the murder of his brother, George Beauregard, five and a half years ago. What do you have to say for yourself?"

"Your Honor," Costello said.

The judge held up his hand. "I'm sure you've coached your client well, Joe. Let's hear what she has to say."

Sheriff Lewis made as if to get to his feet. The state's attorney laid his hand on the sheriff's shoulder, pushing him back down.

Katie licked her lips. She thought of what she had said to Joseph Costello. And what she hadn't.

"Sir," she began. "A friend of mine was charged with George Beauregard's death. Even though she was released and never charged with murder, the after-effects are still haunting her. I started out just asking questions, trying to find something I could offer that would help her get over that terror. One tiny detail led to a second one. There were a lot of pieces that were not in the report."

"How did you come up with the police report?" Judge Pierce asked.

"It was in my grandmother's papers. I don't know how she got it. She's dead. I can't ask," Katie said, honestly. Her palms were sweating. In the room filled with men in suits, she felt at a disadvantage in her flannel shirt and damaged barn coat.

"Why didn't you take your findings to Sheriff Lewis?" asked Morton.

Katie blinked in surprise, then answered honestly. "He investigated the murder because both George Beauregard and Christopher Beauregard are his uncles."

"What?" Judge Morton turned to look at Lewis.

The sheriff seemed to shrivel in his seat, face reddening.

"Ms. Took, I apologize for the county for the way you have been treated for the last twelve hours. I am releasing you at this time. However, you will travel with Attorney Costello or his representative back to your home, where you will turn over the notes your attorney said you gathered. If I have further questions, you will be notified by your attorney when you need to be present. Have a good holiday and goodbye."

A junior attorney from Joseph Costello's firm was waiting outside the judge's chambers. Though what he was instructed to do was not what he had expected, he graciously led Katie to his vehicle.

"Would you like to sit in the back?" he asked.

"No, thank you," she replied.

Chapter Forty

Katie did exactly what the judge instructed her to do. While she gathered her notes, Ruth fed the junior attorney coffee and Christmas cookies. Rick and Stan sat across the table, suit jackets hanging on the back of their chairs. The three men found common ground for conversation in the results of the last World Series and their hopes for the next year.

Unable to face Ruth and Rick, Katie closed herself in her cold bedroom. Even LG was shut out. Then, shortly after lunch, she heard Rick thumping up the stairs.

"Get out here," he ordered. "Your lawyer is on the phone, and he doesn't have all day."

Katie would have liked some privacy, but Ruth, wringing her hands, stood only three feet away. For Katie, most of the conversation involved listening and nodding her head. Ruth nodded when the younger woman did, with no idea what was being said. Rick hung in the doorway, waiting to go down into the basement to feed the furnace fire, but was afraid to leave and not know what was happening. Finally, Katie hung up the phone.

Rick couldn't stand it any longer. "Well," he said, advancing into the kitchen and leaving the door unguarded, allowing Old Tom to sneak past.

"I have to be in Attorney Costello's office next Wednesday at nine," Katie said. Reaching out her hand to Ruth, but unable to look her elderly friend in the face, she added, "The District Attorney is charging Christopher Beauregard with the premeditated murder of his brother, George. I'm sorry, Ruth, it's not over."

"No," whispered Ruth, "but now it's headed in the right direction."

* * *

On Christmas morning, Katie braved the stares of village residents and attended mass at Saint Jude's, sitting between Ruth and Rick. She was wearing her new sweater set, a gift from Ruth, as well as the beautiful Blueberry colored three-quarter-length quilted jacket Marlie had sent her. Rising for the closing hymn, she let her eyes drift around for the first time. Only a few people were still watching her. Near the back of the church, Ginny was seated with Darlene. They shared a hymnal. Two dark heads close together in praise and love. Sheriff Lewis was near the front. The deep gray wool of his Sunday suit stretched across his broad shoulders. The church was more crowded than usual. Arthur and Delia Fortin had scrunched into the end of their pew, with the elderly farmer reaching across to pat Katie's hand from time to time.

When Father Metevier released the assembly to return to their homes and their own festivities, Ruth left the church with her mittens clutched in her right hand. On her left, the sparkle of a small diamond on her third finger caught the light.

Acknowledgements

When I got ready to write this story, the third in the *An It's Never Too Late Series*, this wasn't the book I had in mind. I had a completely different storyline for what was supposed to be the last book. Then, there were all of these questions coming from readers along the lines of social media asking what about Ruth's story? Way back in book one, Ruth showed up on page 5. She was supposed to only stay for a few pages, pack her bag, and walk out the door, never to return. Well, she did pack her bag, but she never left. Over the rest of the book, we all learned she had a black-hole secret that gnawed at her innards. It was right there in Katie Took's face, and people wanted her to deal with it.

Verena Rose, my publishing editor with Level Best Books, and I were having a telephone conversation, and she came right out and asked me the same thing. When I explained that *In the Village Proper* would have been book four of six, but LBB had only taken three, Verena told me to change it up. There would be six books, but Ruth's story would be three. Okay, so that's exactly what happened. I'm not sure why, but so far, this is the most emotional of Katie's stories I have written.

Thank you, Verena Rose, for letting me put these words on pages. Thank you, Harriette Sackler, for inviting me in, and Shawn Reilly Simmons for all the artwork, editing, and question answering in the process. Level Best Books has given me so much. Not only three women who helped me redefine myself, but access to a plethora of women and men, writers, editors, promoters, and readers who have become friends and traveling companions on my journey.

To the librarians and bookstore owners that let me stand in their hallowed spaces and run off at the mouth about what I'm doing, you have my respect and undying gratitude. Fortin cousins, friends who help me research, or read the same chapter over and over, hugs and kisses.

Lisa Mathews, How to Kill Your Darlings Editing, what can I say? Except maybe, should there be a comma here?

Debra Wells, for explaining all the little nuances I didn't understand. English is a tricky language. Kassandra Lamb, for helping me find the path to out there.

To my partner, Glenn, who only asked a few times if I was finished yet, but did dishes, laundry, and all manner of shopping, thank you. I couldn't have come out sane on this end without your help.

P.S. I love you all.

About the Author

DonnaRae Menard began writing in junior high school and has been scribbling since. She is the author of the An It's Never Too Late Mystery series. A 1970's suspense featuring Katelyn Took and 17 cats. The Woman Warrior's series, historical fiction from time periods she remembers, Detective Carmine Mansuer series, set in Boston, Mass. *Dropped from the Sky, It takes Guts, Willa the Wisp*, and several short stories. She splits her time between Vermont and New Hampshire, has an affinity for odd jobs, and rescued cats. She's also always willing to explain about her 450 pound lap pig.

SOCIAL MEDIA HANDLES:
  Facebook – https://www.facebook.com/DonnaRae-Menard-103359971 477217
  Goodreads - https://www.goodreads.com/donnaraemenard
  Bookbub - https://www.bookbub.com/authors/donnarae-menard
  Twitter - @DonnaRaeMenard

AUTHOR WEBSITE:

DonnaRaeMenardbooks.com

Also by DonnaRae Menard

The It's Never Too Late Series:
  Murder in the Meadow
  Murder on Eagle Drop Ridge

The Woman Warriors series:
  Strength of the Mayan Leopard
  In the Shadow of Pharaoh
  WuLee

The Detective Carmine Mansuer series:
  Patterns
  Hunters

Stand Alone:
  Dreams of a Mad Woman
  It takes Guts

Children's:
  Willa the Wisp

Fantasy:
  The Waif and the Warlord
  Burner